one

'Sarah Cupsip,' I muttered to myself as I fumbled through my bag to look for the voucher for the hotel. It's a difficult manoeuvre trying to locate anything in my bag, considering how fast the taxi was speeding to get to my destination. Luckily I was strapped in the back seat, but not being able to find my documents created a slight panic. I thought when the driver came to a stop, I would kiss the ground but I hated the thought of arriving at the checking-in desk without my paperwork. I blamed my late friend, Sarah Cupsip, but just then my hand took hold of the diary she gave me and I blamed myself for not being organised.

I had never travelled before so I was allowed to make mistakes. A plastic cover touched my fingertips and I knew I had the vouchers I needed. Sitting back with relief, I thought about how Sarah would have handled the situation. She had travelled far and wide and I had admired her adventurous spirit for years. She had always travelled alone; her excuse was that she was looking for her soulmate. Sadness came over me thinking about her time in hospital, spent with a body that didn't want to go looking any more. The healthy body she once had quickly diminished, along with her mind that was incoherent towards the end of her life. Sarah Cupsip had mumbled about past lives and realms but I put that down to all the books she had read.

The hotel came into view and I thought about how it was supposed to be Sarah checking in and not me. The trip to Canada from west to east was supposed to be her adventure, but she had been admitted to hospital. I'm not sure why she gave me the ticket, but I took it because I knew my life would be mundane without Sarah in it. I had always missed her when she had travelled, so I dreaded the thought of not being able to see her ever again. Canada was not a place that I ever thought I would visit, as for some reason, I had always wanted to go to Alaska after I had overheard someone speak about the northern lights. The ticket given to me was to take me to Nova Scotia but as it was a once in a life time opportunity, I organised with the travel agent to change the trip to include Alaska. It meant the east side of the country would have to be taken out of the tour but I didn't mind. Circumstances had prevented me from travelling before, so at that moment I was happy to be going anywhere beyond my shores.

A feeling of guilt overcame me as I looked at the luxurious hotel that was meant for Sarah, but my driver only saw another tourist. For some reason, I wanted to tell him about my friend and her sudden death but I put it down to being tired after the long flight, so instead I staggered quietly out of the taxi and pulled my case to the foyer. Not being sure if it was the drive or the flight that numbed my mind, I found myself drifting away on the bed without realising how I got there.

In my dreams, I heard Sarah in her last days repeating the stories of her past lives. Visions of her were vivid and I could see that she had once been a princess and she had spent her lives looking for her soulmate. I could hear her voice as if it was in the room, but I was asleep. The sound became too clear for my liking and definitely outside of my mind. With a start, I woke up to find that my phone was vibrating on the cupboard next to me. I listened to Sarah's voice indicating that it was a phone call from her. Drowsily, I went to pick it up and suddenly found myself wide awake and acutely aware that she was dead. My heart beat uncontrollably until I realised it must be someone else trying to contact me by using her phone. I quickly answered but there was no one on the other end. I tried to ring back but my phone wouldn't work. I tried to access my messages but it had frozen in time. So much for technology; it's only good when it's working. When it isn't working it's bad because then I had to find an Apple store to fix it. Really, I hadn't thought my holiday would be spent in a phone shop but I had planned on using my phone to take pictures. Note to self: if I ever travel again I will bring a camera.

Staggering out of my comfortable bed, I made myself more presentable by brushing my blonde hair before taking the lift downstairs to ask the concierge where I would find an Apple store. Unfortunately, he didn't know so he looked on his computer to find directions for me. A piece of paper was printed out and presented before me, and with a point of his finger I was sent in the direction needed to fix my phone.

I walked the concrete jungle that was Vancouver and took in the beauty of the flowers that broke up the grey. I seemed to be in the industrial side of town as there didn't seem to be many shops. After a while of trying to follow the map I wondered what the time was, as my phone was also my watch. It had then become a necessity to ask for help so I engaged with a well-dressed woman and hoped she knew where the store was. Thankfully, she was able to provide a better set of directions and it turned out that the shop was hidden, which seemed odd but that explained why I hadn't been able to see any shops. I backtracked and found where they were concealed inside one of the grey buildings. The glass doors opened and inside the old building which resembled offices from another era was a modern escalator that took me to the store which had an apple with a bite taken out of it on its sign.

As is typical of Apple stores, it was large and filled with people. I spotted a small stature of a man making appointments in amongst the mayhem. Employees placed customers at their appropriate tables with technicians who had all the answers. With my time slotted and a warning to return early, I left, taking a mental note of the people waiting before me. I wondered how long they had been there and if they would be there on my return, as one lady in particular took my attention. She was pregnant and too sweet to be left on her own with technicians who could talk her into buying unnecessary goods to pay for the employee's next holiday. I felt as if I should intervene, but instead I left to walk around and stare at the shop windows. It was a dangerous pastime as there were too many things to buy, so to avoid temptations I returned to my appointment early.

Faces seemed familiar and as I looked at the clock on the wall I realised why. I had left them only half an hour before, but still I had to repeat my explanation of the problem with my phone. It was after speaking with a few technicians I found myself moved to a table that I then shared with the pregnant lady. Jokingly, I asked if everyone was in the store due to faults with their devices and quickly I was frowned upon. I didn't care as I was leaving a message for the woman who looked as if she was about to give birth. I hoped she would take the hint. I felt as if I had to protect her and made sure to involve myself with fixing her phone problems as well as my own before leaving.

With my phone working and my hotel only a few blocks away, I walked towards the bed that was calling to me. My plan had been to stay awake until late but it was not meant to be. The afternoon nap had not been enough but at least this time I would get to sleep knowing that my phone would not be disturbing me. So I gave in and as soon as I put my head on the pillow I felt the darkness take over.

The deeper I slept, the clearer the voice became. I hoped it wasn't Sarah and thankfully it wasn't. The voice was from the unborn child of the pregnant woman. He was on my mind and no matter how much I tried I could not get rid of him. Giving up, I let the information flow. The boy was about to be born and it would be his last time here on this planet, realm, dimension or whatever. He wanted his mother to know that he was here for fun. The mother was a woman who enjoyed life and although he didn't want her to grieve, their enjoyment would be only short. In past lives he had suffered with an illness that still continued to intrude on his happiness. By the time he would turn eight, he would begin to show his symptoms. His fear was that his mother would try to cure him but he wanted to heal himself, which is difficult to explain when you are so young.

Hours passed with me wondering why I should be given this information as my chances of seeing this woman again were zero. One thing was for certain, and that was the curly fair haired boy with a mischievous face would be here to learn a lesson. Finally, the visions disappeared and I fell into a deeper sleep and slept in.

Thankfully, the ship was docked across the road from the hotel. I was happy to be woken from my sleep, but to make sure I left in time, I had to put up with an alarm sounding in the hotel. I looked down the hallway to other confused guests wondering if we should evacuate or not, but as I was leaving anyway I decided to ring the front desk first to find out how serious it was. It was a false alarm but that didn't stop the firemen coming. Normally I would have laughed at the situation and I was sure Sarah would have joined in on the hilarity of it all. I wondered if she had set up the false alarm as it did get me out of bed. My bag was already packed so I joined in on the controlled chaos at the dock.

My movements were a blur but eventually I made it to my cabin. I have been on my own for many years with only a small number of people in my life. Sarah was my only real friend and as I sat looking at my small room with a single bed, cupboard and ensuite, I realised how insignificant I was. Since leaving my family home to work in the city, I had accomplished nothing. I had spent the last ten years commuting from an office to an apartment I rented in a block that was amongst many other blocks. I wondered how many other people were like me and how many had been saved by a friend. Sarah had been my salvation with her stories of her travels. I was now on her adventure, but if it was she who was here, she would not be sitting on her bed in her cabin feeling sorry for herself.

I stepped out into the hallway looking for adventure but found myself lost in the warren of hallways. I took many wrong turns before I found myself in a room filled with lounges and chairs that faced a wall of large windows. I picked out a particularly comfortable looking chair, and the moment I sat in it, a waiter approached asking for an order. I tried to think of what Sarah would request and ordered a cocktail. Passengers soon filled up the room and it wasn't long before someone sat next to me.

'That looks like an interesting drink,' said a woman with long fingernails that pointed at my half empty glass.

'I've never had one before,' I replied with a smile, 'but it's delicious.'

'What's it called?' she asked as she made herself comfortable.

'I don't know. I'm not usually a cocktail drinker so I asked the waiter to give me what he would order,' I said finishing off my third drink.

My neighbour had just put her bag down when the waiter appeared.

'I'll have what she is having,' she explained while pointing to me.

'Serah Kohw,' I said. 'I'm Serah Kohw.'

'I'm Lizette Leclerk,' answered the woman, taking out a mirror from her bag to check her face. 'Are you travelling alone?'

'Yes,' I replied and went on to explain about another Sarah who had been in my life and how she had given me her ticket to travel through Canada.

'But we are going to Alaska,' said Lizette in an abrupt manner.

'I know. I always wanted to see the icebergs and the northern lights and as it was probably the only opportunity I would ever get

HE SAW one YOU

HE WANTED YOU

HE GOT YOU

HE MISTREATED YOU

HE MESSED WITH YOU

HE GREW BORED OF YOU

HE TALKED ABOUT YOU

HE USED YOU

HE BROKE YOU

HE LEFT YOU

WHATS UITH ALL THE

HE'S GOT A GIRL

to do so, I swapped half of Canada to go on this cruise!' I declared as the waiter placed the cocktail on a small table next to Lizette's chair.

'Thanks,' she said to the waiter and turned back to face me. 'I'm also travelling alone so it looks as if we are together for a couple of weeks; I go on the Canada tour after this cruise as well. We are probably on the same bus trip.'

'What a coincidence,' I remarked as I caught the attention of the waiter to get another cocktail.

An announcement stated that it was time for lunch and as I struggled to my feet whilst balancing my drink, Lizette took my arm to escort me to a room filled with colour. Amongst the tables and chairs sprung flowers of every description and every crisp table cloth sparkled with silverware waiting to be used. An aroma of fresh bread wafted through the entry door and as I took in the pleasant surroundings, I let Lizette request a change to the seating arrangements so we could sit together. Waiters stood in line beside the door, and after a small discussion we were escorted to a table where napkins were placed on our laps.

Normally I look after myself, so it was nice to have someone take care of me. I sat back and looked at the menu, and to fill my empty stomach and soak up the alcohol I ordered asparagus soup, salad, fish, and crème caramel. Sometimes during my lunch break I would buy a pumpkin soup that was claimed to be freshly made by the restaurant in the building but when the asparagus soup was put in front of me, I found out the real meaning of the word fresh. It was as if the asparagus had been pulled out of the dirt to be cooked just to the point where all the nutrients and flavours exploded into one. My body approved of each mouthful and I savoured the taste as it passed through my throat to fill up my stomach. Lizette laughed at my expressions but I told her that she had missed out on pleasing her taste buds by not ordering a soup.

We waited for the salad and as soon as my bowl had been

removed, the plates arrived filled with colour from the different fruits and vegetables. As I put my dressing over my salad I watched Lizette take her first bite. Her groan in delight of eating fresh food found me stabbing at my salad to join in on the pleasure. Not a word was said as we ate our way through the main course and dessert. With full stomachs, we looked at each other hoping every meal would be the same.

I rubbed my stomach and as I got up from my seat, I remarked on going to the gym in the morning.

'I'll meet you there,' said Lizette pulling on the waistline of her pants. 'But what are you going to do now?'

I turned to her with dreary eyes that probably looked narrower than usual. 'Lizette, I don't know if it's the alcohol or jetlag but I'm really tired. I'm going to bed.'

'But you'll miss out on dinner,' declared Lizette.

'Probably a good thing,' I answered before turning my back to her.

We parted company at the stairs and I ambled around to find my cabin. It took a few wrong turns but I made it, and when I lay on my bed I was glad I had made the effort to leave the cabin as now I had a friend to travel with. I thanked the spirit of Sarah Cupsip as I pulled the blanket up around my shoulders.

two

Serah Kohw had always admired Sarah Cupsip but had never been brave enough to travel with her. Her late friend had tried to encourage her, because to Sarah Cupsip, people who didn't explore the planet were not living. Serah Kohw used to listen to the adventures but she was too scared to change. There was a reason why she was held back and it was going to take a trip for her to find out what that was.

As Serah stared at the bright light that shone above her, the realisation hit her. She was on holiday! She had wanted to look at the sun from a different country but then she remembered the light was not from the portal but from the lamp she had left on as there was no window. When she managed to find the clock, she realised that, again, she had slept in. Skipping dinner had its drawbacks as she was now famished and had to rush to make breakfast before the doors shut.

The dining room for the morning was in another area and when she got there she hoped the food would be as good. It was a buffet which meant she had to help herself, but when she looked at the food that was on display, Serah knew that she had to hold herself back. There was too much to choose from so a decision had to be made for moderation. She looked at the pancakes and maple syrup and as she piled them onto her plate, she decided to choose something different each day as a way to keep her portions down.

Looking around for a table of one, she found Lizette seated in front of a few empty plates.

'Don't eat any more than that one plate,' Lizette advised, patting her flat stomach.

'I've already decided on one meal for breakfast,' Serah declared putting her plate on the table.

'I thought the same thing until I decided on a few plates of different foods to taste first,' Lizette groaned. 'I think I'll sit here for a while before going to the gym.'

'Good move,' Serah said before putting the pancakes into her mouth.

'That way,' added Lizette, 'the fitness fanatics will have finished and we will be able to use the equipment.'

'You have a point,' Serah said. 'I was thinking of going later as well to use the showers in the spa area. My shower is tiny and when I tested the spout yesterday, it didn't want to co-operate. Not many would be using the spa, I imagine, so I'll make that my ensuite.'

Lizette agreed. 'Everyone has a plan of sorts and all are different. Just look around you at the amount of different people there are on board. There are gym junkies, old retirees, young families and everyone in between.'

Serah took in what Lizette said and hoped it wouldn't be too busy. When they finally stepped into the gym room, she sighed with the sight of empty treadmills that faced large windows looking out to nothing but sea. Serah had left her phone in her cabin, so listening to music was out of the question unless she wanted to walk the many hallways. So instead she opted to walk on the treadmill anyway, and with one look out to sea she knew she would not be requiring music to pass the time. Whales swam beside them as if giving them a safe passage. She watched in awe and by the time the mammals had decided to swim deeper, she had already walked for half an hour. Serah stepped off the machine feeling energised and she wasn't sure if it was from the walking or the energy she had picked up from the ancient mammals.

The itinerary was a full day at sea, so Lizette and Serah decided to head back to their chairs from the previous day to sit and look out for the whales. The moment they sat, the waiter was there for the orders and as Serah had finished her exercise, she didn't feel guilty when she asked for a cocktail. A promise had been made to herself to drink water between the drinks but good intentions are not always realised, and she blamed the waiter who continually provided her with alcohol.

Due to too many drinks, their whale watching became anything-that-moves watching, which created laughter so contagious, other women were attracted to join them. They were all so loud they missed the call for lunch, but several hours of frivolity later Serah managed to hear the call for dinner, which turned out to be her salvation. The food helped to soak up the alcohol and filled her with sustenance to help her to sleep and she went to bed thanking the spirit of Sarah Cupsip profusely for the ticket.

three

Sleeping in was becoming a habit and again Serah woke up late but she blamed the alcohol and the lack of night time. It was summer and Alaska didn't get dark until after ten in the evening which made it feel like the afternoon. Before going to bed it had turned foggy, so she didn't know what to expect that morning as she didn't have a window to look out of. She sat up wondering what to wear, then she remembered the dream she had had during the night. It was Lizette this time who had been in her thoughts but her appearance had changed to one of a reptile. The vision brought a shudder down Serah's spine so she made another note not to drink so much.

Presuming that the shiver had been an omen, she put on her jeans and jumper to brace herself from the cold, but when she reached the top of the stairs, she was glad she had put a shirt on under her jumper as the sky was clear. A couple of women who she had been drinking with the day before passed her and stated that it was apparently very unusual weather, which reaffirmed Serah's decision about layering her clothes.

Serah had always wanted to see icebergs, and thankfully, due to the cloudless sky, she would get to see every peak through the Glacier Bay passage. In her mind she pictured mountains of ice, but what was in front of her were masses of stone, covered with pine trees and dusted with snow. She found a window to sit at for breakfast and although she tried to stick to an omelette for sustenance, the temptation of French toast was too much to ignore, so instead she piled her plate. Feeling annoyed with her lack of willpower, she punished herself by eating everything on her plate determined not to let it be wasted as she watched the whales pass by for entertainment. Did it really matter if she put on weight? She had no one to look good for. But then she thought of her health, and when Lizette walked past in her gym gear, she rushed back to her cabin to get changed.

Her exercise was out of the way but after the warning of Lizette's bizarre transformation during the night, Serah decided to keep away from the waiter who supplied the cocktails. Instead she went looking for a different room to view the whales; hopefully one that served herbal tea. She bid her senses take her to the tea room, but instead they led her to a room filled with passengers listening to a local ranger who had come aboard to speak about the cycles of the glaciers.

The ranger's story was interesting, but it was the other speaker who really got Serah's attention. The woman was from the local tribe who had lived there for centuries. At one time the glacier was a distant piece of frozen water that provided a vibrant river running through their village. Over the years, they had thrived on the salmon and the tribe had grown. They had kept ancient traditions alive through art, and their totem poles, that were once placed outside their homes to provide an address, lived on. But the time came for the glacier to move, and as it did, the tribe took to their canoes to watch as their home was buried. The speaker didn't mention the name of the ancient tribe but did speak of a lady who refused to move from her home and was frozen into the ice. Her description of the glacier reminded Serah of her own thoughts that she had of something massive. What she didn't know was, if the size related to ice or something else!

Serah hoped to see ice and knew the possibility was there, so when the ship turned into the passage to face the glacier, Serah felt initial disappointment at the size. That was until they stopped by it. The wall of ice that blocked the flow from the mountains was like a castle that had been built with massive blocks. A loud crash of thunder ripped through the air to remind them that the ice wall was capable of falling apart at any moment. The sun shining through the new growth of ice provided a shade of blue that stood out amongst the different greys. Small sections of the glacier fell into the water giving an explanation as to why there were lumps of ice floating around.

The ship turned around, giving everyone a renewed sense of hope that the whales would join them again on the way back as their sprays could be seen shooting out of the water in the distance. Elation rushed through Serah as she felt alive.

She looked up to the sky to reiterate her emotions to her departed friend, understanding what Sarah meant by "living". Again, she felt shivers and joined the many who went back inside to look for whales through the windows to escape the chill in the wind. Inside, she had still hoped to find the tea room but she ended up back at the room where the women were drinking their cocktails. Despite her misgivings she entered the room, and when an entertainer from another room joined them, she felt obliged to stay. A game was about to take place where a tune was played and a person was picked to sing the words. Not wanting to be picked seemed to be a good excuse to leave, but Lizette spotted her and called for Serah to sit with her new friends. There didn't seem to be any other choice so she walked towards them as inconspicuously as she could. She didn't get picked which was a good thing as she was not one to remember her way around the ship, let alone words for a song.

'You know,' said one of the women, 'we can look out at the ice from the spa area.'

Serah was interested as she didn't want another day of drinking cocktails so she prompted everyone to move.

'I think I'll stay here,' answered Lizette who displayed a large tongue that licked the salt around the rim of the glass.

Serah wasn't attached to Lizette so she felt no guilt when she announced that she would join the woman.

'Good,' said the woman who was a few years older than Serah. 'I've had enough of sitting down and I think the jets would do my back some good.'

Serah didn't mind what the rationale was as she was glad to be leaving the cocktails behind.

'I have to get changed so I'll meet you there,' said the woman, leaving her at the staircase.

Serah couldn't be bothered finding her cabin so she headed straight to the spa to strip down to her underwear. There wasn't anyone around so she quickly jumped into the spa and immediately wished she hadn't. It was at boiling point, so not wanting to be cooked, she jumped out and got dressed.

'Don't go in there,' warned a passenger, 'it's too hot!'

'Too late,' Serah answered with a grin on her face.

'Are you cooked?' he asked, smiling back.

'Hope not,' she replied.

'Come on, I'll get you a drink to rehydrate you,' said the man who extended an arm.

Serah was about to move but then remembered that the woman was getting changed to meet her. Could she leave? Without consciously deciding, she looked at the gruff man and left with him. To her delight he took her to a room that offered herbal teas. She was sure the spirit of Sarah was helping and she thanked her as she sat by a window to view the ice and forests that provided homes for bears. The rest of the day was spent listening to her new companion who knew all about wildlife. His mission was to end animal cruelty and she gladly took in everything he had to say, knowing she was learning something about how others lived their lives.

His calming voice soothed her brain and the tea soothed her body. And when he thanked Serah for her company, she blissfully went to bed.

who

Help

I N

four

Thankfully, Serah woke up before the wakeup call. Drinking tea had helped her body clock to function correctly and also helped with her dreams as she didn't have any. Her sleep had been silent and she got up with a feeling of positivity. The ship had docked at Skagway and an announcement warned them that the weather was unpredictable. Deciding to play it safe, she packed her raincoat inside her bag. As she disembarked she was glad she had listened to her intuition as the wet weather hit her the moment she faced the gangway. Staying positive, Serah prepared for the invigorating Alaskan air she was about to inhale but a gust of wind beat her to it. As she choked, she zipped up her raincoat to take on the miserable weather and head out to a street that looked inviting. Tourists kept the eight hundred residents in money, so to keep the economy going she slowly examined the first shop window which provided a display to entice her. Her eyes focused on the topaz, the colour of the bluest ocean, and as she followed the jewellery to the door, she could feel her spirits lifting with the prospect of buying a new ring for her frozen finger. Serah needed something symbolic to remind her of her trip and she thought a piece of jewellery would be something she could admire.

Turning a brass handle in such a low temperature would have normally felt cold but she was too excited to feel anything until she felt a hand on her shoulder and her mood changed to fear. She turned without hesitation and not knowing what to expect, she met the eyes of Lizette.

'Aren't the stones beautiful?' Lizette said, pointing to a pendant. 'But you can't buy the first thing you see. You have to look around first before buying or you'll find something better later on and regret your purchase.'

Lizette was right, but Serah still felt disappointed at being dragged away to the next store which sold novelties. They wandered through the aisles that displayed everything anyone could possibly think of to take home as a gift. Alaska was displayed on each item as a reminder of where the purchase had come from and it was with great willpower that she didn't buy anything. Instead Serah left to look into the next store and as she studied the embroidered high heeled boots, Lizette came to join her.

'Aren't they beautiful?' said Lizette running her spindly fingers over the material.

'They are, but where would I wear them?' Serah questioned, trying to think of an excuse to buy them.

Lizette flew over to the counter to ask for her size.

'Are you thinking of buying them?' Serah asked, sitting next to Lizette as she took off her boots.

'I can wear them on this trip,' said Lizette, 'and I'm sure there will be opportunities for me to wear them when I return home.'

With the zip pulled up, the boots surrounded Lizette's legs to show off their workmanship.

'Are you going to look around first in case you find something better?' Serah asked but Lizette shook her head. 'When you find something like this, you have to buy it straight away or you will come back to the store and someone else will have bought them.'

For a second, Serah felt anger towards Lizette. Her euphoric moment had been destroyed and she looked at her finger that should be wearing the blue ring. A decision had to be made to control the situation, and that was to buy what she wanted and not listen to someone else.

But Serah left to find the next shop window which displayed t-shirts when she should have gone back to the first shop. Secretly, she had hoped the next window would reveal jewellery, but as she looked at the leaves printed onto the material, Serah knew there were only clothes. She could see the beauty in the design and hesitated to look, which was a mistake. Instead of listening to her instincts that urged her to turn around and purchase a ring, she stared at a woman who held open a door with pleading eyes. Serah could have walked away but she blamed herself for listening to someone else so without hesitation she went inside. A black t-shirt with bronzed leaves caught her attention and before she knew it she was paying for it. A bell jangled and she looked over at the door to see Lizette wearing her new boots. 'What have you bought?' she asked still looking down to admire her purchase.

For a moment Serah saw a different Lizette, but she put it down to her eyes playing tricks on her due to her negative emotions. She told herself to be thankful for the holiday and with a more positive approach, she grabbed Lizette to visit the next store.

The sign on the window announced that the shop was run by a family and the pair watched one of its members use tweezers to put together tiny pieces of glass that became pendants. Carvings were in abundance but bears and totem poles only came in sizes to fit in a suitcase. She had learned from Sarah's trips that small ornaments were dust collectors. If she was going to dust something then she wanted it to be substantial. Besides, it gave her a good excuse not to buy and not go through the questioning about whether the item would ever arrive in the post. She went back to watching the man hunched over the pieces of glass and as she glanced over the road, she noticed an interesting building.

'It's haunted,' said the man, putting down his tweezers.

'Really,' said Lizette joining in the conversation.

'It's an old bar,' he said taking a stretch. 'The ghost is named Lydia.'

Serah stared at the building thinking about the spirit of Sarah. She wondered where she was and if her spirit was still around. Was she with her on the trip?

'Come on,' said Lizette who grabbed her hand.

Serah turned to thank the man but there was no reply as he was back to concentrating on his job.

Although Serah wasn't hungry, she was used to eating at lunchtime so she followed Lizette to the saloon. Apparently, it was supposed to be haunted but when Serah looked around, the only spirit she could see was behind the bar. However, she didn't complain as she was out of the cold, the atmosphere was lively, there was paraphernalia all over the walls to increase her knowledge, and the pizza looked good. The waitresses and staff at Klondike Kate's were dressed as prostitutes from a bygone era with one woman in particular who stood out.

She was not the most attractive but her personality was colossal enough that she stole the attention from the others. Men tipped her for a photo and when Serah aimed her phone at her from a distance, she noticed. Serah expected her to ask for a tip but instead she wanted Serah to take a close up. Everyone laughed so Serah took a menu to hide behind but the waitress joined her.

'Be careful of your friend,' whispered the cheeky waitress who shook her rounded bottom before leaving Serah behind to comprehend what she had said.

Lizette ordered a couple of whiskies to warm their insides while they glanced at the varieties of pizza, but Serah could only wonder why the waitress would give her such a warning. She looked over at the solid woman flirting with the men and decided that she was only teasing. Letting go of the information, she sat back in her chair and ordered a vegetarian pizza and another whisky.

With high spirits and full stomachs, they left to banter with the shopkeepers in the next store who seemed to be quirky. It might have been due to the alcohol, but Serah began to enjoy the attention she had taken away from Lizette who ignored her as she chatted with the staff. Information was provided about the blue stone she had fallen in love with at the first shop window, which apparently was in abundance. The store they were in mainly sold statues so her jewellery options were limited but the jade statues were intriguing and after a brief conversation they found out that jade was actually from Alaska.

She was sure she had been told that it was from Asia somewhere but the staff member was adamant so she left with the knowledge and continued through to the next store to receive more information about a painting of a bear on the wall. Immediately Serah whipped out her phone to take a photo and was promptly told that the picture had to be deleted. She was about to tell the owner that she had taken a photo of the totem pole standing next to the picture when a man appeared who changed the subject by chatting about the northern lights.

He placed his arm around her shoulders, which emphasised his suit from the seventies, to explain about the lights only being visible in the darkness. Serah walked with him thinking it was obvious that it needed to be dark for something to shine through so brightly. But there was no argument as his voice was soothing so she continued to listen as he read her mind. At the doorway, she felt the force of his arm as he turned her around to face him. He explained about the lights on the ship being too bright and how the brightness distorted the green ghost-like figures in the sky. She tried to visualise the colourful sky, but all she could see was the blue in his eyes that reminded her of the ring that she wanted to buy. She was letting go of herself and could have quite easily fallen over if it had not been for the man holding her back. She wasn't sure how he manoeuvred her but she realised she was outside when she felt the cold air hit her face. She had questions but all he could tell her was that the blue stone would protect her from the ghosts.

Staring at the ring in his shop window, she wondered why she hadn't noticed it before and went to walk inside.

'Come on,' said Lizette barging through the door, 'we have to go.'

Serah turned to thank the man but he was gone.

A bus was waiting for them so she hurriedly followed Lizette to join their tour guide who enthusiastically explained that they needed to sign a waiver as there was no doctor in town and to get one would cost twenty-five thousand American dollars. He was a character so she didn't know whether to believe him or not but she signed the form and passed it to the front of the bus as they drove along dirt roads. They had left civilisation so quickly, by the time she had adjusted to looking outside, she had to wonder how far they had actually travelled. Serah couldn't believe the wilderness had been so close and she had not noticed it. She needed to focus, and so to take it all in she sat back in her seat and enjoyed the passing show of nature until they stopped with an abrupt halt.

Their tour guide called out for them to get off as they needed to change vehicles. Apparently, it was too wet for a normal bus to handle the roads that were before them so they all stood in silence as they watched their bus leave them inside a dense forest filled with Christmas trees. Thoughts of being stranded took over her but were dismissed when another vehicle came into view. Others also sighed with relief and it wasn't long before they were again sitting down, anticipating the sight of two hundred dogs that would welcome them.

The smell of the pine filled the air as they moved past buildings made from wood. They knew they were close and the chatter filled their vehicle once more with the excitement of seeing the huskies that would pull them in a sled. Once stopped, they quickly made their way out only to be silent. Everyone had expected dogs that were thick and fluffy but what was brought out were thin and sleek. The musher who owned the team of dogs explained that they enjoyed pulling the sled as they had been mixed with greyhounds who loved to run, and the dogs having thin coats meant they didn't get hot, which made sense. However, as they stopped near a pile of diarrhoea, Serah wondered how healthy they were.

The sled took off as the sixteen dogs pulled it along a track they knew by heart. Serah expected a long ride through the forest, but instead the bumpy ride ended after just one lap. Despite the disappointment, she didn't complain as she was glad the dogs could rest before the next lot of tourists arrived. Serah patted one of the dogs as she contemplated whether they enjoyed their life or not, but her thoughts were put to an end when the tourists were called back onto the vehicle. Serah assumed the vehicle was going back to the main street but after a short ride back down the hill, they stopped to cuddle some puppies. This, of course, made everything else irrelevant. The mother of a litter sat on top of her kennel as the puppies slept. Serah wanted to cuddle them but hated waking them so instead she stood still, watching them sleep.

'Look,' said Lizette with a white, fluffy pup in her arms.

'Where did that one come from?' Serah asked as a woman put a white, fluffy puppy in her own hands. She was annoyed that they had been woken, but when her body connected with the animal, the baby fell back to sleep. The puppy's tiny heart beats brought on a feeling of relaxation and as the tiny paws placed themselves on her arm, the puppy sank into a slumber. A woman from the tour group watched on hinting for a cuddle, but Serah was not going to wake the small animal again.

Before leaving, the puppy opened her blue eyes so Serah handed her over hoping she would get a peaceful sleep and not be bothered again for a few hours. The large, blue eyes played on Serah's mind as she got back on the vehicle that would take them to their bus. Sitting in her seat, she wondered how she got there without stumbling as she was not thinking straight. Even the grey colour of the cloudy sky that appeared between the dominating green scenery was blue in her mind.

'Everybody off,' stated the tour guide who motioned for them to get onto the other bus.

As Serah walked over, she looked up at the patch of blue sky that was trying to break through. She took it as an omen and told herself that she would be buying the ring as soon as they got back to town.

'There you are,' said Lizette sitting next to Serah. 'I didn't see you on that last contraption.'

She turned to look at Lizette but all she could see was blue. The colour had distorted her vision, so with a different outlook, she went to speak but stopped. The Lizette she was used to looking at had changed—or was it because she had not really looked at her before. She was used to looking at her clothes as Lizette was always immaculately dressed. Now for the first time, she was really looking at her and all she could see was a tall, skinny woman with a face of a lizard. Her skin was cracked to the point that it reminded Serah of scales. She was surprised that she had not noticed it before. Lizette stared at Serah with dark eyes and she quickly looked at her boots.

'Can I get your attention everyone?' called out the tour guide who started with the advertising. Serah wasn't interested as she had a chore of her own to tend to but at least it meant that they were nearly back.

The guide had been advertising a brewery, but what Serah hadn't realised was that they were being dropped off there. Her vision of buying the ring was deteriorating, but not giving up, she asked how far away they were from her destination. They were in walking distance so she left everyone to sample different beers as she took off at a fast pace to where she started when she got off the ship. A few of the shops were closing, which made her heart beat too quickly. Hastening even more, she felt the panic of missing out and cursed herself as she relived the events of the morning.

The shop at the beginning of the main street was in view so she continued on in hope but to no avail. The door was locked with the closed sign firmly placed on the window. She was not meant to have the ring. Lizette had stopped her and she relived the messages she had been given during the day, warning her. One warning had been to be careful of Lizette, the very one who had stopped her from buying the ring that was meant to protect her. Panicking, she wondered what she should do. Would she be safe if Lizette knew that she considered her dangerous? Would it be better to play along with the friendship? Or was it all in her imagination? She didn't know, but the weather was worsening and with the ship in sight she took off to the safety of her cabin.

An announcement came that dinner was ready as she lay on her bed contemplating the day. There were other restaurants she could eat at but the food selection was not as extravagant. And if she didn't turn up for dinner then Lizette would know she was on to her, so she had no choice but to continue on. Serah walked the hallways thinking about her late friend, Sarah Cupsip, and how she would have handled the situation. Was their friendship a mistake and was it supposed to be Sarah Cupsip who crossed paths with Lizette? There were too many things to think about, so Serah erased them from her mind and walked up to her table with a brave smile as she sat next to Lizette. Another chair had been added to their table which turned out to be a lifesaver.

The agitated man had more problems than the whole table put together, which was evident as soon as he sat down. Serah didn't need to speak to Lizette, or anyone else for that matter, as the overbearing man took centre stage when he started to complain about the placing of the cutlery. Loudly, he bellowed for the waiter so he could express his views on etiquette. As Serah listened to him, she looked at her cutlery and how they were in the right positions. She wanted to tell him that he shouldn't open his mouth unless he knew what he was talking about but thought better of it.

His voice took them through their orders and their soup. No one dared say a word; not even Lizette. Instead, they watched in silence as he dragged his spoon towards him to eat his soup then place the spoon on his napkin. With his meal finished, he called out with his mouth full for the waiter to come and remove his bowl. Serah couldn't help herself and made a point of putting her spoon in the bowl the correct way, and to sit back in her chair in silence for the waiter to collect it. The others on the table followed suit and sat back staring at him as the waiter came to collect the bowls. After many thanks were given to the waiter, the man left, realising how ridiculous he had been. Once he was gone, they all laughed and Serah was glad of the entertainment he had provided, but without the presence of that diner Serah was vulnerable. She needed to leave straight after dinner, so once the dessert was over, she proceeded to fake a few yawns and to excuse herself for the rest of the night.

five

The next morning, her wakeup call didn't work, but luckily she woke up early. The ship had docked in Juneau and apparently it was going to be warm, but Serah chose not to believe the announcement and layered herself with a t-shirt, jumper and jacket. She took off to get breakfast and that was when she saw the rain clouds. Instead of going to the gym, she decided to give herself some sustenance and ate heartily, then after shoving her raincoat, hat and gloves into her bag, she took off towards the gangway. The rain hit her face the moment she stepped outside and she wondered how the announcer could get it wrong—surely he must have been looking at it while he was speaking. She didn't care as she had a ring to buy, so Serah put her raincoat to use over her jacket, hoping it would keep her dry as she ran over to the safety of the shops.

A bus waited in the distance to take them on another tour but she had deliberately been early so she could explore alone. The first shop lifted her energy as it sold jewellery, but once inside, her energy subsided as there was not one ring with the blue stone in her size. She walked along looking for another jewellery store but it was not meant to be. What she was meant to do was head towards the bus. Since the raindrops felt lighter, she took off her raincoat, then noticed her wet bag. She probably should have been looking for a waterproof bag instead but there was nothing that would diminish the feeling of hopelessness. So with a heavy heart she dragged herself to the bus where a woman commented on the rain and how they would be looking by the end of the day. Serah didn't have a mirror in her bag but she didn't care about her appearance anyway. Just then, Lizette ran towards her with an umbrella and Serah wondered if she would make it through the day.

'Where did you get to?' called out Lizette.

'I went to look at the shops!' Serah called out, getting into the bus to find a single seat.

'Did you find anything good?' she called out as others let her through to get closer to Serah.

'There was only one street of stores and they didn't differ that much,' said Serah.

'Here's a couple of seats,' Lizette said, taking her arm. 'It's surprising really that the capital of Alaska wouldn't have more shops.'

Serah shrugged her shoulders and looked at her finger lacking the stone that would protect her. She had to stop being negative and try to look at the positive: she was on her way to a close encounter with whales out at sea. She had watched them from the ship but now she was going on a boat so she could see them close up. She tried to forget about everything else and focus on enjoying the whale watching tour.

Lizette laughed. 'We probably won't see any whales. Probably see dolphins, if yesterday's tour is anything to go by. Honestly, yesterday I thought we were seeing huskies not greyhounds.'

Serah wanted to switch off but then the guide announced that a full refund would be given if they didn't see any whales. Serah laughed along with others who had listened to Lizette.

The boat, encased in glass, rocked by the dock waiting for the hundred tourists. With a now dry sky, they eagerly left the bus to stumble into the boat all seeking the best positions to look for humpback whales. The sight of a girl promoting a woollen headband sold by the company reminded Serah that she had a woollen hat in her bag but it was probably wet through. But she soon forgot about that when she spied a few blows of spray which appeared above the water.

'Probably have a few divers underneath pretending to be the spout,' whispered Lizette.

The whales remained out of sight so Serah took off with most of the group to run upstairs, risking freezing her body for a better view. The rest stayed put below and once the whales were in view everyone enjoyed the show provided as the school swam around the boat. Serah was cold but she was away from Lizette and she could listen to the information being given without any added commentary. Whales appeared in full glory and the information stopped but Serah could have sworn she heard someone speak, despite no-one being close by. There was an inner dialogue going on and another warning. Someone was messing with her head— but who?

The whales took off and the next bit of information was to do with items for sale so she bought a nice dry headband and a shawl. Feeling the warmth heal her body, she tuned in to the information that she wasn't sure was quite accurate. They were told of an eagle that had picked up a salmon which was too big, causing the fish to fall onto a plane. The pilots then reported what had happened, and because of the story, the company decided to name the plane "salmon 4 salmon". Apparently, it was the most decorated plane in the world with a picture of a salmon painted on it to commemorate the event. Everyone was impressed with the picture of the plane but how did a salmon really fall onto a plane?

Before anyone could ask, the announcer was telling them how Alaska was bought by the Americans from Russia who had thought it was only covered in trees and wildlife. But then gold was found in Alaska, creating the town that has no way in or out except for planes or boats. The information continued with them being told that the land mass was the largest in USA. Some had questions but the guide didn't stop. Serah presumed it was a diversion while the whales were not appearing. The announcer went on to tell them of how a whale's tongue weighs a tonne and how it uses it to push out the water while the hair-and-nail-like part of their mouth filters in the fish. She was sure he was trying to think of other information to give them when he was rescued by the appearance of a whale that seemed close enough to touch. Finally, the microphone was put away as further whales appeared and entertained the group until it was time to head back.

Their coach picked them up from the blustery dock to take them to a park that had the most amazing glacier. Amazing was the only word Serah could think of but it didn't give it justice. The glaciers through the passage were impressive but the glacier at Juneau was spectacular. The rain returned to a drizzle but that didn't stop all of them walking through the dense forest and over bridges covering the numerous running streams. The tourists were determined, persevering along moss covered stones and ducking branches until finally rewarded by the vision of a mountain of tree tops fading in the mist. They had been told that the view was better with the clouds, as it allowed the blue colour to reflect from the icicles recently frozen. Once they spied part of the glacier, they could see that the blue brought the massive mound of ice to life. Every glimpse of the mass through the trees brought on a feeling of insignificance.

The end of the track brought them closer to the glacier which provided the perfect backdrop to the waterfalls that thundered next to it. Water from different directions led to a lake, taking the broken parts of ice, the size of houses, along their journey. It was as if they had reached the edge of the planet; or it was as if the world was as new. Marvelling at the formation had to be cut short as they were not allowed to be late for the bus, but Serah would have been quite happy staring at it for the rest of the afternoon.

Tourists had been left behind in the past and had had trouble getting back into town, which probably explained why there was an extra person on their coach. The talk on the way back was about the Red Dog Saloon, so when they got there, they stuck their heads inside the establishment and were soon shown to a table. Serah sat, taking in the surroundings that were filled with memorabilia and trophy bears, and up the stairs was the head of the largest moose she had ever seen. Across from her sat Lizette who she had been able to avoid during the walk. With their group squished together around a tiny table, she noticed how crowded the rest of the room was, as everyone who stuck their head in was pushed towards a seat. The staff wanted as many customers as possible, not wanting to miss any in the line of tourists at the door who didn't mind waiting. Soon they were joined by their guide who they thanked for getting them in, especially when they noticed that the line had almost stopped moving as the room was full to capacity. But the entertainer was so amusing, many stayed in the queue or tried to squeeze themselves in when the staff weren't looking and stood around the walls. The comical man played old time tunes on the piano and sang songs that everyone knew and could sing along. He only stopped whenever someone got pulled through the entry door. 'Look who is here!' he kept calling out and although no one knew the person, everyone looked over and cheered.

When the food arrived, it was tasty and satisfying. The owners had made the most of the passing tourist trade by having a merchandise shop in the path to the exit. The logo initially seemed to be an upside-down Alaska but it turned out to be a Scotty dog; the original owner was from Scotland and happened to own a red dog. The dog was on Serah's mind as she walked out with her new t-shirt, and as she closed the door behind her she nearly bumped into a woman walking a husky. Striking up a conversation with the owner, Serah learned the dog's name was Daisy. She was beautiful and liked the attention as Serah patted her soft, thick fur.

There were a couple of hours left before they had to be on the ship, and as they had been dropped off at the end of the street, Serah decided to try her luck with the search for the ring. As she had witnessed in the morning, the stores mainly sold ornaments, but there was nothing else to do so she took off to be alone and wandered through the aisles that would eventually lead her back to the gangway.

The stores mainly sold the same items but there were a few that had handmade products which made everything else look as if it was a reproduction from China. A small totem pole with a story of mankind from a raven to an eagle stood out, but when she walked past another handmade one that was taller than she was, she had to rethink her options. Whilst thinking, Serah came across another one made from a whale bone that put all the others to shame. The price was astronomical so she decided she would look for the maker on the internet to cut out the middle man. Of course she knew she never would, but it did stop her from spending money she didn't have.

The sculptures made of whale bone had an advantage as they were light, so when she came across one in a shape of a bear it brought up the whole scenario again of what to buy. The sculptures distracted her from the ring, but in the end she didn't buy anything and only managed to get back to the ship with just minutes to spare. However, there wasn't a need to rush as thirty-three passengers were running even later than she was and had not yet returned.

Dinner was a formal affair that she nearly missed as her feet were tired from a full day of being on the move. She lay on her bed listening to the announcement that lobster was included on the dinner menu, so she put on her high heels to walk to a dining room she still had trouble finding. Lizette was already there with a couple of women from their group who visited the glacier. Thankfully, the Asian man with the bad manners had been replaced by an English couple. Serah sat down looking at the menu, trying to be inconspicuous, but her Italian dress—a present from Sarah Cupsip—stood out.

Comments were made regarding her colourful clothing but the attention soon turned to Lizette who was commenting on the lobster. The others followed her choice, but since she had stolen the conversation, Serah decided to retaliate and chose the fish instead. Surprisingly, despite the spite, her choice had been a good one and she was sure her taste buds moaned when she finished the dish. With the meal over, satisfied diners discussed their disbelief of how it was possible for the staff to serve twelve thousand meals a day that were hot, fresh and full of flavour.

The dining room emptied and, after chatting to the couple from England for two hours, they parted so Serah could go the library to write down the day's events. She was happy to end the day with writing as she was sure if she had waited until the next day then she would have forgotten moments she wanted to remember. With the last sentence, she looked around at the empty room. The clock on the wall showed it was nearly midnight so she looked out of the windows of darkness to see if the green ghost was there, but all she could see was the raindrops on the glass. Not wanting to give up, Serah downloaded a picture from Google images and found out that she was travelling at the wrong time of year to see the spectacular event.

six

The next day, the stop was at Ketchikan which apparently was the first town in Alaska. Serah had heard so many stories that varied from town to town, she was not really sure which one was accurate. But there was one thing she knew for sure and that was Lizette was happy to leave her alone. When she had left the dining room the night before, Lizette had not followed, so Serah put it down to her fascination with the English couple. Finally, she was going to be rid of the messages and there was no need for her to buy a ring for protection. Feeling better about herself, she headed for the gym to try to burn off the intake of food from the previous meal.

With her exercise finished, she headed down the gangway to find an Aquaduck where a comedian of a tour guide assured her that the stories he was telling were true. Really, Serah didn't care, but she climbed on board as she listened to him tell of an ancient tribe. He spoke of them as if they had gone, but Serah was not sure if that was accurate as they seemed to still be around. Why was he not able to see them? She didn't ask and let him continue with the story of the Americans who came looking for gold and had created towns and brothels. The gold rush, the cannery of salmon and the logging industry came and went, leaving behind only evidence of deterioration, but the brothels survived. Fortunately, there were tourists who provided compensation for their lack of income, but unfortunately the locals could not see the full opportunity that existed. During the quiet times on the Aquaduck, she heard a familiar conversation amongst the passengers. They all wanted something unique or authentic to the area to take home as a souvenir. So far, every stop sold mostly the same things that looked as if they could be bought at a junk shop. Every now and then something stood out but it cost thousands of dollars. There was definitely a market there for Alaskan products, so why weren't the locals creating them? Again, she didn't ask but she probably should have put it out there! But it wasn't necessary as the tour guide must have read her mind. He went on to explain about the tribe that made authentic totem poles which were sold at the end of the road.

As the weather was fine, a group of them disregarded the comments made by other tourists that it rained every day in Ketchikan. They watched others put on their raincoats as the duck hit the water but, like Serah, they continued to leave their coats in their bags. The sky was blue and she felt the warmth on her face, but it was short lived, as moments later she felt the wind and knew the weather would change. The temperature had dropped quickly but thoughts of being cold left her when she saw the eagle sitting near the salmon factory waiting for the dregs to be thrown out. Younger eagles sat near their mothers as they watched the mature birds fly about the water's edge. Without the narration, she would not have known that the younger birds were related as they were larger with brown, fluffy feathers and a face far less aggressive.

The commentary continued, providing an answer as to why there were staircases of a hundred or more steps between the houses. It turned out that they were considered streets that had names. As most people didn't need cars, they were used to walking everywhere, including the stepped roadways. It was a steep climb along the stairways to get to the houses and as the narrator said, you only forget your keys once! Serah didn't know how they did it, especially in the winter and as it rained most of the time, they would be permanently inside a raincoat. It was an eye-opener as to how others lived, and for a moment she felt grateful for her life in Australia. At the end of the tour she found other people looking for the tribal carvings so they all took the bus, and twenty minutes later they were at the end of the road on the outskirts of town.

The smell of wild flowers and cut timber filled the air. Although the information centre was closed, a small wooden box provided a map of the walk through the forest to where the totem poles were placed. With directions in hand, Serah took in the breathtaking scenery and walked alone along a trail surrounded by the new growth in amongst old trees that towered up above. Green moss covered what had fallen providing something colourful in a dark place. It was a peaceful walk and when she inhaled the smell of the cut down timber, she knew she was close to the building that was used by the locals. The information on the map told of a building that was created with cut down trunks and was large enough to hold a totem pole that was as tall as the trees in the forest.

Serah's imagination ran wild as she followed the signs to where a large structure stood out between the enchanted forest. With eyes lit up, she took in the changed surroundings and wished the doors were open, as inside the construction was a pole which was being restored. The pamphlet explained that a totem pole will start to deteriorate after seventy-five years, so she tried to imagine someone carving into the large trunk all those years ago. From what she could see, it looked interesting but it was closed and no one was around. So Serah followed the trail to find other totem poles standing high in the air, covered with symbolism. The walk was interesting but not long enough as she found herself back at the start without any sign of the shop that the guide had mentioned.

The others who had taken the trail waited at the bus stop but Serah was agitated and needed to explore some more, so she walked around the corner and finally found the building that sold the carvings. She had begun to think it didn't exist but was glad to find it did as it looked interesting, but when she walked towards the door she found the shopkeeper closing up. He had just turned off the lights and didn't want to turn them back on. There were at least six sales he could have made as she knew the others were looking for something authentic, but he wasn't interested and continued to ignore her as he locked up.

A voice calling out alerted her to the arrival of the bus and she climbed aboard to get a first-hand look at the locals. Serah generally took people as they came; after all, everyone was different, even in Serah's small life. However, she was pushed to the limit with this bus trip. Firstly, one girl kept getting on and off the bus because she couldn't make up her mind where to go. Then another man who was so huge he took up two seats, refused to move for elderly tourists. She thought she had seen the worst of the locals but then another girl used her baby to push her way to get to the back of the bus instead of asking to be excused, while a couple argued very loudly about not having any trust. For a moment, she wondered if it was part of an act but then she spotted the shopkeeper hiding at the back of the bus, probably because he had closed the shop early.

Despite the ugliness of the bus ride, Alaska was the place of beauty she had seen publicised on the television. Tourists viewing the place with fresh eyes could see the splendour, but it seemed that most of the locals were stuck. There was a feeling of negativity beyond the tourist town which made her wonder what they really thought of the outsiders. As with anywhere, there were exceptions to the rule and some locals were positive, but even Serah's energy level lowered when the beauty of the trees opened up to show everything that had been left to deteriorate. Beyond the forests were homes that were not maintained and whatever was put down on the ground was left there. But then it was impossible to have any pride in their belongings when there was none for themselves. She hoped that things would change for them so she decided to help the economy by buying fish and chips before shopping.

In the morning, she had smelt the vinegar and salt in the air on her way to the Aquaduck, but when she got to her destination she was disappointed to find yet another shop shut. The smell still lingered so, still craving seafood, she headed to the Fish Pirate Saloon. The lift that took customers up to the restaurant promptly returned down to the ground floor without allowing anyone to get out. Unperturbed by the faulty contraption, she went back up to find it also closed for the night. Giving up, she decided to head back to the ship for food, planning on returning to the town to shop later. As she sat down to a three-course meal, she forgot about the smell of the fish and chips. Instead she watched the rain hit the windows and sank into the comfortable chair to consume a meal she could not fault. Serah looked around the room, sipping on her wine, thinking about how her eyes had been opened to a different life. She had lived in her own little world and hadn't thought there was anything different outside of her own space.

There were many nationalities on board, and to recognise whether peculiarities pertained to the person or the whole civilization was difficult. This was especially so when a group of Polynesians were allowing their children to run wild. There was no consideration for the other diners, which she found hard to understand as there was a lido deck for kids to eat and play, so why did they bring them into the dining room to bother others? She observed as the bored children ran and yelled while others glared. She waited for someone to say something but they didn't. The whole situation had become her entertainment so she opted out of shopping and continued to sip on her wine until her eyelids could no longer stay open.

seven

It wasn't necessary to wake up early the next morning as the ship was at sea. They were on their way back to Vancouver and it seemed as if the captain had put the ship into top gear. An announcement was made to remind them that they were not at port and she was sure the crew wanted them to sleep in because a mention of whales not being around was included in the information. Serah didn't believe him so she had her breakfast outside.

The grey sky turned to blue, filling her with hope, and as she looked out to sea, she watched as whales came alongside them.

'I knew they would be here,' said Lizette as she pulled on a chair to sit opposite Serah.

Serah acknowledged her, knowing that their time together was coming to an end.

'When we get to Vancouver another adventure begins,' Lizette said, staring out to sea.

'What adventure?' Serah asked, despite knowing she shouldn't encourage her.

'We take the bus tour to Calgary,' Lizette announced, touching Serah's arm. 'Have you forgotten?'

Serah hadn't forgotten about the tour, but she had forgotten she would be on it with Lizette. There was no escaping her. Some things couldn't be escaped. Then Serah remembered the family who she had considered badly behaved, yet apparently that was normal for them. Suddenly, she felt judgemental as there must have been others who found her to be odd. She looked at Lizette with different eyes and reverted to seeing her as she did when they first met. The face of a lizard disappeared and she went back to seeing her good fashion sense. Serah was not going to avoid her any longer and she was not going to let this woman dictate her holiday. Serah had her own mind and she was going to use it.

'I have to go,' said Lizette standing up. 'I'm late for a seaweed wrap at the spa.'

'Sounds interesting,' Serah said, sipping on her coffee.

'I had a seaweed bath in Ireland at the beginning of the year,' said Lizette. 'I visited a spa where you slipped into a bath where seaweed sat as if in a teacup. Sounds strange, doesn't it, but putting up with the slimy feeling was worth it because I glowed for days.'

Lizette left as Serah wondered what should be on her own agenda for the day. There were options; she could have sat around and relaxed or she could experience something new, so she went to the spa to enquire about a seaweed wrap.

For some reason, she expected the receptionist to say they were booked out, but instead she asked Serah to follow her into a room to lie on a massage table. A green substance covered her body as she lay there wondering why she would copy Lizette. The feeling was unpleasant initially, but she had to remain still so she closed her eyes and listened to the sounds of the whales coming out of the speakers. They helped her to relax as she allowed herself to be pampered. Her scalp was massaged and reflexology was performed on her feet. Serah could have stayed there for hours but someone else was booked in after her so she had to get up and take a shower to remove the green substance that had dried like mud to her body.

'Very relaxing,' Serah mentioned to the receptionist as she walked past to leave.

'It is, isn't it?' she answered. 'The solution sinks into your skin and makes you feel fantastic.'

The receptionist was about to give the sales pitch so Serah stopped her before she could go on. 'I meant the background noise of the whales!'

'There was no background noise,' said the receptionist, looking at Serah with confusion.

'I thought I heard something when I was in the room,' Serah said feeling stupid.

She shook her head and replied, 'Just silence.'

'Must have been my imagination,' Serah said, leaving before the girl could say anything else.

The discussion played on her mind as she headed back to the cabin but was forgotten when she remembered she was leaving for another tour and would require clean clothes. On the ship, she had not thought about washing her clothes as there was a service available, but she knew that travelling by coach would be different. The present moment was her only opportunity to do the washing so she went in search of the laundry.

What she thought was an easy task ended up being a comedy of errors as everyone else had decided they needed their clothes washed at that same time. With three laundry rooms and a lot of disorganised guests there was bound to be a problem, which she realised when she hit the first laundry and found it full. Still being calm at that point she strolled with her bag of clothes to the next one where a woman ran in front of her and placed one item in the last machine. Still unperturbed she headed for the third laundry and managed to get a machine, but she didn't have the right change. Serah knew it was likely someone would steal her machine, but then again, she hadn't taken the one that the woman had placed one item in. She had to risk it, and luckily her clothes were still in the machine when she got back.

With her washing done she thought she would have nothing further to do, but it was becoming one of those days where nothing ran smoothly. Serah vowed to herself if she ever travelled again she would be more organised with the washing and do it the day before, because when she got back to her cabin, she noticed that some of the clothes weren't as dry as she had thought. So reluctantly Serah had no choice but to head back to the laundry to throw them back in the dryer.

After trying all three laundries, she realised there was no way she would be able to find an available dryer. Her opportunity with the machines had passed, so she had to come up with another plan. Back in her cabin she took out the hangers in the small cupboard and found as many places as possible to hang up her clothing. Her cabin had now become a Chinese laundromat. As she closed the door to her room, she hoped they would dry in the stagnant air as she couldn't visualise the clothes hanging in the coach.

Glad to be away from the room, she made her way to the secluded spot to sort out her vouchers for the following day. When she had first looked at them at the beginning of the trip, she had spent too long going over which ones she needed to keep and which ones she could throw out. Seasoned travellers would have been organised but she was new to the game so she wanted to be ready for the following day and have all the vouchers she needed in order.

Feeling more organised, she sat back to take in the surroundings of the people enjoying their last day at the bar when she was joined by two couples who she had associated with on and off during tours from the docks. They were characters, and she gladly sat listening to them tell her stories of their lives back in New York and Florida. One of them pointed out how the same people on the cruise kept interacting with each other although there were over a thousand passengers. It was odd that they hadn't really had a routine, yet they crossed paths with the same faces. That was when she noticed that Lizette wasn't at the table. Lizette was an experienced traveller so Serah thought she would be completely organised but maybe she was busy filling out the form that was being handed out. Serah hadn't expected a survey and wanted to throw it away. She spied one woman with a pile of brochures who was looking for a quiet place to relive her experience. Serah knew that some passengers would take it seriously but she had had enough of looking at papers, so she pushed hers aside as she lifted her glass of wine.

'Not filling out the form?' asked one of the group, lifting up her glass.

'Maybe, but not now,' Serah said, taking a look at the menu of snacks.

'It's the fourth of July,' stated the rambunctious man from Florida, 'and we should be at the dining room.'

At first Serah thought it was too early but time had passed quickly, so she followed her American friends to find a dining room filled to capacity. Alcohol-infused diners entertained the room as she looked at a menu with too much to choose from.

'Service will be slow tonight,' said the wife of the man from Florida.

'I'm not in any rush anyway,' Serah said. 'I can't decide what to eat. I feel like trying everything because it's the last night but I'm worried I won't be able to fit into my jeans tomorrow. I did manage to get to the gym today and I put the treadmill on the highest incline but I don't know if it's helped.'

'You're on holiday,' replied the woman with a nudge. 'Order the lot!'

Unfortunately, she had managed to influence Serah because when the waiter came, she ordered too many dishes including a spicy dish that burnt her mouth. She was sure she ate nearly every bread roll on the table to help her taste buds regain composure before her chatty friend gave her some nuts to help with the heat.

With more food than normal to sample and the banter of her American friends to occupy her, she hadn't noticed how quickly the time had gone by. The last time she had looked out of the window it had been a blue sky but now it was pitch black. It was her last chance to see the northern lights and Serah looked up into the darkness but saw nothing.

eight

The disembarkation process was unexpected as they were rounded up through hallways and corridors and lined up like sheep to pay their bill for the alcohol and then show their passports to re-enter Canada. Being Australian meant Serah had to line up in the large queue which gave her time to think about all the money she had wasted on drinks. She needed to be careful with her money for the rest of the trip or she would end up without any.

Eventually her passport was stamped and she was set free from the ship. That's when déjà vu hit her. As she walked across the road from the dock to her hotel, she couldn't believe that a week had gone by so quickly. The building she had stayed in was undergoing a facelift when she had left and now a week later, it was just about done. So much had been achieved but what had she done? She felt like doing something exciting, and after watching the seaplanes continuously land and take off she went to find out about taking a ride in one.

The concierge passed her pamphlets over the bench but as it dawned on her the experience would involve heights, her need for excitement diminished, so she informed him that he could put them away. She needed to do something else so she decided to watch the planes for a while at a closer distance to see if her courage could be sufficiently mustered to get on one. She watched them take off from the water as she walked along the concrete path that took her beside the water's edge. The blue sky highlighted the surroundings of mountains in the distance which would provide a magnificent view from the plane's window. As Serah got nearer she listened to the people chat in excitement as they waited in line to take their flights. There was no reason for her not to go but as she sat in a chair to contemplate her actions, she knew it wasn't going to happen. Being up high had always been a struggle. For some reason, she always felt a need to jump to her destiny below. Instead of a plane trip, she probably would have been better with skydiving but her fear was too great so she sat firmly in her comfortable chair to observe the planes from the ground instead.

Serah's attention was caught by the unusual shoes on the woman sitting beside her, and as there were such a variety of people in Vancouver, she didn't think anything about striking a conversation. So far everyone had been friendly, but this woman didn't want to continue a discussion. Maybe she was contemplating taking a flight, so Serah turned away from her, but as she did she was struck with the realisation that this woman was not like everyone else. Serah heard the chair scratch the floor as the woman went to leave, but she wasn't expecting her to put her hand on Serah's shoulder to tell her that the shoes were comfortable and that she should be careful and not turn her back on anyone. Serah wanted to respond but the words wouldn't come out and before they had a chance to, the lady had gone.

Serah felt this was her cue to move on so she walked around the gas light district with historical buildings which helped to distract her. The more Serah walked, the better she felt, and when she found a shop filled with cowboy boots, she completely forgot about the woman and her warning. Boots of every shape and colour stood in rows, and with the mention of them being half price, Serah knew she had to get a pair. This time she didn't have Lizette telling her to wait for something better or beating her to the purchase, so she let her instincts take over and picked the pair that drew her attention first. The black suede fitted comfortably around her foot and with the boot being cut off at the ankle, she wouldn't get too hot if the temperature increased. Serah looked down at the pointed toes and embroidery as she walked around the shop, and she left them on to head back to the hotel.

Feeling good about herself, she walked the long way back to the accommodation and as she had spent many hours walking, she felt she deserved a soak in the jacuzzi that looked so inviting. It didn't take long for her to get there, but once her foot was immersed, she knew she would not be soaking. Disappointed, Serah tried again but it was at boiling point. She sat back on the lounge to take in the sun instead, knowing she should have told a staff member. A woman went to put her children in and Serah told her that if she put an egg in it, it would cook. Despite the warning the mother still contemplated it, so Serah knew then she had to warn the staff.

By the time a sign had been put up advising people not to use the jacuzzi, it was time for dinner. Down the street was a variety of restaurants filled with people. Tourists blended in with the locals, all overflowing onto the streets. Vancouver was a beautiful city with plants everywhere, covering shops hidden inside old buildings, and a mountain of snow standing in the background. Someone took care of the city, but no one took care of the homeless people—they were everywhere. Their stench filled the air, giving the surrounds a negative outlook. Serah needed a change of scenery. She knew it was not possible for her to help the situation; what was really needed was a homeless shelter.

She ended up in an Italian restaurant that certainly changed her mood. The smell of the filth was replaced by the delicious odour of garlic, and the owner, who was quite a character, provided the entertainment. Music filled the atmosphere and the laughter of others brought a smile to her face. Gigantic meals were served, but were unfortunately followed by an astronomical bill, which she only realised after she had placed her order. She couldn't eat the bowl of pasta and when they offered a take away bag she should have taken it as she could have given it to one of the homeless. However, the thought didn't occur to her until too late. Before retiring to bed, she made a note to herself to next time order soup and as she slipped under the blankets she felt herself drift away towards another dream-filled slumber.

By the time morning had arrived Serah had already foreseen a change, but she told herself it had only been a dream. So with a packed bag she checked out of the Fairmont Hotel to move to the Renaissance Hotel as per the booking of the next tour. The Renaissance was only a few streets away, so with her cowboy boots on she walked along, excited about the adventure up ahead. However, when she found her new accommodation, she felt as if the standards had been lowered and hoped that it wasn't a reflection on the tour. The hotel would have been nice in its day but an attempt to renovate it hadn't worked. The saying that 'you can't make jam out of pig poo,' came to mind, but then who was she to judge? Outside, the contrast was evident with Lamborghinis and Ferraris speeding through the clean streets that were filled with colourful flowers. Women were dressed immaculately and dogs of all sorts were everywhere, but surprisingly there was no poo anywhere to be seen. She shouldn't judge a book by its cover so she went inside with an open mind to find a welcoming lobby. The receptionist greeted her with information about her tour, and as she wasn't due to meet the guide until the evening, the girl provided her with information of things she could do to fill in her day.

With a map in her hand, she headed to a place that hired bicycles. As she walked, her enthusiasm dropped when she realised she must have taken a wrong turn. The beauty that Serah was previously admiring had disappeared. There were still the upmarket shops but every now and then she was struck by a bad odour as she passed a homeless person. One man did have the honesty to hold a sign stating that he wanted money because he was lazy. Serah put away her map as she didn't want to look like a tourist and eventually she found herself near the bike hire shop.

Half of Canada was out, which apparently was normal in the summer. With her hired bike, she walked over to take off on a ten-mile trip around an island that had many pathways for bikes, people and roller-blades. It had been a while since she had ridden a bike, and she wished she had a warning sign on it for others to read as she was sure she would crash into someone. There were too many people to wait for a large gap so she braved the track taking in the coastline view which was spectacular. A breeze cooled her face as she rode the paths that took her through different areas including a public pool with slides, a beach area with logs for bonfires, gardens filled with flowers, and parks. The ride took her back to the hire shop where she was glad to give back that means of transport due to her aching body.

The walk back to the hotel was a welcome relief after hours on a bike, but she was still sore. At the time it had seemed a good idea to go for a bike ride and her brain had agreed but her body had been against it from the start. So she suffered and when it was time for the talk by the tour guide, she wasn't sure if she would be able to sit. Instead, Serah came up with another plan, and made a late entry to stand at the back of the room. It seemed plausible and would have worked but as soon as she entered the lobby, Lizette called out for Serah to sit with her. Lizette was there early to get a good seat and insisted that it was important for Serah to join her. Begrudgingly, Serah did as she was told whilst feeling angry that she couldn't make up her own mind; but Lizette had saved her a seat so what was she meant to do? Like a lost lamb, she followed Lizette inside a room filled with people. Fortunately, the chairs had comfortable cushions, Serah observed as she followed her companion to the front of the room like a sheep to the slaughter. Lizette had reserved two seats by throwing her jacket and shopping bags on them. Once comfortable, Serah looked around the room at the rest of the group which comprised of a variety of people. They weren't what she expected as she knew the tour held adventurous activities and some didn't look up to it. The guide, a man in his thirties with a fit physique, made himself known and started off by discussing the bike tour in the morning. Serah didn't know what to think, but she knew that the part of her sitting on the cushion was not impressed. She looked around to see who was moaning and smiled at the ones who were in worse shape than she was.

nine

It was early morning when they left Vancouver, and with heavy eyelids Serah followed Lizette to a coach where everyone had already claimed their seats. Somehow Lizette had managed to take the front seats which became apparent when Serah finally got to leave her suitcase with the driver to climb on board. Lizette was looking right at her as she moved up the stairs, so there was no other choice but to accept the hand gesture for Serah to sit next to her. It was not for Serah to complain, as she did have a good view of the scenery that grew wilder and more beautiful the further out they drove.

Although she had to endure Lizette's company, she didn't have to listen to her as they had a guide who was providing a continuous commentary. She sat back into the padded seat and listened as he mentioned that the bike tour had been cancelled. Cheers brought the sleepy passengers back to life and once the noise had subsided, he then went on to state that they would be changing the seating arrangements the next day. Lizette let out a groan along with the other couple that sat across the aisle who had gone to great effort to commandeer their seats.

Their first stop was at an old mine that was now a museum. It was tastefully displayed and authentic looking, which explained why it was a popular location for making movies. It had also been used as a background in the television show, X files, and she could see why as they got on the rickety old train that took them into a mountain. She had expectations of going down underground, but the tour organisers had taken into consideration the people who had phobias. The darkness and small surrounding tunnels showed an interesting way of life from the past and brilliant colours of blue from the water running over the copper brought back a vision of her protective ring.

It had been an interesting visit, but with more to see they left to visit their next stop. The sinking seat on the coach provided comfort and with the life of a miner and the topaz ring on her mind, the time passed quickly. She had heard the mention of wilderness but wasn't focused on the scenery, so when the tour guide stated they had arrived at their next destination, she was surprised.

Whistler was unbelievably beautiful with mountains that held large slopes of green. During the winter, the slopes would have been covered with snow but for now they were being used by people on mountain bikes. Up above the activities, the snow remained on the highest peaks and chairlifts ran for people who wanted to catch a lift to the gondola in the sky.

The guide explained that part of the tour was to ride in the gondola that took the tourists from one mountain to another. Unfortunately, there was an electrical storm on its way so they couldn't go on, which was fine with Serah; there was no way she was going up there. Instead, the bike ride was back on, which seemed a better option to Serah and thought others would have agreed.

'You would rather ride a metal bike in an electrical storm than go on the gondola,' said a chubby man in a sarcastic tone.

Serah had obviously drawn attention with her relief of not being able to go to the top of the mountains. 'I definitely would,' Serah replied with a grin.

Quickly, Serah found her raincoat, which was needed as the raindrops were beginning to fall. A couple of ladies backed out, blaming the sound of thunder, but others thought it was because they were wearing dresses. Some who had complained the night before about the ride being cancelled were on their bikes and with Serah's sore behind, she put her foot on the pedal and joined in on the ride. She could have joined the ladies with the dresses but she was glad she didn't because the track was smooth and the wilderness around the lake was incredible. There was only one casualty which was a woman who crashed into the trees, but apart from that they all made it back, albeit covered in mud.

As a reward for putting up with the weather, they were given extra time outside to explore the place where the winter Olympics had once been. The authenticity of the place was inconceivable as it looked as if it had been removed from a Swiss ski resort and dropped in Whistler. The shops ranged in prices and people from all over the world blended in with the bike riders of extreme sports. Although there were only a few rubbish bins, the streets were clean. Locals walked their dogs which were welcomed everywhere. In one shop, a lady tried on shoes while the dog guarded her bag. Serah imagined the disgusted reaction of people back in Melbourne if a dog had appeared in a supermarket. It was certainly interesting to see how others lived.

Avoiding a rain shower meant that Serah had been able to escape Lizette for a short while, but being on a bus tour was different to the ship as they were now like one large family. Many of the others had stopped for a chat whilst Serah had looked around, and she hoped they would be a distraction when it came to Lizette. So far, her companion's attention had indeed been diverted. Even inside the coach, Lizette had to be quiet as Serah, along with everyone else, was listening to the information the tour guide was providing. It was a good change, but it ended when it came to dinner.

Serah thought the meals would be at restaurants where they would be provided with what was on the menu. She was no longer on a ship that catered to her every culinary whim, which had been dangerous for her waistline. With some trepidation she sat in what looked like a normal restaurant, but the food that came out was as if it had been made on the ship. It was a welcoming feast for the group, but it was a reality that she would definitely need to diet after the holiday.

Going to bed on a full stomach was not what she wanted, so she made a mental note to herself again to stick to soup or salad at dinner. However, when she woke in the morning she knew that her willpower would weaken, which it did as chocolates were passed around on the coach. Giving up, Serah chewed on a sumptuous selection as the coach made its way towards Kamloops where gradually the scenery changed from green trees to mountainous rock. The ice had melted, creating falls of fresh water that gushed beside and underneath them towards lakes of brilliant blue. The weather was warming up outside but the water would have been freezing. She looked outside the window from a different aspect as everyone had been given new seats on the coach. Along with the change of scenery was the change of people surrounding her. She had become accustomed to the young woman who spoke as if a peg had been put on her nose and constantly used the word 'like' in every sentence as she laid back with her phone to take photos of herself. Today there was a new personality to contend with in a form of a teenage boy whom Serah made the mistake of telling that she was looking for bears. Being someone who knew everything, he continually pointed out things to her that were not bears. After a while she focused her attention on the man across the aisle, an older man who constantly chewed on a toothpick. The only time he didn't chew was when he was quizzing people. At the mine he had asked so many questions, everyone thought that he was looking at running his own dig, then he lost all credibility when the demonstration at the table became too much for him and he went from asking questions to grabbing items. At the time the group had waited in expectation that he might jump over the table, and now Serah waited back while be got off the coach so she could be sure to avoid him.

Apparently, the jade was mined locally and although the statues in the shops were expensive, the tour guide assured them that they were cheap to produce. He told the group that a community of monks in Thailand had commissioned a huge Buddha to be made from a single piece of jade and that the monks requested the shipping to be included in the price. Since small statues were selling for thousands of dollars, everyone presumed that it would have cost at least a million for the Buddha to be produced and transported, but apparently, it was only in the hundreds of thousands of dollars. Was he trying to tell everyone that it should be cheaper to buy a small one? Their confused faces must have prompted him because they found themselves back on the coach and in search of cheaper statues.

The coach pulled up opposite the shop that sold the jade where it was mined but it was closed. A member of the group noticed that there was another establishment a few blocks down so, ignoring the heat they took off in hope of a bargain. It was open. The wares inside included statues of bears, but unfortunately they cost thousands of dollars, so Serah decided she needed to look at wooden carved bears instead. Her statement prompted the discussion back to live bears which everyone searched for as they drove to their next stop.

Serah looked at her cowboy boots as she got off the coach and knew she would fit in when they stopped at a ranch that was owned during the gold rush times by the MacLean family. The guide explained that MacLean was a Scotsman who had married a native girl and had built the ranch for his eleven children. As years went by it had changed from a home to a hotel for the travelling workers. A day's pay at that time had been a dollar, and to sleep in the warmth you had to part with your pay. At the bar, a small glass of alcohol would have cost twenty-five cents and as the workers were short on cash they would leave one bullet from their gun instead as it was the same value. That, claimed the guide, was where the saying "give me a shot" came from.

There were many rooms left in their original condition with one room being more extravagant than the rest. In that particular room was an old bed that had a chest next to it with a rounded lid. It had belonged to a wealthy gentleman who did not want trunks put on top of his so he had cleverly devised a lid that was not flat. The house held many stories and in the dining room, one hundred-year-old dishes still sat on the table in perfect condition. They had been transported in molasses to stop them from being damaged and then, once cleaned of the syrup, were put to use. Mr MacLean died and despite everything he had done for his community, his wife was not accepted because she was not pure Anglo Saxon. So sadly, she sold the ranch and her children went in different directions. After that, the ranch changed hands every ten years until the Canadian government took it over and opened it as a museum.

The property apparently looked the same as it did in its day. A stage coach pulled by two Clydesdales turned up to carry the group around the grounds. The horses had been rescued and now were a picture of health. Serah climbed to the top of the coach from where she got a view of the other horses and a miniature donkey named Frazzle. He was a stallion who was always getting into mischief. As they paused for a look around she desperately wanted to cuddle Frazzle. With a carrot in her hand, she made her way to the fence as close to him as she could get but he wouldn't budge from his shade and she didn't blame him.

After leaving him, she joined the others to listen to a native who spoke about their heritage. His story was the same as the American Indians but that was because they were all tribes on a chunk of land that originally came from Siberia. He told how when the English wanted to escape the lifestyle of England, they ended up in America and they would have died of starvation if it had not been for a tribe showing them how to grow corn and how to live off the land. The new people integrated but at some point, war started and the Indians were forced into Canada to escape. Tribes were still in existence which made Serah wonder who the real Canadians were. There were many who looked as if they were crossed with American Indians and Asians. Then there were Anglo Saxons, especially females who had olive skin, blonde hair and seemed to be taller than others. But then again everyone at home was mixed so why not there! So far, everyone seemed to get along in Canada so that's all that mattered.

With historical information being the topic of conversation, they took off again, leaving Kamloops behind with also an explanation for the heat. It was part of the valley that went through Death Valley in the USA, down into Mexico. The temperature was hot, but apparently, the week before it was hotter. She hoped the heat was trapped between the masses of rock as the next day they were moving up into the Rockies where it should cool down.

ten

Serah was getting used to getting up early and leaving her suitcase by the door to eat breakfast. Lizette and some others had saved her a seat but it wasn't necessary as the food was non-existent. This was unexpected as up to now they had been spoiled with a range of foods, so after a bowl of cereal, a demand was made for a stop at the next restaurant. Not wanting a mutiny, the tour guide managed a short stop at a quiet café on the roadside that instantly became full to the brim due to the group's lack of sustenance. Thanks to her forward friend, Serah was one of the first out with a bacon and egg toasted sandwich. Lizette had her benefits at times, so Serah couldn't begrudge her wanting to walk together to explore an antique shop made from large logs.

The building was a pickers' dream with an overflow of stuff spilling out onto the grass at the front. Every second-hand ornament imaginable filled the interior, which excited Serah as it brought the possibility of stumbling upon a carved bear. Thoughts went through her mind as to what was in store but the images had to stay inside her head due to a sign on the door that stated it was closed for a few minutes. Not being able to buy something led Serah back to food and they made their way back to the café with minutes to spare to get a coffee and cake to go.

Once inside the coach, a few told of how they had managed a quick look inside the antique shop. It had opened while some were buying their coffee and cake. Serah cursed that she had not waited, but was glad when she heard that everything was too expensive. With relief, she sipped on her hot drink as they headed off towards Jasper.

Luckily a lid had been put on her cup; she had a feeling the coach driver was not impressed with their breakfast stop as he drove erratically, all the time complaining about being behind schedule. He blamed the slow vehicles on the road, especially the RVs which he called "road viruses". They listened to him grumble but in the end, it was for nothing as the group made it to the waterfall on time.

Placing her empty cup in the bin, Serah took in the sound of the water falling. Lizette had already gone on with the others but Serah was in a trance. The sound spoke to her and again she heard the warning to be careful. Her mind was playing tricks on her and she was not going to let it stop her from enjoying her holiday. Lizette had become bearable since Serah had changed her outlook on life so she refused to let anything else interfere. So to stop the sound, Serah hurried on to join the others who were watching the waterfall that fell into a large crack. She was not sure if the water had dug it out or if it was that they had driven so high into the mountains that a small crack could look like a deep opening. Either way it was unexpected and spectacular to witness, and as they listened to nature's fury, the guide rounded them up like sheep to get to their next stop on time.

As the destination was for lunch at Robson there were no complaints about rushing. There was something about moving water that brought on hunger but all thoughts of food disappeared when, arriving at the restaurant, Serah looked up at the large, steep rock that reached into the clouds. Mother Nature had put on a display that outdid the waterfall. Serah watched in awe as she swallowed her lunch, wondering how the formation could have been created over the years. It was mind boggling and after a while she felt a stiff neck that complained about looking up for far too long. It was time to get back on the coach and back to swivelling her head from side to side to look for bears.

Their time spent searching paid off as they found a moose, an elk and finally, Serah saw a brown bear in the distance. The others wouldn't believe her as the coach had stopped in front of the tree that the animal was behind. Bear spotting had become a comical sport that infuriated the driver who was making too many stops due to everyone telling him to pull over whenever they thought they saw a bear.

It was a situation where the hilarity only made things worse, as the driver's frustration at getting behind schedule escalated. However, when they were pulled over by the police for a safety check, the driver gave up. There was no choice but to wait as the coach was checked over but Serah felt sorry for some horses that had to wait in the trailer on the other side of the road. Luckily the trailer was set up with windows for the horses and once opened, they provided the group with entertainment as they stuck their heads out to see what was going on.

The stop had been longer than necessary, according to the driver, but somehow it made no difference as they ended up at the white water rafting yet again on time. Life jackets were handed to them as they despatched from the coach, and after a quick safety talk they were placed into rafts. The surroundings looked calm with water that ran from the ice, and as her body sank into the raft Serah took in the clear shade of blue that blended into the green surroundings. The guide explained of the eighteen hours it took for the water to get to the river, and how a few years previously a large chunk of ice broke loose and created a tidal wave that ran down the river and covered the tree tops. Serah looked up at the trees and visualised the water being that high, thinking the life jackets would not be able to save them if that happened right now.

She was being negative, but was saved by a boy who screamed with delight every time they hit a ripple. Everyone laughed along at his excitement that lasted for over an hour. When the ride was over, warm towels thawed their bodies, and with a deep breath of fresh air, Serah went back to the warm coach to head to their hotel.

The staff at their accommodation were expecting them, and with a chef to oversee the proceedings, everyone knew they were in for a feast. After dinner, with full stomachs the group sat back in the comfortable chairs to listen to a woman speak about the bears. She explained about Jasper being a national park with a town in the middle, and of the forest that covered eleven thousand acres and held only two hundred grizzly bears. Locals were working on helping the bears to exist, but their latest problem was the picnic sites. The sites had been cleared of trees allowing in the sunlight which helped the berry trees to flourish. These berries were a staple diet for the bears who required twenty thousand of them a day to help produce the fat that broke down into liquid during the winter months as they hibernated. The public spaces were filled with berries, making them unsafe for humans as the bears came in search of food. But Serah couldn't understand why there would be a concern, as to her it was obvious. All that needed to be done was to fence off the picnic sites to protect the people from the bears and open up other areas where the berries could grow, helping the bears survive. It was their domain so why should they have to suffer because of some picnickers?

That night, Serah went to bed still angry that the bears had not been put first, but she woke up in a better mood. The coach was already there so she scrambled out of bed to fit in some breakfast before taking off to a lake that was surrounded by woodlands. There were no tracks to access the camping grounds, so it was a case of paddling a canoe if anyone wanted to set up a tent in the wilderness. They were lucky as they had a boat that took only forty minutes to get to the next dock.

In the distance, the large rocks stood stretching out towards the sky, and one in particular held a glacier which was only a fingertip of an icefield that was in the shape of a hand. The trees called out to Serah so once the boat docked, she walked alone, taking in the surroundings of what the world would have looked like before the destruction started. Energy flowed through her body and cleared her brain. The air was clean and filled her lungs that sighed with relief from the rejuvenation. She could have stayed there and continued on the path, but she had to go back to meet the boat. A small shop occupied those who didn't want to walk, but not many purchases were made as the souvenirs were the same as all the other stores that they had visited.

Back on the coach everyone wondered where they would end up next as they seemed to be in a forest with nothing else around. Rocks appeared through the gaps in the trees every now and again and when they finally did stop they were shown a path along a waterway. With the trees in the background they walked along, taking in the smooth rocks that had been shaped over the years. At the end of the path were a few different options. They could go on another walk through the woods but most opted for a walk to the shops instead.

Serah hoped for Canadian shops instead of tourist shops, but still found there was no change. She was determined to buy something different to take home to remind her of her trip, so when she found a carving of a moose that she had not seen before, she grabbed it. Serah spoke with the shop assistant who explained that if she wanted something different, she could go to the charity shop down the road. Serah couldn't believe her ears and headed off on a wild goose chase, only to end up back at the coach. Apparently, others had also looked for it and couldn't find it.

Serah sat quietly next to Lizette wondering if the shop had been hidden inside a building, but it was not meant to be so instead she joined everyone else in looking out the windows to find bears. Within twenty minutes she knew it was going to be the day for animal sightings when, from the back of the coach, a woman screamed to stop. Something so simple brought so much joy and they thanked the woman for spotting the moose they had all missed. The driver feared to move as endless photos were taken of the large animal eating at the side of the road, oblivious to his fame.

Five minutes later, someone else called out to draw attention to black bears hugging the bushes to eat the berries. Then as the driver took off, he had to stop again for a viewing of horned sheep licking mud off cars. It was explained to the group that apparently, they were not too bright, because they would smash into each other with a force of a car for up to twenty hours before one of them realised that his head hurt. It was done to impress the females, and that piece of information brought about comments from the male travellers.

'Explains a lot,' said Lizette who was becoming comical with her comments.

eleven

The previous day had been enjoyable with watching the animals, and as Serah pulled back the curtains to look out at the car park, she saw with shock, an elk with her baby standing amongst the cars. A man was taking photos and she wondered if she should go outside to join him. The baby was curious, and Serah didn't want to miss a moment, so she stayed in her room to watch the youngster roam around taking in all the attention from bystanders.

At breakfast, Serah told of her view from her window and learned it was lucky she hadn't ventured outside because the mothers attack if they feel threatened. How she would love to hug the wild animals but she knew she couldn't. Still, it was tempting when she saw the bears on the side of the road. She was safe in the coach and she accepted that she could only watch as their journey took them past more bears. Many passengers wanted to stop but had to also accept that their driver couldn't stop every time they called out requesting it. The bears were everywhere and ranged from light brown grizzly bears to an enormous black bear with her baby running after her. They created visions that would stay in her memory for a lifetime.

Inside the coach was warm but something was telling Serah that the temperature outside was dropping. Luckily, she had put her coat in her bag because when they got to their next stop, she had to put it on. Mt Edith Cavell intrigued her but she had no idea as to why she found the glacier so fascinating. Serah was drawn to it and her eyes stopped roaming when she saw in it the shape of a sleeping dragon. She knew at some point it had been real and the shape was left as a reminder of what there once was. Why, she didn't know; but she knew it was a reminder frozen in time.

There were different shapes in the ice that stayed the same for years which was surprising because the ice moved a few feet a day. Normally, humans see the images of faces in a lot of places because people were conditioned thousands of years ago to look for others. Some of the group found them in the ice but all Serah could see was the dragon. A trance took over her unexpectedly as she was not a person who would normally ponder, but here she would have stayed indefinitely if it had not been for Lizette dragging her towards the icefields.

A one million dollar, specially designed truck took them out onto the ice which was thirty metres thick. Before getting off the bus, the group were warned that the temperature had dropped to minus ten degrees Celsius, but nothing could explain the pain Serah felt in her face as she braced herself to step out onto the slippery surface. She pulled her scarf up around her face and sipped on a drink of whisky mixed with maple syrup to warm up her insides. The empty cup came in handy to catch the falling water melting from the snow up above. Normally, she didn't drink water without a bit of flavouring but the taste was pure and just what her body needed. It was water as it should be and her body craved it.

The field of ice was remarkable to Serah especially as it was something that she had never seen before. The guide explained about it being summer which was something she had forgotten. She tried to think of winter and listened as he further explained about how the temperature would drop to minus fifty degrees Celsius. How was it possible to live in such conditions? She imagined everything frozen, including the lakes they had visited, but she couldn't. The ice was hard under her feet and she looked at it thinking she might never see such a thing again.

Once inside the coach, Serah unwrapped herself and watched as the view of the landscape changed from rocks and ice to trees. Somewhere there was water, and they looked for it in anticipation of the canoe ride they were next to endure. The group had been warned in advance that when they got off, they would be going on a canoe ride and to head over to the canoes in two lines. Lizette was eager to be first, so when they finally got off the coach, Serah found herself not needing to line up as Lizette had already held a space for her. The wind blew and she contemplated going back for her scarf but the instruction had begun for the canoes so she had no choice but to brave it. They waited for the life jackets and safety talk but instead they were informed that taking a canoe out was going to have to be their decision due to the change in weather. The wind had just flipped over two canoes sending their paddlers into the cold water. The decision was easy: they all went for a walk along the lake's edge instead.

The backdrop of the rocks towering above them looked as if someone had chiselled them in sections to provide a surface for the snow to fall. There had been many avalanches and the force of the snow was able to break the ice that sat on the rock. Serah was beginning to think that being in the wild was dangerous but she was already half way around the lake and had no choice but to continue on. She was learning a lesson and that was to take it as it comes, which was a new concept for her as her world at home was safe.

The next stop was back into cowboy country. Banff looked as if it was straight out of the cartoon movie, Cars, with its main street and giant mountain at the end of the road. They were let off the coach to explore the town where she found a shop filled with shirts speckled with rhinestones and heavily embroidered boots. They were expensive and she was glad she had picked up her boots in Vancouver for half the price. There were a lot of steak restaurants, and as Lizette dragged her into one for a burger, she looked out the window to see her first cowgirl, complete with hat, boots, buckle and pink shirt. The sight brought a smile to Serah's face as it was nice to see a different life.

When she woke up the next morning she felt very confused due to a change in their itinerary, compounded with the weather.

At one of the meals, she had spoken to some tourists who hadn't made it to their destination and had to turn back as the roads had been closed. Canada had experienced a lot of rain and there were many mud slides. Her new philosophy of "who cares", led her to take in the information and let it go. It wasn't necessary for the others to know so she decided not to mention it. She was determined to ignore the itinerary and accept the changes, which turned out to be a good decision.

Every night the guide had given instructions and for some reason she had thought he had said they were leaving at eight o'clock in the morning. Naturally, she presumed the bags would have to be out an hour before, so when the wakeup call rang, she went into action. But when Serah put her suitcase out, she saw she was the only one. The other bags must have already gone, so she rushed with her bag in tow to the lobby—and that was when she noticed the schedule on the wall. Yes the itinerary had been changed, but it changed to staying in Banff for another night. At breakfast the others laughed hearing that she had put out her bag, but they did agree things were getting confusing.

After being rounded up, they put on their riding gear to head off to a ranch for a trail ride. On the way, they made three stops to view a lake, waterfall and mountain. At first everyone had rushed out to take photos of the lake but by the time they got to the waterfall, the enthusiasm had dropped. Serah looked out of her window and watched the water cascade but as her view was clear, she could see no reason to leave the comfort of her coach. Others stayed with her and by the time they got to the mountains, the novelty had worn off.

The only time people jumped from their seats was when someone yelled out 'bear'. As soon as Serah heard that word her body went into automatic mode and sprang towards the best viewing window to see the cute animal. She needed to see another one to feel alive again and thankfully they did get to see one before arriving at the stables which raised everyone's spirits. When the coach pulled up, the atmosphere in the bus was the same as if they had witnessed a wild animal. Emotions were high with the sight of a ranch that looked as if it was from a movie set. A wooden house and cabins surrounded the corals that held their horses. Dotted throughout the enveloping fields were over two hundred horses that were involved in the huge operation.

Horses who knew the drill stood still, waiting for the group of twenty-four riders. As the tourists waited to sign waiver forms, Serah spied a grey and black mule. He was tall, and as she stroked his face he closed his eyes with enjoyment. His ears were large, and when she spoke to him, he pushed them forward to listen. The distraction had lost Serah her spot in the line so she ended up being the last one to sign the waiver, but it was worth it to speak with a mule.

One by one everyone was allocated a horse and she ended up with a chestnut named Kenny. All she could think of was South Park and how Kenny was always killed. Not wanting it to be an omen, she spoke softly into his ears to let him know they were going to be alright. The cowboy on hand overheard her so he informed Serah that she was on a good horse and there was nothing to worry about. He held the animal as she mounted, but she should have been worried more about the saddle than the horse as she hit herself in the stomach when she got on. Serah had always thought western saddles would be comfortable but nothing could be further from the truth as she felt discomfort the moment she sat onto it. The large pommel had distracted her at first, making her wonder how she was going to get off, but the moment the horse moved she knew that she had to manoeuvre herself to find a comfortable position. She hoped the ride would be short, but it was going to be two hours.

She needed a distraction to help make the time go faster so she took in the woodland beside a river. Other tracks were for hikers and bikers who all stopped to see the convoy of horses following each other. She inhaled the air and moved her body around and even took her feet out of the stirrups to put them in front of the saddle but nothing helped to ease the discomfort. For a moment, she contemplated getting off the horse to walk beside him but just then the cowboy turned up on his mule. He had noticed her struggle with her aching body so he took evasive action by riding next to her to include her with singing "Home on the range".

It worked for a while but then she stopped singing when she was distracted by the man riding behind her. He was making funny comments because he didn't want to think about his wife who had abandoned the ride in the first five minutes due to fear. Serah wished she had joined her, but then she would have missed out on chatting with the handsome cowboy who kept her entertained for the rest of the ride. He had managed to distract her from the pain and the thought of dismounting. It wasn't until the ride came to an end that she remembered the pommel. He grabbed her horse and waited but she didn't move. Instead Serah asked for a crane to lift her out of the saddle but he thought she was joking and before she could say anything else, he grabbed her and stood her back on the ground. His cheeky grin diminished all the pain in her body and she stood still as he took her horse away to be looked after.

She should have gone with him. She could have taken the tack off and given Kenny his food and water, but instead she was pushed along with the crowd heading back to the coach.

There was an option for a helicopter ride but Serah didn't feel like floating through the air in a glass ball. What she wanted was to go to the mineral baths to soak. Her aches became more apparent with time and when the coach stopped at the hotel, she wasted no time getting changed to slip into the water. The minerals helped soothe her body which, once submerged and finally comfortable, refused to move, even when the others came back from their trip with stories to tell and pictures to show on their cameras. Their experience had given them a different perspective of the mountains, but her body was happy to have stayed in the healing pool. She thought about staying where she was even longer when the guide announced they were going five pin bowling, but she was intrigued. She had never heard of such a game. It turned out to be a fast-paced challenge where a team continually bowled using a small ball within a time limit. She had made the right decision to go as she hadn't laughed so much in a long time; if ever.

twelve

The next day they were off to Calgary for the stampede and Serah was up before the alarm. She thought the cowboy boots and the encounter with the cowboy had swayed her and she looked forward to what she would experience at the rodeo. The youngest boy in the group was also excited and yelled out, 'Yee ha,' every few minutes. His energy was contagious and soon everyone was in the mood. A few of the oldies found him too noisy but said nothing as everyone around him soaked up his enthusiasm. Cowboy hats were handed out and they arrived to see t-shirts printed with: There is nothing like a woman scorned so don't mess with Mother Nature.

Calgary had been flooded out a week prior, but luckily the rain had stopped and the water that filled the grandstand had now disappeared. The only affect it had was on the stadium where a band would have played. Apparently, it was beyond repair so with great expectations, they entered the ground that was a little disappointing; Serah had expected a huge site and not a show that compared to a local event. However, her new outlook was one of optimism, so she tried to remind herself of that as she went into the grandstand for the afternoon show. The atmosphere was electrifying and their seats were in a perfect viewing position. The whole tour group sat and listened as the commentators joked their way through the bucking horses, bucking bulls, barrel races, roping, and an event Serah had never seen before.

She watched with interest as a small pony ran out of the shoot. Three young children tried to slow him down by holding onto the rope around the pony's neck as one of the kids tried to jump on his back. To achieve this meant that three kids were dragged along behind the pony. It didn't seem nice to laugh at the kids being dragged but they could have let go if they wanted to. With the afternoon show over they went back to the hotel to rug up as the temperature was beginning to drop. The evening show was to start in a couple of hours and everyone was excited to see what was in store for them.

When they returned to the show, the first item involved the appearance of horses. Serah thought they would be the enormous Percherons that were in the stables but instead Thoroughbreds were used to pull the wagons. It was interesting, but after a few heats it became monotonous. The organisers did break up the show with short films of inspiration showing what went on behind the scenes. They spoke about the animals as if they were loved, which was nice to hear, and they broke up the last heat with kids pulling wagons on toy horses.

Then the performance area was cleared, and as the programme didn't say what to expect next, everyone was very curious. Tractors pulled pieces of equipment into the arena and an enormous tractor pulled a stage bigger than a house to put the final piece of the jigsaw puzzle into place. With the stage put together, the group thought it looked like something fit for Lady Gaga but instead everyone was entertained with a group of kids who came onto the stage singing and dancing. Although it was quaint, some people started to leave so Serah asked the women around if they wanted to go to the fairground with the others.

One stated that they should stay and as Serah didn't want to go on the rides alone, she also stayed to watch the outcome. Rugging up, they sat and watched as slowly the quality improved with effects, costumes and acrobats. The stage began to come to life and then the stage lit up as, to their absolute amazement, the famous band Kiss came out onto the floor to perform. Serah couldn't believe it. She had been a teenager when she last saw them. The tourists huddled up to see what else was in store for them and they watched on to hear a woman whose singing sent chills down Serah's spine. Serah didn't say anything as she was sure the others would think it was just the cold air. A man behind her didn't care what others thought as he expressed his opinion that the talent was lacking. At first she had agreed with him, but when the show started to take shape, it really came into its own. The horse theme came through with the native Indians performing a dance telling the story of transformation from animal to man, while up above them glowed strips of steel that were made to dance around by men inside glowing metal horses. They ran above everyone in the darkness before a finale of spectacular fireworks came to life before their eyes.

At the last blast of colour, they had to leave to catch the coach back to the hotel. The only problem was they were not the only ones leaving. After twenty minutes their coach had not moved very far. Serah asked if anyone would like to play a game to pass the time as she didn't think they would get back to the hotel until one o'clock in the morning, which was another hour away. With that in mind, their tour guide decided that the game would be who could guess the closest to the time of arrival at their destination. The tour ended on a humorous note with everyone trying to get the driver to drive slowly, take short cuts or speed through the gaps. It didn't matter how the time was spent because if you want it to go fast it doesn't and if you want it to go slow, it goes too fast.

The tour was coming to an end and Serah dreaded the thought of going back home to her mundane life. She ate her breakfast thinking about the next day when she would be home and all of her trip would be a memory.

'What are you thinking about?' asked Lizette, putting her plate of bacon and eggs opposite Serah.

'I don't want to go home,' she replied glumly.

'Then don't,' Lizette said, picking up her knife and fork. 'Come with me on my next tour and see the rest of Canada.'

'I can't do that,' Serah said wondering if she could.

'I have the number of the tour guide,' said Lizette. 'All I have to do is make a call. It isn't a tour like this one. It is a spiritual tour that the guide himself has actually prepared, instead of a company. It wouldn't be difficult for the guide to fit you in.'

Two paths stood before her and she didn't know which one to take.

'I'll tell you what,' said Lizette. 'I'll ring him and if he can fit you in then you can come and if he can't fit you in then you were meant to go home.'

'What about my flight home?' Serah asked not knowing how things worked.

'Easy, all I have to do is ring the flight company and explain and they will change your details.'

It seemed too simple so Serah allowed fate to make her decision as Lizette made a phone call.

Stabbing her food, Serah wondered about her fate and her destiny. There was no destiny waiting for her back in Australia, but what if her destiny in Canada turned out to be one she didn't want? Could she choose her outcome in life? She had so many questions that needed answers, and that was when she saw a vision of Sarah Cupsip. Had it been fate or destiny that had ended Sarah's life which in turn had sent Serah Kohw on a trip to Canada? Was she meant to meet Lizette?

Sarah Cupsip was a spirit but she looked real as she appeared in front of Serah Kohw. The sounds of the others preparing to end their trip faded into the background. Silence surrounded Serah as she concentrated on the message that Sarah Cupsip was trying to convey. She could feel her energy and finally she managed to hear her when she stated, 'The end is always the same regardless of the path that you take.'

Her path had changed and she watched the spirit of Sarah disappear as a hand touched her shoulder.

'You're booked in, so it looks like you are coming with me,' said Lizette Leclerk who quickly left the table to advise the tour guide of the new plans for Serah Kohw.

thirteen

Serah had no idea of the consequences of the choice she had made. It was possible for her to return home and feel safe but she had lived her whole life on a path without passion. The holiday had been unexpected and her eyes had been opened, so for once in her life she was going to be impulsive.

'Bye Serah,' said an American man as his wife hung onto him, relieved that the trip was over. It had been nerve-racking for her, facing many of her fears, and Serah could see why she would be happy to return to her safe life at home.

All around the room, people were leaving their breakfasts to say goodbye before taking their relevant transport back to their ordinary lives. Serah sat back with her cup of coffee and watched them, wondering if any of them had encountered what she had in the past couple of weeks.

'Bye Serah,' said another lady putting on her jacket in preparation for boarding the bus that was to take her to the airport. 'I hear you're not coming with us.'

'Change of plan,' said Serah hoping she was making the right decision.

Within her turbulent head, she could hear the screams telling her it was not too late to go with the woman.

'When an opportunity presents itself,' said the woman who placed her hand on Serah's shoulder, 'then you should go for it.'

The words were comforting, and as everyone left, Serah looked around at the empty space that was once filled with tourists. The only sound remaining was Lizette's voice, still on the phone. The words were muffled so Serah sat back to let the waitress fill her cup with coffee. Inhaling the aroma of the beans lifted her spirits. Just as she took her first sip, a man entered the room and Serah presumed he was the next tour guide to take her on her journey.

Lizette hugged him, making Serah wonder about their relationship but all such thoughts had to be dismissed as they both turned to look at her. It was an uncomfortable feeling and one that she would have to get used to. Not knowing what to do, she stood up to shake his hand but the closer he got, the more he outstretched his arms. Within seconds, the formality was shed as she felt his embrace. Being hugged was a strange feeling and one she was not used to. His smell reminded her of incense. It was unusual for Serah to sense anything and it dawned on her that she had spent her whole life not feeling anything. It was as if she had now been awakened.

Serah took in his attire of a cotton shirt and loose pants as he let go. 'I'm Francis and you must be Serah.'

'I am,' she replied and felt the energy as he took her hands.

He glared into her eyes making her feel uncomfortable, but this was a time of transformation so she stared back and saw the green of the grass that filtered through his stare.

'Where is your luggage?' he asked, still holding her gaze.

Serah manoeuvred herself from him and took hold of her case to pull it behind her as she and Lizette followed him to the minibus.

She had been used to the big comfortable coach and giggled to herself at the white van that was in need of a wash. Standards were going to be dropped and she wondered why Lizette would pick such a tour as she had been the one who had complained the most on the last trip. Not wanting to know the details, Serah went to the back of the bus and placed her suitcase in a gap, then with her handbag on her shoulder, she looked inside for a seat. The bus was small but there were plenty of spare seats, and that was when she realised that being added to the tour had been a blessing for the tour company.

The perfumed smell of the last transportation had been replaced by sage, and as Serah took in the aroma of the herb she looked around at the women who would be her companions for the next week.

'Now that everyone is on board,' said Francis, 'I would like for you to introduce yourselves to one another.'

Serah looked around to see who would speak first. As she was at the back of the bus with Lizette, she presumed they would be last. Her stomach jumped into her throat as Francis announced that he wanted everyone to also mention something about themselves and why they were on the tour.

'Let's start with you.' Francis pointed to a stout woman sitting at the very front. The woman went to stand but Francis told her to remain seated, so instead she turned to face everyone as she told about wanting to connect with nature. Her name was Akasha which sparked a conversation with the others as they wanted to know how she ended up with such an unusual name.

'I'm sorry, I don't know because I don't have any family. My parents died when I was young and I've spent my life in foster homes. That's why I'm here. I feel unattached and I need to be connected, so I thought that being with like-minded people might help me.'

Silence filled the bus as everyone suddenly felt sorry for Akasha. Francis took in the mood and decided to change it by pointing to another woman to tell her story.

'I'm Celeste and I am also alone. My parents are still alive but I don't see them as much as I should. I'm here because I'm interested in the stories about the planets and how they are meant to be aligned within the next seven days.'

Serah looked at the young woman with long, red hair, intrigued by her comments. Studying planets had not entered Serah's mind but it would be an experience and she looked forward to it.

Francis pointed to the next person who fiddled with her bag. 'I'm Leila,' she said nervously. 'I'm here because I've always wanted to travel but I've always been too scared. I thought being on a small tour would be a good way for me to start and being with spiritual people would help me to feel safe.'

Smiles covered the faces in the bus and must have had an effect on Francis' heart because he told everyone to send love to Leila. Serah joined the others in doing so, although in all honesty she had no idea what she was doing.

'Who is next?' smiled Francis as he looked at the back of the bus.

'I'm Lizette,' came from the seat beside Serah, taking away the suspense. 'I have a mission.' Serah suddenly cringed from a vision in her head of falling to her death. The vision was so vivid, she felt the jolt in the pit of her stomach and the lightness in her head. 'My mission is to know my path in life,' continued Lizette.

The dread swelled up inside Serah but she wasn't sure if it was due to the vision or because she was next to speak. She was the last person left and all eyes were on her. Bravely she spoke. 'I'm Serah and to be honest with you I don't know why I'm here.'

'Thank you for your honesty,' said Francis, 'and thank you to everyone for sharing.'

After a few acknowledgements, the tour guide turned his attention to the driver and left the women alone to contemplate each other. Serah could only think about her vision of falling which reminded her of the warnings she had received from others in recent days. She had been told not to trust Lizette and now she was on a bus to who knew where with her. Serah felt she had made a mistake. There was still no reason why she couldn't go home, but as she looked around at the other women, she hated the thought of disrupting their trip. Instead she looked at each individual and tried to determine who would protect her.

fourteen

A distraction was needed and it soon appeared in a form of a large tepee. 'We are coming into Medicine Hat and this is a place that has a famous story,' announced Francis, fuelled with excitement.

Serah could not think of any story and wondered if the others were thinking the same.

'This is where a young couple in love were sent out by their tribe to get help during a long winter. Their food supplies were short and because the boy had a wolf for a friend, they believed he would be the one who would be able to connect with nature to provide food. The wolf took them to a place where water spirits go to breathe air. On arrival, they were met by a serpent named Lamia who respected the boy for looking after the wolf. To show his love for his people, he had to provide an offering to the serpent. It was expected that his wife would be given but the boy offered his wolf. In the end, the boy learned it was love that had to be sacrificed and he was forced to sacrifice the girl. Once she was given, the boy was rewarded with a hat.' Francis pointed to the tepee through the window, and it seemed to Serah it represented the hat he was talking about.

'The hat was filled with knowledge,' continued Francis. 'Knowledge is wisdom, but in those days it was magic. To the tribe, it was medicine because when the boy wore the hat, he was able to provide herbs from the ground that would heal his tribe's ailments.'

The bus pulled into a parking spot and together the tourists followed their leader to the city hall. Serah looked around at the street filled with boxy buildings and pictured a coffee stop, but the thought of a café filled with pastries had to be left behind as there was something Francis was eager to show.

'Wow,' said Celeste, 'the story is true.'

'I don't know if a mural makes a story true,' said Lizette.

The brick wall showed a picture of a boy holding a hat to a serpent and whether or not the story was true became irrelevant as everyone, including Lizette, went up to touch the wall.

'Fantastic,' said Francis making everyone look at him. 'You are all on the right tour. This is a week of touching stones, but as none of you has a message, I think it is going to be a week of learning for all of you.'

Serah looked around at the others nodding in agreement and wondered if they could see what she could.

The moment she placed her hand on the wall, she felt the vibration. It was as if the energy from the boy was running through her. There was a glitch with the story she had been told because what she was getting was that the boy had taken the knowledge from the serpent. The serpent wasn't happy as it was actually a woman who had been scorned. Quickly Serah took her hand away, wanting to go to the café instead.

'Maybe you shouldn't drink so much coffee,' said Francis taking her hand. 'There is a fear you have to face and I don't think coffee will help you.'

Serah stormed off with the others in tow. They had not heard the conversation and thought that Serah was leaving to go to the next stop.

'Where to now then?' asked Lizette eagerly.

'The end is near enough,' answered Francis, 'but for now we are back on the bus.'

With their orders given, Akasha took Serah's hand to lead her to their transport.

Once again, they were looking out at the scenery while Serah sat in fear of making a wrong decision. This wasn't the tour she was expecting and as they pulled in to their next stop, she thought about leaving.

'What were you expecting?' whispered Akasha as they clambered down the steps. Serah looked at her in shock that she could read minds. 'I was expecting another street of shops,' Akasha said with a grin that crinkled up her face.

Serah looked around at the majestic river that reflected the mountains. Taking a deep breath, she inhaled the clean air; she felt the chill that cleared her mind and brought her back to her senses. Calls came from the water by the rock that Francis had already picked out.

'This is where I want you all to meditate,' he said sitting on the large stone with a flat top.

Everyone sat and closed their eyes. Serah had never meditated and didn't know what to do, so instead she closed her eyes and listened out to what had called her.

It was a voice of a female that spoke to her. Pressure filled Serah's ear as she listened to the soft voice that held back anger. The serpent living in the water was real. She had once been a beautiful woman who had been in love with an immortal. She had betrayed him and he had turned her into a serpent. Her only companions were the whales that swam deep in the water, but she longed to be in human form again. When a boy had come asking for help, she had given him the knowledge in a shape of a hat so he could reverse the spell that was put on her. She had trusted him but he had become angry about the sacrifices he had been forced to make and had taken off leaving her to remain in the water.

Serah tried to communicate with her but was unable to, so once the flow of energy had been distorted, there was nothing else to do but open her eyes. Everyone else was still meditating. She watched as they sat taking in the energy from the stone, but as she looked at them they opened their eyes.

'Sorry,' said Serah, 'I didn't mean to disturb you.'

'Don't be sorry,' said Francis. 'Everything happens for a reason. If we are meant to come out of the meditation now, then that is what it is.'

The others stretched as Francis got to his feet and took off his pants and shirt and walked into the icy river. With all eyes upon him, Serah wondered if the others would follow. She was determined to stay well back from the serpent that lived underneath.

'Come on!' he yelled but it was only Lizette and Leila who responded.

Akasha, Celeste and Serah stood and watched before being lured by an unusual smell.

'What is that?' asked Celeste.

'Don't know but let's find out,' said Akasha, leading them back to the bus.

The bus driver was pouring out a brown substance into cups and the sight of the approaching women brought a smile to his unshaven face.

'Smells good, I think,' said Serah.

'It's milk with cacao and honey,' he said.

'What's your name?' asked Celeste.

'Ricardo,' he said, passing the cups around.

Serah took a sip before asking him where he was from.

'I'm from Italy. I am studying to be a geologist but my fascination with rocks has taken me to mythology. I've come on this tour to find out about the sleeping stones.'

Akasha interrupted, 'But you're driving the bus.'

He smiled making everyone smile. 'I'm driving because I get to go on the tour for free this way.'

The substance continued to be poured as the conversation changed to reveal Ricardo's dreams of rocks protecting knowledge.

Serah was about to speak about her experience with the voice from the water when the others arrived to dry off their feet. The chatter stopped for the handing out of towels and warm drinks, and once Francis was dried off the conversation returned to the experiences that everyone had had whilst in meditation.

Akasha spoke first telling of how she had experienced peace with the quiet of the wilderness, of how she could feel the connection with the rock she sat on and of how she could hear the nothingness in her head. For a moment Serah thought that Akasha was going to tell of a voice but felt disappointment instead, realising that Akasha was not the person she had anything in common with.

'What about you?' asked Francis pointing to Celeste. 'Any planet information?'

She shook her head. 'Nothing but peace and quiet.'

Serah listened on disappointed with the experiences that involved being at peace. How she wished she had also heard nothing. When it was time for her to tell, she contemplated telling the same as the others, but if anyone was going to help her then it was going to be Francis. She had to trust someone. A shocked group of faces listened to her encounter.

'Why can't something like that happen to me?' asked Celeste.

'I'm sure it will,' interjected Francis, 'but first you have to be able to let go of everything that blocks you.'

Celeste's face turned a shade of red to match her hair. 'I am not blocked.'

Ricardo filled her cup with more liquid.

'Well I can see that the cacao has brought us out of our shells,' said Francis as he put on his clothes to escort everyone back onto the bus.

'Where is our next stop?' asked Lizette as she sat down.

'We are going to a place named after a princess,' he said sitting next to Ricardo.

There was no itinerary stating where the stops were, so the destination remained a mystery as no one could think of such a place.

'If I had my phone I would be able to look it up,' said Lizette annoyed that all phones had been confiscated.

'I suppose phones or any electrical device would interfere with our communication,' said Leila.

'What communication?' asked Serah wondering what on Earth she had let herself get in to.

'The communication with Mother Nature,' stated Akasha.

Not having a phone didn't bother Serah as she was not one for technology. Her phone had doubled as her camera, but this wasn't a trip that needed photos. She was on an adventure that would be locked in her mind and not one that required photos to jog her memory. She thought back to her life at home and her acquaintances who would look at her pictures. They wouldn't appreciate what she was experiencing. There was no need to show anyone else as the experience was her own. As the scenery hadn't changed, she laughed to herself as to what the photos would show anyway, and that was when it dawned on her that the bus was following the river in the shape of a snake.

The gasp attracted the attention of Leila who was sitting in front of her.

'I'm alright,' whispered Serah. 'Just thinking about snakes.'

Leila smiled. 'Snakes mean a new beginning. You are shedding the old you for a new you.'

'Thanks,' said Serah. 'I needed that.'

Leila went back to looking out the window but Serah wondered what the significance was with the reptilians. Words were entering her mind that she had never uttered before and she wished she knew what it all meant.

fifteen

Regina was a place that seemed to be very flat. Serah wasn't sure how she had not noticed the change in scenery but knew there would not be any secrets hidden as everything was on display. Trees, buildings and people were in abundance as the landscape seemed to go on forever and for a moment she let down her guard.

'You have a caring soul,' said Francis as he sat next to her.

She looked at him wondering why he would say such a thing.

Francis pulled his hair back into a pony tail. 'You have to let yourself go. Let whatever it is happen. Do you know that cows are sacred to many people? Your family name is Cow, isn't it?'

'Well, it's K-O-H-W,' replied Serah.

Francis ignored her emphasis on each letter. 'Cows are princesses in the animal world. And did you know that Serah also means princess? Names are important because they give you a clue as to why you are here.'

Serah went to speak but Francis was already walking to the front of the bus.

'So!' he bellowed, 'has anyone figured out Regina?'

Blank looks from the group gave him his answer so he proceeded to tell everyone the meaning of the name. 'Regina is Latin for queen. The town was named Regina to honour Queen Victoria because her daughter, Princess Louise, lived here.'

Leila interrupted, 'Why didn't they call the town Louise?'

'There is a Lake Louise,' stated Lizette.

Serah knew there was no escaping the water and wondered if the serpent, Lamia, had been at the lake when they were meant to go canoeing on their last tour. Why had the weather changed on their arrival overturning paddlers?

'Who knows of another famous Regina?' asked Francis.

Celeste spoke up, happy to provide information that no one else would know. 'Juno Regina. She is the queen of the gods and the daughter of Saturn.'

Outside, the surroundings were changing and the stories of the past were left behind.

A street lay ahead with glass buildings that towered opposite each other and with the positioning of office blocks came the notion of a coffee stop—or a hot chocolate stop at the very least—but it was not meant to be. The small bus continued on through streets of older buildings and shops that beckoned for them to enter, but still Ricardo did not pull over. They were heading out and finally their stop was beside the water's edge.

The river rippled making it look like the skin of a snake that slithered along the top of what it had to protect. Serah knew there was gold underneath the water, hidden in the tunnels, because she could hear the whispers in the air telling her, despite not knowing why. She was not a treasure hunter and had no desire to be one. The tour was enough of an adventure for her, so when Francis announced that they would be meditating with their feet in the water, she declined.

'You don't like the water,' said Ricardo setting up a park bench with sandwiches, cakes and drinks.

The others called out for Serah to join them but instead she turned to Ricardo. 'I don't mind the water but . . . '

'But what?' he asked, pulling out a flask and pouring the whisky into a cup.

She took the cup and threw the drink into her mouth. With eyes opened wide she wished that she hadn't swallowed it all at once as the burning sensation was too much for her. Feeling responsible, Ricardo grabbed her to sit opposite him on the bench and fed her nuts to break up the alcohol.

Serah grabbed her throat.

'Oh no,' panicked Ricardo, 'you're not allergic, are you?'

She smiled as she shook her head. 'If I tell you something, will you promise not to think I'm crazy?'

Then it was his turn to choke on his drink. 'Think you are crazy, when I am the one that believes in stories about rocks being alive!'

'You have a point,' she said and proceeded to tell him about the voices she had been hearing and the warnings she had been getting about Lizette.

He took her hands and placed them to his lips. 'You are not crazy. There is something strange with that woman. She reminds me of a lizard.'

They both laughed, staring into each other's eyes. At that moment, she wished Ricardo was the tour guide and Francis was the driver. They were both so different in their demeanour and also in their appearance. Ricardo with his rugged, handsome face was much more pleasing to the eye than Francis who had a face that would never stand out in a crowd.

'As for the voices,' said Ricardo. 'I think you should listen to them and if it means you have to stand in the water to do so then I think you should. I'm a big believer in things that are meant to be. Everything in life is for a reason.'

He stood up, still holding her hand. 'Come on, I'll come and stand in the water with you.'

With him holding on to her, she felt braver and allowed herself to be taken away from the others to a shallow inlet of still water. She removed her shoes and stepped in with him. Once the ripples stopped, she looked at their reflection. He was watching her but she couldn't look at him. Instead she continued to look down, hoping to find a reason as to why he was still staring. Her life had been robotic with only parts being broken up by her late friend Sarah Cupsip. She had never taken notice of her appearance before, and although she was in her late twenties, no one had ever complimented her, let alone held her hand. Energy ran through her, making her wavy hair messier than normal. She tried to pull it back from her face with her free hand and that was when she noticed in her reflection that her eyes were sparkling. Her features became more prominent but when she suddenly realised that the sparkling eyes were not hers, she jumped, nearly pulling Ricardo into the water.

'What is it?' said Ricardo taking her into his arms.

'I thought I saw something,' she said trembling.

In the distance, a roar could be heard from the group but Serah didn't care. For the first time, she felt safe and nothing was going to move her away from Ricardo's embrace.

'The others are going to the table,' he said. 'Do you want to go?'

'I'll stay here for a while,' she replied as she moved away from him, 'but you can go. I'll be alright.'

He didn't say anything but continued to stare.

Not knowing how to react, she stayed still and let him move so close that she could feel his heartbeat. She knew he was going to kiss her.

'Ricardo!' bellowed Lizette. 'I need your help up here!'

'Lizette needs me,' he said.

'Of course she does,' said Serah sarcastically as she moved away to let him go.

The dark brown eyes of the Italian stared at her as he moved but he didn't turn towards the others. Instead he moved closer to Serah to kiss her.

All fears that Serah had stored in her mind disappeared, and after what seemed an eternity they separated to take in the noise that was being made by the rest of the group.

'Come on,' he said, dragging her back to the table.

Lizette was the first to speak, 'This is a spiritual tour not a match-making trip.'

Francis intervened, 'It happens from time to time.'

'Not with me,' defended Ricardo after receiving a glare from Serah.

'Other bus drivers,' stated Francis who grinned, crinkling up the lines around his green eyes.

'Anyway, what do you want help with, Lizette?' asked Ricardo.

She held up his flask. 'I need someone strong to open up this.'

'That's mine,' he said taking it from her.

Akasha felt as if the mood needed to be changed so she asked about the next stop and if it would involve meditating in the water again.

'We are going to a place where there are stones to touch,' said Francis.

'Not more guessing games,' replied Leila.

Francis shook his head and explained about stories of a mason who had worked on buildings in his life times. He wanted to know if anyone could pick up on the knowledge that the mason had been given.

'This one really interests me,' said Ricardo. 'You know I believe in the stories from the rocks but I would love to hear from the stones that had been used by this man.'

'Who is this man?' asked Leila.

'Brandon,' answered Ricardo.

A chill ran down Serah's spine. For a moment, she felt as if someone was with her. There was a hatred for this man that she didn't want to know about, which meant she would be missing out on the next meditation as well.

A plate of sandwiches was placed in front of Serah. 'What is on your mind?'

'I don't think I'll be doing the next meditation,' whispered Serah. 'I haven't even touched the stones yet and I'm getting weird feelings.'

'You have to,' said Ricardo moving in close to her. 'I'll be there with you and I promise I will not let anything happen to you.'

She went to speak but he kissed her again. Serah would be touching the stones and would be explaining herself to the other women later on when they were alone.

The silence was deafening to Serah as everyone sat in the bus and waited for their driver and tour guide to put everything away. There were questions that needed answers but no one wanted to speak in earshot of the men outside. Instead, everyone sat quietly and only moved when Ricardo climbed the steps to sit in the seat and turn the key. Quickly, he looked over to see if Serah would like to be closer to him but her face that had turned red was enough of an answer.

Francis was the one to clear the air with the announcement about the accommodation. They were to stay at a guest house that had a ghost. Life was brought back to the group with the excitement of meeting a spirit from the past. Questions spat out from everyone except from Serah who continued to look out the window. She wasn't interested in being alone with a spirit and the exhilaration from the others did nothing to ease her mind as they drove along.

'Here we are,' announced Francis, but time had gone too quickly for Serah's liking, so she allowed everyone else to get off first to prolong the inevitable entrance to the unknown.

Ricardo was taking the bags from the back of the bus and waited for the eager women to leave before taking Serah's bag to her.

'You're worried,' he said.

'I shouldn't have come on this trip,' she said, going to take the bag.

His dark features became prominent as his face became a picture of confusion and disappointment.

'Sorry, I didn't mean you,' she said. 'I mean the things that you can't see.'

He kept hold of her bag and pulled it behind him as they started to walk.

'Do we sleep in a dorm or individual rooms?' she asked feeling the anxiety creep through her.

'You are in your own room, but if you are that frightened, I can stay with you,' he said pulling her towards him.

'Are there two beds in the room?' she asked.

He shook his head.

'So would you sleep on the floor?'

Again, he shook his head.

'What would the others think?'

He shrugged his shoulders. 'Who cares?'

The conversation ended with Ricardo taking her bag to her room and informing her that he would be back with his. The decision had been made and she dreaded to think what the others would say. The discussion was needed so she left her room to go into the lounge room where the others were sitting in front of a fire place.

'Alright, spill the beans,' said Leila as Serah entered the room.

Serah looked around to see if they were out of earshot of anyone else before sitting with the four women who wanted to know all the details.

'I don't know how it happened,' stated Serah. 'One minute we were talking, and then he was hugging me.'

'Kissing you,' stated Lizette.

'You're just jealous,' interjected Celeste. 'I am too.'

'So does that mean he is off limits now?' said Akasha.

'I suppose he's sleeping with you tonight!' blurted Lizette.

Serah nodded. 'Only because I'm afraid of the ghost.'

A woman nearby wearing pants and a woollen jumper was feeling the cold and had come to start the fire. The mention of the ghost had caught her ear and to put Serah's mind at ease, she told of how the ghost was a friendly one. He had been the one to build the house and he loved it so much he couldn't let go. He liked to listen to the comments made about the house which got everyone remarking on how beautiful the building was.

'Dinner will be in the dining room tonight,' announced the owner, 'so why don't you take advantage of the time and take a walk through the beautiful woodlands we have here.'

'She's right,' said Ricardo walking into the room. 'Let me take you away.'

Laughter filled the air, with Ricardo trying to accentuate his Italian accent.

'They're laughing at me,' he said as he took Serah outside to be alone.

'I don't know you,' said Serah taking her hand away, 'and you want me to walk with you in the woods alone.'

'Really? You are scared of me?' he said in a shocked voice.

Serah's heart was beating too quickly and she didn't know if it was because she was scared of being alone with him or because she wanted to be with him. Either way she was going because he had taken her hand again and was dragging her towards the entrance of the forest.

Once inside and surrounded by walls of tree trunks, she loosened her grip on her persistent partner to take in the ambience. Conversation would have ruined the surroundings that provided homes where wildlife chatted. Listening to the creatures brought on a sense of peace that Ricardo also picked up on as nothing passed through his lips. The crunch of odd leaves under their feet occasionally drew their attention away from up above, but not for long. There was activity that most didn't notice in the treetops and the couple savoured every moment—until a sound echoed from the distance.

The rest of the group had entered the woodlands from the other side. Their loud voices carried under the rooftop of branches allowing Serah to hear their opinions of her spending the night with the bus driver. It hurt her to hear them criticise her.

'They aren't going to connect with nature with that sort of negative crap,' steamed Ricardo, 'and on a pathway in a forest as well.'

'Shall we turn around?' asked Serah.

'No,' Ricardo declared as he took off to face his enemies.

The women realised their voices had carried when they saw Ricardo's fuming face, and they stopped with embarrassment.

'I'll make them apologise to you,' fumed Ricardo, but Serah didn't want a confrontation so she tugged at his hand.

Surprised by her pulling, he turned to look at her and calmed down when she kissed him so passionately it made the group turn around and head back to their accommodation.

The surprise tactic had worked, with the topic at dinner being about the ghost and not the romance that was developing on the tour. An abundance of food was shared by the owners who also provided their own spirits to sip on as the stories about ghosts intensified. It was an entertaining evening that ended on a positive note and saw the guests going to their rooms with the anticipation of meeting a spirit. Luckily the women's fascination of the affair had been diminished and Serah was left alone to be carried into her room by Ricardo.

sixteen

Brandon looked like any other town with its street of buildings ranging from old to new. The only exception was that it had an enormous mountain watching over it. The giant rocks that watched over the towns had inspired Ricardo's imagination, and he would have been quite happy to be left to walk to the top, but he was the driver with a job to do. It had been only days since he started his employment with Francis, but there was a new position that was becoming his priority.

He watched Serah through his mirror and smiled. She had stolen his heart and he didn't know if he could let her go at the end of the tour.

'Alright everyone!' bellowed Francis, full of excitement. 'We are stopping any moment now. Are you ready to touch some stones?'

Everyone except Serah joined in with the excitement by responding with vigour. The energy grew, and by the time the bus had parked the women were at the door, ready to find out what would be revealed to them through the stones they were to pick up.

'Not excited?' asked Ricardo watching Serah slowly walk down the steps.

Her lack of energy was obvious as it expressed itself through her hair which, at this moment, was flat. 'I really don't want to do this.'

Scrambling out of his seat, he took her hand as she stood on the walkway. Having him with her would help, but still the anticipation grew as she followed the others to the building Francis had picked out for them to absorb some spirituality from.

Serah squeezed her protector's hand. 'I have a feeling I'm going to fall through the wall.'

'If you do, then I'll be with you,' he said with a grin on his face.

It was early in the morning and a sleeping town had no idea that a group of people were going to meditate down an alleyway.

'Don't worry about where we are,' stated Francis. 'There won't be any activity here for a couple of hours, so lean against the bricks and let go.'

With a deep breath, Serah put her hand against the wall and relaxed to let her forehead take her weight. Once her mind was connected with the stonework she saw a vision of a man. At first, she wondered if she was thinking about Ricardo. He was handsome, rugged and strong, but his name was Brandon Macfarlane. The more she took in his detail, the more she noticed his white skin and thick hair with copper highlights. He was trying to tell her something with his Scottish accent. Although she was terrified, she felt safe with him in front of her so she let go of all other thoughts to listen to what he had to say.

It was another warning, but this time not about Lizette. He warned that a fall was inevitable and a choice would have to be made. There would be cause and effect with the decision, and for her to live the life she wanted, the right decision would have to be made. He told of the lives he had lived; he had made a discovery and used it for the greater good but still had not been allowed to be with his soulmate. There was more he had to do and other lives he had to live before being with her.

Serah sensed that in their connection he had now finally got what he had longed for, but being with her soulmate was something that had not crossed her mind.

Brandon Macfarlane came closer and Serah was sure she could

smell the pine that scented his clothing. 'I'm not speaking to you, Serah Kohw; I am speaking to Sarah Cupsip.'

The scream from Serah as she fell back brought everyone out of their trance. Ricardo still had her hand and only just managed to stop her from falling to the concrete.

'What is it?' asked Ricardo pulling her into his arms.

Shaking with the realisation that Sarah Cupsip was with her, she told him about seeing Brandon Macfarlane.

'You saw him?' interrupted Leila. 'So did I.'

Francis intervened, 'No, no, no, girls. That wasn't Brandon Macfarlane you saw; it was the Duke of Brandon.'

None of the others had seen anyone so they listened with interest to the story of Brandon's ancestor, Lord Selkirk.

Francis waited until he had everyone's attention, including the shaken up Serah who was still in the arms of her protector. 'Thomas Selkirk was born in Scotland in seventeen hundred and seventy-one. He wanted to change the world for the greater good. Highlanders joined him in his cause but he didn't do very well in politics and ended up here in Canada to supervise the Red River colony. He was a great man and that was who you would have picked up on.'

Leila turned to Serah and whispered, 'I saw Brandon Macfarlane not Thomas Selkirk.'

Glad that someone else had seen her vision, Serah let go of the embrace to speak with Leila. 'The man I saw was Scottish and wore clothes from the past. He did mention doing something for the greater good but he also spoke of being with his soulmate.'

The energy was strong as it ran through Leila's hair that was abnormally messy. Leila ran her fingers through it to try and clear the knots as she spoke. 'The man I saw did mention his soulmate but he told of scrolls of information. They had been hidden in a vault in Italy but the building had been destroyed.'

Ricardo listened with interest after hearing his home country being mentioned.

'Maybe you know some more about this, Ricardo,' said Leila. 'The scrolls must have been important and maybe Thomas Selkirk was sent here because he knew about the information that was kept in the vault. Do you think that because things didn't work out for him in his home country, he was given the opportunity to come here to bring his vision to life?'

Serah listened as she wondered what information was held in the scrolls.

'Do you know about the information?' Leila asked Ricardo.

He shook his head.

'I wonder if the scrolls are the treasure that has been put underground in Nova Scotia,' said Leila letting her imagination run away with her.

'Impossible,' said Ricardo, 'the vault was only destroyed a few hundred years ago.'

'So you do know,' said Serah giving him a push.

'No,' answered Ricardo glaring at her, 'I know nothing about the scrolls. I only know about the vault because you are not the only one who gets messages from the stones. I thought it was the Templars who put their treasure underground in Nova Scotia. If the scrolls were put there as well then wouldn't Thomas Selkirk have been sent to retrieve them? I mean, since he knew all about them then doesn't that make sense?'

Leila twirled her hair, creating a ringlet as she contemplated. 'If the Templars put the treasure there before the vault was damaged then why would you put the scrolls in the same place?'

'Maybe we are all here for a reason,' stated Ricardo with raised eyebrows. 'We might be going to a place where the scrolls are hidden and it might be up to us to retrieve them.'

'Where are we supposed to be staying in Nova Scotia?' asked Leila.

'I know the accommodation is on a property where a tree is used for meditation,' replied Ricardo, 'and I did hear that a hole had been opened up under the tree.'

Leila squealed with delight at the thought of the adventure ahead.

'Can we keep this to ourselves?' asked Serah. 'Or Lizette will be pushing me down the hole to get to the treasure.'

Ricardo grabbed Serah around her neck to pull her in close. 'No one is pushing you anywhere, understand!'

Leila laughed but she was the only one. Serah wasn't as animated and left the conversation to listen to Francis.

There was an argument going on. Francis was keen to go to the next stop at Thunder Bay but Celeste, Lizette and Akasha wanted to go shopping. The stores were opening up and the women had noticed the windows displaying items they wanted to buy.

Ricardo and Leila joined Serah who stated that she was keen for a break from meditation, and after she informed everyone that she was likely to speak with Zeus at Thunder Bay, Francis threw his hands up in defeat. He didn't want another episode where someone could get hurt, so to bring some normality to Serah's life, he conceded that they all could go if they promised to be back at the bus by lunchtime.

Lizette, Celeste and Akasha had already headed for the store with the clothes on display, which left the others wondering what they should do.

'Do you want to look at clothes?' Leila asked Serah.

'I probably should, but I would like to go to a café first,' Serah replied.

'Well, I'm going back to the bus for a sleep,' said Francis. 'I didn't get much sleep last night. I kept waking up thinking that the ghost was in my room.'

'Do you mind if I join him?' asked Ricardo, 'I didn't get much sleep either.'

Serah shook her head as Leila laughed.

'What's so funny?' demanded Serah.

Leila explained how everyone had been dying to ask at breakfast about the night with the Italian. There had been a brief discussion about it before the couple had entered the dining room but after the anger they had witnessed from Ricardo the previous day, they had decided not to ask.

'He didn't get much sleep because I was the one waking up thinking the ghost was in the room,' said Serah. 'There wasn't a ghost and honestly I think there isn't one there at all.'

'I agree,' said Leila walking off so Serah would follow her to the café. 'But really, you didn't do anything at all?'

Serah stopped in her tracks.

'Sorry,' said Leila stepping back to grab her. 'It's none of my business.'

They walked passed other buildings that had stories to tell until they reached one that called to them with the aroma of coffee.

'I don't know what it is, but I love the smell of ground coffee beans,' said Leila.

'So do I,' said Serah, taking a seat overlooking the street.

A waitress took their orders and as they sat back to watch the rest of the group walk to the next shop with bags in their hands, Leila considered what the outlook would be like if they were sitting in a café in Italy. She had never been and wanted to know if her companion had ever travelled there, not knowing that up until this trip Serah had never been anywhere.

'Fear stops me from travelling,' said Leila accepting a cup of latte. 'I was supposed to come on this trip with a friend but she had to go to hospital. It took a lot of convincing and a lot of medication to get me on this tour alone. I honestly didn't think I could do it, despite desperately wanting to come. But now I'm glad I'm here. I would be at home working otherwise and not drinking a good cup of coffee with a new friend.'

Serah smiled to hear she had a friend. And Leila was someone she could relate to. They both had visions, they both were interested in Italy and they both had hair that reflected their mood.

'Do you think our hair gets out of control because we have more energy than others?' asked Serah.

Coffee spurted onto the table. 'Wouldn't that be funny if we could identify with each other by the style of hair?'

Serah mopped up the coffee with a napkin as Leila wiped her face.

'Most people have tidy hairstyles but then there are others that are out of control,' Serah said, not finished with the process. 'Look at the other three and how their hair is always neat but they don't get visions. Our hair changes with our moods. Doesn't it make sense?'

'Putting it like that then maybe,' agreed Leila. 'Would you like to go to Italy? Do you think you will go there with Ricardo after the trip?'

The change in conversation intrigued Serah who wanted to know why there was a sudden fascination with the country. Ending her relationship with Ricardo was something she had not given much thought to and nor did she want to think about just yet. Was Leila hinting to go there?

'I want to go but I don't want to go alone,' said Leila looking at her friend in hope. 'Lizette did mention that she would like to visit Pompeii which has always been a destination of mine. But I would rather travel with you. Wouldn't you like to see what's left of the old city?'

Serah wondered what the airline company would think if she rang them to say she was changing her flight again. It was an impossible thought as Serah had a job she had to go back to, a home that needed her there to collect the mail and other things she couldn't quite think of.

'Come on,' said Serah finishing her drink, 'let's go for a walk around the town.'

seventeen

Thunder Bay was a stop that was heard before being seen. The bus parked to let its occupants out near a giant crack with water running through it and trees growing high into the air. As Serah stepped onto the ground, she heard the water move along the vertical rock formation that rose out of the lake. There was movement under foot, and the thunderous sound of the water flowing terrified her.

A hand on her shoulder made her jump, but then she looked at her bus driver and calmed down.

'It's a sleeping giant,' he said. 'I've been looking forward to coming here. There is a story of the rock once being a man who sacrificed himself to protect the Lady of the Lake.'

Many thoughts went through Serah's head. Was Ricardo her protector? Would he sacrifice himself to help her when the time came for her to fall? Was the Lady of the Lake the serpent she had encountered? Was she going crazy? She needed to be back in her box, inside the safe building she called home, but then she looked at Ricardo and couldn't imagine life without him.

'What is it?' asked Ricardo. 'You have to tell me what you're thinking.'

She replied by telling him she was glad she had befriended Leila as it was nice to have a piece of normality in her life. The times that Serah had strolled the shops with Lizette had been unpleasant, but with Leila it had been enjoyable. There had been no warnings when Serah had gone looking at clothes with Leila before meeting up with the others. Francis had done his best to get the women on the bus but they had been too hysterical to move. Their laughter brought on by the purchases they had made had been contagious and all control had been lost with them modelling each other's clothing and jewellery. Serah smiled thinking about the situation and wished it could take place again. But as she looked around at the surroundings of trees in the distance she knew it was a different experience that would be coming up.

The disturbing thoughts that plagued Serah's mind diminished during the bus trip to their next destination. Leila's excitement took over any negative thought that tried to come to fruition and Serah started to relax. When Ricardo next pulled over, Serah was one of the first to get off but as she heard the water in the distance she thought about getting straight back on the bus. Ricardo went to provide encouragement but it wasn't necessary as Leila was by her side, pushing her towards the next vision that was to come. Serah knew there was no other choice so she walked as she inhaled the scent of pine that brought on the memory of the Scotsman who had got her attention.

If the rock had been a man at some point, then he would have been big. The closer they got, the smaller Serah felt. A flat area of rock waited as everyone made themselves comfortable leaving only a small spot for Serah who was last to arrive. As she edged her way through the gaps, she found one that would allow her to lie down and she bravely closed her eyes. Panic soon struck with the sensation coming from her hands which had not even touched the stone. Too terrified to look, she succumbed to the feeling of someone being with her. She thought of Sarah Cupsip and tried to find comfort in knowing that a good friend was with her, but the feeling of another energy crept up her arm. Snakes were her vision. She would have to open her eyes to stop one from slithering around her body. It wouldn't be long before she would be crushed to death. Was it Sarah Cupsip's intention for her to die so they could be friends together in the afterlife? She didn't know what to think and screamed to put an end to it.

With her eyes opened, she sprung up to a sitting position to look for the snake—but it wasn't there. Instead a hand was on hers. It was Ricardo that she had felt. Her fears had taken over and as she saw the eyes of everyone else upon her, she felt the heat of her cheeks turning red with embarrassment.

'I'll take her back to the bus,' said Ricardo pulling her to her feet.

Serah objected as she didn't want him to miss out on the experience he had been longing for.

'It's alright,' he replied. 'I've already got my message.'

She wondered how long she had been in a trance as it had only felt like seconds. If Ricardo had received a message then the trance must have been longer. She felt weak and was glad Ricardo was there to help her.

Once she was seated in the bus and a flask of whisky put in front of her to sip on, she was able to make light of her overactive imagination. She needed a normal conversation but it was not provided by Ricardo as he explained about his message from the rock. He was told that he needed to go back to Italy to find out about the giants first. Not realising she was rolling her eyes to his statement, she found herself being pulled over to sit on his lap.

'So you think I'm crazy do you?' he said with an Italian accent.

She nodded in agreement as she listened to him tell her that Italian men were lovers and not crazy. Laughter filled her once more which erased all fears and as the emotion intensified, she found herself being thrown to the back seat which was wide enough to seat four passengers.

With Ricardo on top of her holding her hands behind her head, she was unable to move so instead she pleaded for forgiveness.

Normally, it would have worked but he had already gone one night of not being allowed near her and he was not going to let the opportunity be missed again. The others were meditating and with no one around, he ripped off her shirt to feel her against him. Still holding her arms, he was able to kiss her neck and move to her stomach. She tried to struggle but really didn't want him to stop. Her mind was completely focused on him and she would have let him do anything to her. Even death was not a fear as she would have died feeling happy in his arms.

'I've ripped your top,' he said letting go of her to sit up. Quickly, he took off his jumper and put it on her.

Serah rearranged her clothes when Ricardo indicated that the others were walking back to the bus. They were chatting loudly and luckily Ricardo had heard them because Serah had not. Not wanting to draw attention to herself, she moved to her seat as Ricardo flexed his muscles in his t-shirt.

With a wink, he was back in the driver seat before the others could enter the doorway.

eighteen

Timmins was a place that sent chills down Serah's spine. The feeling of falling had intensified and with the next stop being filled with old mines, she worried it would be there that she would fall to her death. Ricardo had promised to protect her but she knew her destiny was inevitable. Would it mean she would be always with him if he didn't let go? She tried to think of something else and concentrated on the white houses that appeared through the mass of trees. She wondered what type of life the occupants had and if any of them received visions or messages from the many lakes that surrounded them.

Francis was getting excited in anticipation of the next stop. There were a few stories he wanted to tell. Serah hoped it would be a distraction, but the moment her feet touched the ground she felt vibes from the river that ran alongside them. It was a higher vibration and one that was telling her to keep away from the gold hidden underneath. A battle was raging inside with warnings coming from different directions. Now that she had accepted Sarah Cupsip was with her, she knew one of the warnings would be from her but was surprised at the idea that Sarah thought her persuasion would be going towards the gold.

After a few moments of the group stretching and inhaling the fresh air, they turned their focus on Francis. He was stretching through a few yoga moves and when he realised that all eyes were upon him, he motioned for everyone to follow. Serah thought they would head towards the water but this time their tour guide took them to a place where a mine had been filled in. With relief, Serah observed the mass of dirt, grateful there were no holes for her to fall into. And to seal the feeling of being safe, Ricardo put his arms around her shoulders as they listened to another tale from Francis.

'Is anyone interested in meditating in another country?' said Francis to a group of astonished faces.

It wasn't what the group had expected and they stood around trying to comprehend the question.

'Why?' asked Leila.

'Lately I've become fascinated with the story of the city of gold and I'm thinking about meditating near where the site is supposed to be—hopefully the messages will take us to the gold,' stated an excited Francis. 'Maybe Serah and Leila might like to join me since you two seem to pick up on things quite easily.'

Serah knew she wouldn't be going but Leila was intrigued and was about to ask questions when Lizette interrupted, 'We are not here to discuss another trip. We are supposed to be here to meditate.'

Francis stared at the woman and changed his tone. 'There is a connection with what I'm saying and where we are. This was a town where people came to dig for gold. Where we are now is an old gold mine and our meditation spot. I'm interested to see if anyone picks up on anything different as we are well away from the rocks and river.'

Leila interjected, 'What do you know about this city of gold?'

The tour guide looked around to see if there was anyone else who was interested and with all eyes on him, he told of Percy Fawcett who went looking for a civilisation in the Amazon jungle.

'The people they searched for were meant to be spiritual beings who had built a city. Within the buildings was meant to be a pyramid that held a myth of transformation. Percy was considered an excellent mapmaker and was given a job to map out borders in

South America. As a youngster, he had found some old Roman coins in a cave which started his thirst for adventure, so with the job offer and with the story that lay within the large rainforest, he became intrigued and felt it was his destiny. There were others who went with him but slowly they deserted him due to either disease or fear of the native tribes. For some reason, Percy was untouched. Apparently, there had been a nagging feeling for him to continue on alone and look for the advanced civilisation in the Amazon. Once he was by himself, he was able to connect with trees that told him of the Inca ruins and of a man-made path that took him to an empty city filled with fantastic, large halls and columned buildings made from black stone. He had marvelled at the grandeur and the ruined statues that confirmed there had been considerable wealth there. Percy had already pictured the city of stone buildings when he was younger thanks to his spiritualist mother who had had an enormous influence over him. His brother was also spiritual and had studied the beliefs of advanced people, including priests still living with their past DNA who were looking for what was lost.

'Percy was a man with a mission and luckily his endeavours were documented. His missions took him towards Brazil to find the Shingu River. He was meant to go alone but he decided he needed help and took two men with him. It wasn't long before the storms set in and the two men took off. Percy spent three months alone but had to return to England when his food ran out. His desire to return to the jungle was strong and he managed to persuade the Royal Geographical Society and newspapers to support him, in return for him forwarding writings of his adventure. He knew the readers would want to follow his footsteps. He set off again, this time taking his son, Jack, but alas they were never seen again. In the last letter to his wife he wrote that 'she was not to fear failure.'

'I don't think I want to go to the Amazon,' said Leila breaking the silence following the story that had a sad ending.

'Are you going to look for gold or are you going to look for Percy and Jack?' questioned Celeste.

Akasha joined them with their questioning. 'Percy would have died of old age but what would have happened to Jack?'

Serah felt a shiver run through her spine. It stopped at her head making her shudder. Something inside her wasn't happy hearing Jack's name. Desperately she wanted to speak with Sarah Cupsip; she knew Sarah would be able to answer the question of the son living with the ancient civilisation. Having been distracted with her thoughts, Serah didn't notice if Francis answered any of their questions, and only heard him concluding. 'Anyway, if you feel like an adventure, I might be following in Percy's footsteps.'

'Can we meditate now?' asked Lizette with a tone of disapproval.

With the demand to end the discussion, they all touched the wall of dirt and closed their eyes.

Serah didn't know what to expect. She believed the stones held a vibration but dirt was part of the earth and not an energy that she expected would reveal any secrets. Not knowing why she felt that way, she lay back feeling better in her belief that no information would be given. The soil had hardened over the years but still managed to mould around her body as she sunk into it. It was a warm and comforting feeling that helped her to relax even further, and once her eyes were closed a vision appeared. She expected apprehension but there was nothing. Her only feeling was to take in the man that stood before her. He was difficult to see as he wore a large Stetson hat that covered his face. His body was covered with leather boots laced to his knees, beige pants and a cotton shirt. He lifted his head and that was when Serah felt an anger she was sure was from her deceased friend, Sarah Cupsip. She thought the spirit inside her had risen from the dead and was ready to explode. Serah had to battle with the energy to keep the spirit under control until a face appeared that dispelled all of Serah's emotions.

It was a face that was too handsome to be human. She was not one who believed in angels but that was the only thought that came to mind when she saw the man with striking chiselled features, blond hair and eyes as blue as the sky. With a focused vision, she watched as the man conversed with the people who appeared around him. It was initially a pleasant discussion but soon started to turn ugly. There was a problem but she couldn't hear. She knew he was going away but she didn't know where. She pushed her body forward to try to hear but everything dissolved, including the anger from Sarah Cupsip.

'Damn!' exploded Serah, startling those who were still meditating.

She stood and walked away not wanting to disturb the others any more but it was too late.

Leila followed her to question her on her vision and was surprised to learn they had seen the same man.

'His name is Jack,' said Leila.

'The son,' interjected Serah. 'But he was taken away.'

'I know,' said Leila, 'and you won't believe where.'

Serah listened with interest as Leila went into detail about him not wanting to leave because he had a loved one at home who he wanted to return to. There was a higher being and Leila had sensed that the being was the Lady of Life although she had no idea who that might be. Leila had watched as Jack had been taken from the human realm to a dimension that was full of gold.

'Honestly,' said Leila, 'their gold is our bricks. It was everywhere.'

Ricardo laughed as he joined them. 'Don't tell Francis what you saw or he will want to find the dimension.'

Their laughter drew the attention of the others who joined them wanting to know what had been experienced. As usual the others had not encountered any visions, but when Leila mentioned the Lady of Life, Celeste had something to tell. 'The Lady of Life has come up several times in my research of the universe and its planets. It seems she was in charge of souls in ancient times and when things got out of hand, she blocked the portals between life and death which erased past memories over time.'

'You don't believe that do you?' demanded Akasha.

Celeste glared at her. 'Think about it. How would you know if something had happened, if it had been forgotten? We know about certain events but not all.'

'What do you mean?' asked Ricardo.

'We know about the ice age,' said Celeste. 'But was that made by someone to end a civilisation? There are things from the past that present themselves today and are unexplained. What we call modern technology has been used in the past but why don't we know about it?'

Everyone, including Francis, couldn't answer. She had given them something to think about.

'You said that the Lady of Life was in the past,' said Serah, 'so does that mean there is no one now?'

'Juno Regina,' said Celeste looking up to the sky. 'She is the one who controls the gods and therefore was given the job of ruling the universe. She controls the destiny.'

'Do you believe that a destiny can be controlled?' asked Serah.

'I don't know,' said Celeste still looking up above.

Serah joined her to stare beyond the sky. She hoped that if Juno Regina was real then she would intervene and help to stop the end that was coming. Quietly Serah asked for the ruler of the universe to stop her from falling into the earth.

'Enough,' whispered Ricardo as he took Serah away from the others. 'You've gone from getting information from stones to asking for help from the universe. Next it will be aliens. Don't get too involved with Celeste.'

She turned to pull herself away from him. 'You can talk,' she said. 'You talk to stones and want them to answer you back!'

'That's different,' he said. 'I'm a geologist.'

'I don't care what you are,' she answered pointing at him. 'You are no different to any of us here.'

He rolled his eyes at her but she had already stormed off. He could have let her go to simmer down but his Italian genes made him emotional. He needed them to argue so he could get it out of his system and with the rising frustration he took off after her.

'Don't speak to me!' she demanded as she kept walking.

'My work is real,' he said trying to catch her arm so she would face him.

'Yes, it is,' she said turning to him voluntarily, 'so go and drive the bus!'

His emotions grew to the point of exploding and he was about to retaliate when she surprised them both by kissing him. A calming feeling simmered his emotions, erasing his need to argue and leaving him to sink into her lips.

nineteen

Saint Jerome was their next stop and the place where they would spend the night. Akasha complained as they walked back to the bus. She had become bored with the meditation stops, café stops and guest house accommodations. She had thought that a meditation tour would have helped her to connect with nature but it hadn't, and sitting in the bus for hours had made her put on weight. Akasha had always been a little overweight but was already feeling concerned about gaining more when they weren't even half way through the tour. Flicking her waistband, she was glad to have brought stretch jeans with her. The focus of the accommodations had been eating dinner with the owners— which she enjoyed— now she longed to check into a luxurious hotel that had a spa she could benefit from. Some agreed that a change would be nice and hoped the next stop would provide such a request as they took their seats.

The drives seemed to be getting longer with even the short ones feeling too long, but when the women saw the sign announcing they were in Saint Jerome, they eagerly looked around for a grand hotel.

'There's an interesting building,' said Celeste leaning over from her seat.

Everyone turned to look at the grey cathedral with roof and towers that shone white in the sun. It was a beautiful building and Akasha was sure they would end up meditating in it later, but for now she wanted to be pampered.

'Okay ladies!' announced Francis. 'Something a little different.'

Akasha looked at him hoping her prayers had been answered.

'We can stop at the shops,' said Francis. 'Since you had fun shopping last time I thought I'd give you some more time to shop to break up the spirituality chatter that nearly caused our couple to have a feud.'

Ricardo smiled as he looked at Serah through his mirror.

'Is there a spa near the shops?' asked Lizette looking over at Akasha.

Francis shook his head. 'But there is one at the accommodation tonight.'

'I don't know about all of you but I would like to go to the spa instead of going to the shops,' declared Akasha looking around for a unanimous response.

An agreement among the women became clear to Francis who relented and told Ricardo to take them to the manor.

The word manor being used instead of guesthouse brought magnificent images to the minds of the women. Expectations were running high with visions of grandeur and butlers. Pictures of what could be were being discussed when they noticed their change of environment. The shops were replaced by farmland and with that, hopes dropped of a luxurious building being hidden in the trees. Sheep munched on grassy pastures and as Akasha watched them she pictured herself with the owners grazing at the food on the table. Minutes dragged by until, when the bus turned into the driveway, a manor in the true sense of the word did in fact await them.

A renewed excitement filled the bus and the women anxiously waited to depart the vehicle to receive their rooms. With everyone given an explanation about what was on offer, there was no hesitation with the ladies booking in to receive massages, body scrubs and bath robes. Downtime was not to be spent eating and drinking but by soaking in the hot spa that easily fitted them all in.

After stopping to fix himself a whisky, Ricardo was the last one to arrive at the hot spa which contained the five chatty women and their tour guide. He had never given much thought to his appearance but when the banter changed to taunts and teasing due to him taking off his robe, he suddenly felt self-conscious. There were two choices in front of him; he could either jump in the spa and hide or stand there to endure their jeers. Serah was obviously finding amusement with the situation so he decided to flex his small muscles until the novelty had worn off. With the entertainment over, he jumped in creating a splash which was retaliated with a group of women throwing water at him. He needed to escape and dove under to end up next to Serah.

She continued to laugh.

'What's so funny?' Ricardo asked. 'You like seeing me getting attacked by a bunch of women!'

'It's funny,' she said, 'that you come to me for help.'

He glared at her, about to protest, but she kissed him knowing she was in control of his emotions.

'That's not fair,' he said pulling away from her. 'How can I win an argument?'

She kissed him again.

A wave of water hit the couple alerting them to the others.

'I think you two need to go to your room,' said Celeste whose face had turned a shade of red to match her hair.

'There's nothing to do in my room,' said Serah to alert the others to the fact that she wasn't intending to share a bed with him.

Ricardo pulled Serah in close as he whispered, 'There is plenty to do in my room.'

She smiled but didn't respond.

'I was the perfect gentleman when we slept in the haunted house,' he declared, 'and I gave you my jumper to cover you up when I attacked you in the bus.'

She stared at him without saying anything.

'What do you want from me?' he whispered.

'I haven't had sex before,' she said waiting for his expression to change.

There was no emotion on his face that gave him away, but he slowly let his feelings be known by moving in and kissing her neck. Serah didn't know what to do as she could feel all eyes upon her. She wanted to stop him but her heart beat faster and her breaths became heavy. He rose and held out his hand to her and she took it knowing he would take her to his room. If the others were making any noise, she didn't hear it. Serah didn't feel the robe being slipped back onto her body. There was no sensation; she was numb. The only sense that came to life was the taste of his tongue that entered her mouth when he kissed her.

She had tasted whisky on several occasions before and it had always been sour, but the taste of it on his tongue was sweet. She had never tasted anything like it and wanted more. Sucking the alcohol from him made him moan, and with her acceptance came the tightness of his grip holding her next to him. Falling in love had not been something Serah thought she would encounter on the trip, and for a moment she wondered if the spirit that was with her had anything to do with it. Her friend had spent a lifetime looking for her soulmate—could it be Ricardo she wanted? Serah didn't know what to think, but stopped thinking altogether when she joined Ricardo to be together for the night.

*   *   *

The breakfast room sprung to life when the couple came down the stairs together. Celeste put down her toast to ask if they were feeling alright and if Ricardo would be able to drive the bus.

'You lucky thing,' said Leila pouring a cup of herbal tea from the pot.

Francis smirked but didn't say anything as he knew that Akasha was bursting to comment: 'You missed out on an unbelievable massage.'

'No, she didn't,' said Ricardo pulling out a chair for Serah.

'Why did you say that?' whispered Serah but he only answered with a grin.

'Well, I'm not hungry any more,' announced Lizette who left the table in disgust.

Leila watched her leave before announcing she thought Lizette's behaviour was getting worse.

'Don't worry about her,' said Francis who passed over a basket of wholemeal toast to the starving couple. 'Today we head to Victoriaville. There will be lots of messages to come through there in meditation so that will draw the attention away from the lovebirds.'

Ricardo wanted to defend his honour but Serah shoved a piece of apple in his mouth before he could speak.

'Is there a spa at the next accommodation?' asked Akasha pushing away the tempting cereal.

Reluctantly Francis told her that there would be no more manors and no more spas. A devastated Akasha then devoured a bowl of cereal along with three slices of toast.

A peaceful mood took over once everyone was settled in the bus. The massages and relaxing hot spa helped to calm the body and brain. Akasha was wondering if she had come on the right tour as she was thinking she might have been better off staying at a health retreat. Meditation had helped calm her soul but her body was much happier after being pampered. Driving along in silence allowed everyone to reflect on their lives. They were half way through their trip and wondered what they would feel like when it was time to leave. Serah was feeling torn. She wanted to go home and back to a life of normality but she didn't want to leave Ricardo. She knew he would want her to go with him to Italy but the premonition of falling to her death still played heavily on her mind.

Scenarios flowed through Serah's mind of how her life might be. In such a short period of time her life had changed dramatically and she wasn't sure if she could take any more. She needed to know the end and whether it was her imagination making her think she would fall to her death. But then it struck her that her reality was to return home to a safe place. So with her mind made up to play it safe, she decided she would tell Ricardo at the next stop, but she caught a glance of his stare in the mirror and knew it was going to be difficult.

The bus stopped and with a heavy heart she waited to be last off, intending to tell Ricardo of her decision while the others took in the natural beauty of the river. The hand that took hers belonged to one who also wanted to be alone but for different reasons.

'I want you to come back to Italy with me,' said Ricardo with a hopeful face.

She wondered if he knew what she had been thinking, but couldn't back down. 'I have to go back to Australia.'

'Why?' he demanded.

'I have a home, a job, responsibilities—'

Ricardo interrupted her, 'You don't have to go back. Stop paying the rent and someone else will rent your place. Stop paying your bills and they will stop sending you mail when they realise that you are not there. You can email everyone, including your employer, to tell them that you are not coming home. You have no excuses so you are coming back with me!'

'Your accent gets stronger the more determined you become,' she said trying to change the subject.

'Stop it!' he demanded.

'Or what?' she said with a grin.

'I will put you over my shoulder and force you to the altar!' he screamed.

There was a moment of silence with them both realising what he had said.

'Now you've given me more to think about!' she said trying to break free of him.

'You drive me crazy with your thinking!' he yelled back. 'Stop, thinking!'

'I have an important decision to make about what I am doing,' she said in a calmer tone.

'I've made the decision!' he said still raising his voice. 'You're driving me mad!'

'Maybe we aren't meant to be together then,' she said but he kissed her, causing her to question again what was the right direction for her to take.

Slowly the tension subsided and an exhausted Serah admitted to being frightened.

'I'll be with you,' said Ricardo holding her tightly.

Feeling the strong slow heartbeats from his chest helped as she calmly explained that Leila had asked her to accompany her to Pompeii along with Lizette, but a feeling of dread had stopped her from making a decision.

Ricardo laughed as he took her face in his hands. 'I know why you are scared. I bet you Lizette wants to visit the temple of Isis to redeem her sins.'

Serah's eyes widened as she looked up at him for an explanation.

'You don't know about Isis, do you?' he asked with a loving grin. 'People went to visit the temple to ask the Goddess Isis for forgiveness in this life because they believed that Isis was the only one who could arrange for them to live a better life next time.'

A smile grew across Serah's face. 'I could understand Lizette needing to do that, but why did I feel dread when Leila asked me to go with her?'

'Probably because you knew that if Lizette did go with you then she would sacrifice you to make sure she would get a better life next time around,' he said putting his forehead to hers.

Francis decided it was time to make a move and led the others quietly back to the bus so there could be a peaceful separation between the intense couple.

Victoriaville was in view and the drive had provided ample time in the bus for the couple to think about their futures. Serah was unaware of the discussion that was taking place in the vehicle. There had been chatter about conspiracies ranging from royalty to aliens. Her mind had not wanted to take in any information as she had enough to think about, so she had turned her back on the others to stare out of the window. The scenery was a blur and she wasn't sure if it was because Ricardo wanted to get to the next stop as quickly as possible so that they could continue the argument. A decision had to be made. Small stops along the way due to wanting to go to the toilet or spotting wildlife were brief. Not wanting a confrontation, she closed her eyes and pretended to be asleep. Contemplating the next stop, she wondered if she could continue the pretence in order to be left alone, but she knew that when they stopped at Victoriaville there would be nowhere to hide and she would have to face him.

Civilisation was becoming more apparent, so with a fake stretch Serah joined in on the conversation that was now about maple syrup. Francis was explaining about the town being the place for the syrup and how good it tasted in whisky. Serah looked over at Ricardo thinking about his flask of the alcohol. But her quick glance in the mirror was a mistake. She knew the argument wasn't over by the look she saw from his dark eyes staring at her. The vision of a traffic accident flashed in her mind, so to get his eyes back on the road, she looked ahead in awe.

'What can you see?' asked Celeste, noticing Serah's expression of fascination.

Ricardo was back to watching the traffic as the others waited for an explanation from Francis but none was forthcoming.

A building as square as a castle stood in its enormity amongst the trees. Windows of old stood tall overlooking the water below that pulled at Serah's heart. There was a feeling of déjà vu as she looked across the water that confused her mind with the sighting of a serpent. The bricks that shone in the light called out to her but then she remembered that Sarah Cupsip was with her and maybe the building was part of Sarah's memory. She tried to let her go but couldn't and had to fight with herself to stop her body being forced to take over the bus.

'What are you looking at?' asked Ricardo as he looked over to her staring through the windscreen.

'You really need to go back to your seat,' said Francis suddenly thinking about his liability insurance.

Whispers in the background made Serah turn around to face the others. 'Can't you see the building?'

'There are lots of buildings,' said Akasha. 'We're coming into town.'

'The building in the trees,' said Serah pointing to a direction away from their sight. 'The one that overlooks the water.'

The others couldn't see what she could and as she fell into the front seat to look back out of the window, the magnificence was gone.

Ricardo spotted an empty car park spot in front of a bar and quickly took it. He announced it was time to try the whisky with maple syrup and there were no objections. As soon as the door was opened the others left to find a table inside to gather around and discuss the actions of their companion as Ricardo grabbed Serah to stay with him.

Lizette had not been centre of attention on this trip, which was unusual for her. As she was the one who had previously spent the most time with Serah, she felt compelled to be the one who should be interrogated.

'Here you are, ladies,' said Francis handing out glasses from a tray.

The interruption was welcomed by Lizette as she had to choose her words wisely. From the moment she saw Serah, she had been overcome with a feeling of distaste. She had befriended her with the intention of taking her to Nova Scotia to end her life, but she didn't know why. There was no way she could tell the others of her feelings as she would be a suspect if the event took place. There was a part of her that tried to keep away from Serah as she didn't want to end a life but there was another part of her that was strong and determined to act on the urge. What the reward was after the death of Serah, Lizette had no idea, so she changed her mind about the discussion. She took a gulp of the drink in her hand and restarted the subject of conspiracies that Celeste had been passionate about in the bus.

Everyone had already taken their seats in the bar when Serah went to stand up in the bus, but she was quickly pulled back down when Ricardo put himself into her seat and made her sit on his lap.

'I've been thinking,' he said trying to remain calm. 'We have a whole lifetime in front of us so let's take it slow. Come with me to Italy for a week. I can show you around and then I'll go with you to Australia and you can show me around.'

She went to speak but he stopped her with a kiss to her forehead.

'If we can come to an agreement about where to live after being in both countries then we can get married,' he said quickly then kissed her mouth before she could respond.

'If I agree to this, can we not speak about marriage until I'm ready?' she asked as she stood up.

'Promise,' he said taking her hand to join the others who had drunk too many glasses.

Somehow the conversation had changed from conspiracies to anything they could think of. It was a discussion that belonged in the gutter and Ricardo wasn't sure if he wanted to hear what they had to say but the laughter was music to Serah's ears. She didn't care what they had to say as she needed a bit of nonsense. Knowledge was something she didn't need and to make sure her head remained empty of all thought, she grabbed a glass and filled it from the bottle that sat on the table and drank.

Ricardo went to join her but as soon as his glass was filled, it was taken away from him.

'You're our driver remember,' said Leila with a slur.

He needed something in his hands so pulled Serah over on to his lap to hold her as his shield against the chatter.

'So,' said Francis, 'Victoriaville was named in honour of Queen Victoria.'

'I know something about the royals,' said Leila standing up. 'King James rewrote the bible!'

Celeste scoffed with a mouthful of drink. 'The royals wrote the bible but it was the Anunnaki who rewrote it . . . unless James was one of them.'

'Every action has a reaction,' declared Celeste. 'Who knows what the Holy Grail is and why were the Templars sent out to find it if they didn't know what it was and who are the Merovingian line?'

Lizette smashed her glass to the table as she stated that everyone was after the gold.

'That's right,' stated Leila who decided to sit down. 'They run the world for their own gain. That "gold and child" lot—'

Celeste interrupted, 'Queen Victoria is an illegitimate child of the Rothschild family!'

'No,' said Lizette slamming the glass on the table again, 'it's all about the gold.'

'The gold under the rivers,' slurred Serah.

'That's a secret,' said a voice that was not from the others.

Serah rubbed her eyes as she tried to focus on the woman who had joined their table. Her clothing was more of a costume with her large dress made of cloth that shone of gold and embellished with jewels and lace.

'Sarah Cupsip,' whispered Serah looking directly at her face. 'Is that really you?'

'What you are saying, maybe in a drunken state, but it is still a secret. It is only Mary who controls the secrets. You must not mention the gold that hides from view.'

Serah took in her voice that broke through the barrier of the noise around the table but it didn't make any sense.

'Are you Sarah Cupsip?' whispered Serah in disbelief.

'I am and I am not,' she stated. 'Now I am Queen Mary, the queen who ruled when women had never ruled England before, the queen who had survived when her siblings had died before her, the queen who had been promised a hand in marriage by so many countries.'

Ricardo turned Serah to face him but she turned back, wanting to know if the spirit of her friend was still present.

'I've appeared to warn you,' said the vision. 'You are not to trust that things will continue on as you believe. My father, King Henry, was a man of good but then changed when he fell off his horse and hit his head. What was meant to be, didn't happen. Instead he divorced his wife and another became princess. It was Mary who was the Princess of Wales.' The spirit moved through the table to stand in front of Serah and state in anger that she had been turned into a servant and had been disowned. But then circumstances brought her back to the throne.

Jewelled hands sat on top of Serah's and as she stared at the garnet ring, she took in the sound of a familiar voice that seemed to be in despair. 'Sarah Cupsip found magic that took her from a life of a servant but all she ever wanted was to be a princess. It was a life that was always taken away from her. Mary had always been given a title because she had secrets but she was no better than anyone else. Why do you think she was known as Bloody Mary?'

'Bloody Mary!' yelled Serah.

'What a good idea!' stated Celeste putting her hand in the air. 'Bloody Marys all round!'

'No!' shouted Serah. 'I don't want one. I think I've had enough to drink.'

Ricardo turned her around. 'I think you have as well. Who were you talking to?'

She thought about telling him but the realisation that he hadn't seen the woman meant it would be a difficult question to answer. 'To myself!' Serah declared suddenly feeling sober.

It was an acceptable answer that allowed her to rejoin the conversation which had changed.

Leila's voice had changed and Serah wasn't sure if it was her hearing or because Leila had drunk too much whisky. 'Serah will always be a princess because she is the daughter of Mary Magdalene.'

'Time to go I think,' said Serah who got to her feet. 'Where are we off to next?'

'Our next town is Levis!' declared Francis who stood up with a drink in his hand.

Akasha joined him as she declared that she needed a new pair of jeans.

Ricardo had had enough of being sober and had enough of listening to the silliness. 'Levis is where the rocks are and not where they make jeans!'

'Then let's go,' said Serah moving towards the door.

'I want to sleep,' said Lizette looking out at the darkness through the windows.

'How long have we been here?' asked Serah as she pulled on the iron handle.

'Too long,' replied Ricardo who was busy getting everyone out of their chairs. 'The accommodation isn't far so let's go.'

With everyone, including Francis, rounded up, Ricardo was able to drive to the guesthouse and escort each of them to their rooms. It had been an exhausting time, and knowing that everyone was asleep helped him to let go and sink into his bed. The blankets covered his body, instantly giving him a feeling of warmth and with a soft pillow under his head he was able to clear his mind. It would have been an enjoyable day if he had been able to participate in the drinking of the spirits. Nevertheless, he had the next day to look forward to, and that was drawing closer. The spirits that awaited him were the ones that were meant to speak from the stones in Levis, so with closed eyes he slipped away into the darkness to rest.

twenty

Levis became the discussion around the breakfast table as no one could remember Victoriaville. Their dehydrated bodies begged for water, which was continually running out. After the fourth jug was brought out, the owner became curious. 'I thought last night you were tired from the trip but now I'm starting to think there was another reason for the drowsiness.'

'Too much to drink,' said Ricardo handing around the basket of toast to soak up the alcohol.

'They don't need bread and water,' said the robust woman holding a jug of water. 'They need a Bloody Mary.'

A shudder ran through Serah's spine. She had gone to bed affirming that she would no longer encounter spirits, so the last thing she needed was a reminder of one she had met. Serah opened her mouth to put an end to the advice but it wasn't necessary as objections were already coming from the others.

With their bodies hydrated and minds reapproaching normality, they headed off and listened to a story from the past that didn't involve royalty. Francis spoke of a woman who managed a business while raising ten children. Her dealings with money had been an inspiration to others, making Serah realise that much could be achieved in the real world. There was no need for Serah to be involved with spirits. She was going to leave the spiritual tour and explore a land that had no ghost stories. Italy was a country of real history with no conspiracies—or so she thought.

'Who cares about what others have done?' called out Ricardo with a grin on his face. 'I want to hear about the stones and their spirits of the past.'

Serah sank into her seat with all hope lost of seeing the real Italy. She knew if she went with him, they would end up continually seeking stones to converse with. She needed him to be normal, so when they stopped to look at a wall of water thundering down in front of them, she took him aside.

'Don't you want to climb down to see the water from the bottom?' he asked pointing to where he wanted to be.

'I do,' she answered holding him still, 'but I need to know now, when we go to Italy, we will go to where normal tourists go.'

'Of course,' he said nonchalantly as he walked away.

'I mean it!' she called out behind him. 'I'm not going with you if you only want to look at rocks. I want to go to the Leaning Tower of Pisa and places like that!'

He turned to face her, expecting her to follow, but she didn't budge.

'I want you to promise me that we will go to tourist spots. You have to promise me that we will go to Pisa to see the tower!'

'Okay,' he said putting his hands up in the air.

As she caught up with him, he reminded her that the tower was made of stones but she was not impressed.

At the bottom of the path, the others stood feeling the spray from the water as it smashed into the river below. The smooth rocks looked man-made and if the crashing sound hadn't been so deafening, Celeste would have made a comment about the rocks being carved out by aliens. Serah wanted to think logically and told herself that the rocks had been smoothed out by the water over the years. Taking on a rational outlook, she thought about how the trip could make her a stronger person. If she was weak then she would not be able to get rid of her spirit friend. Sarah Cupsip had always been the dominant one in their relationship and would not have left the human realm if she didn't want to. With everything that Serah had to deal with she was beginning to think it was meant to be; she was learning how to deal with things that were out of the ordinary, which would make her stronger. She had been able to make a rational decision about the rock formation and if she continued to do so then she would be able to tell the unwanted spirit to leave.

Feeling better about herself she went back to the bus to wait for the others to join her.

'Eager to leave,' said Celeste as they got to the bus.

'I could have stayed a bit longer,' said Akasha looking over at Serah. 'I was just starting to hear things.'

Serah reminded herself that it was the water that Akasha had been listening to and the voices were her imagination.

'Did you see how level those rocks were?' Celeste asked anyone who was prepared to listen.

'We could go back down,' said Leila. 'I think Ricardo will be there for a while. He's sitting down on the rocks with his eyes closed.'

Serah reminded herself that he was in her life to make her stronger. She had to let him do what he wanted without it having an effect on her. Determined not to give in, she went to a nearby rock to sit down and wait. The others were heading back down to the water but Serah was a woman with independent thought and had made a decision to stay put.

'It's easier for Lamia to connect with you if you are near the water,' said a voice in Serah's head.

She put it down to the spirit that Serah didn't want and ignored it.

'If you don't like the thought of the serpent or the Lady of the Lake then what about the whales that hold the knowledge? They can tell you about the underground tunnels that have been filled with gold.'

Serah refused to listen and tried to think about something else, but nothing would emerge. She began to hum instead, but the voice became louder, 'Minds have been erased of a life that once was. There are tell-tale signs here and there but only some are intrigued. Some are beginning to remember and are beginning to wonder about how the past was like the future. No one will find the gold because it is under the rivers and well protected. No one thinks to dig anywhere else except for the ground. There is one who remembers but needs to be released. I told you of my soulmate. It is he who needs our help. That was why I could never find him because he had been trapped away from all eyes.'

'Stop it, Sarah Cupsip!' threatened Serah. 'I am not doing anything so you can leave. I know what you are up to and I won't be your slave.'

'Don't you want to know about the future?' asked Sarah Cupsip in a hissing noise that slid from Serah's spine into her mind. We all have curiosity. It is a trait in our DNA that comes from the reptiles we once were. You know there was a different future at one point. You know about the American soldiers who were stationed in England: they came across the spaceship that was from the future. The spaceship wasn't from aliens; it was from us in the future. You know it was real. They even left coordinates of where to go so the civilisation would rise again to make the planet safe. You can't deny it.'

Serah knew of the story and tried to look at it rationally. The location that was given was one of a land that had sunk and as she thought about it, it could have been put to the bottom of the ocean for good reason. It could have been that the soulmate Sarah Cupsip longed for was responsible for a world that once was. Was it that someone intervened to make the planet safe, and as a result he was trapped? Yet, she thought, there was peace in the world and if it wasn't broken then why should she try to fix it. Love had blinded Sarah Cupsip to the truth and Serah was not going to let the spirit interfere in her life any longer.

Ricardo was coming to her rescue. He believed in spirits and as he walked towards the bus she ran towards him to ask for help.

'Do you know how to get rid of a spirit?' Serah pleaded as she grabbed his shoulders.

Celeste interrupted, 'I do.'

Francis listened in as Akasha stated that she also thought there was someone else with Serah.

'When we get to Nackawic,' said Francis, 'we'll do it there.'

'Why there?' asked Celeste wanting to get rid of the spirit straight away.

'There is an axe,' he said. 'It is an axe that will cut the connection.'

'Is that the next stop?' asked Serah wanting to get it over and done with.

'Saint Leonard is the next stop, then we head for Nackawic,' said Ricardo unlocking the door for everyone to enter.

Spirits and ghosts were the topic on the bus, but Serah didn't want to hear so switched off to look outside the window.

'You can't get rid of me,' said the voice inside Serah. 'I was a witch in one of my lives and magic is still within me.'

'I'm not scared of you,' Serah answered quietly as she covered her mouth so the others couldn't see her speak.

'You should be scared of Lizette Leclerk,' said the spirit. 'She is the one that will end your life.'

'If mine is ended then so is yours,' whispered Serah.

'I have magic. I am stronger than others and I could try to go into Lizette. She maybe unattractive but she has the same feelings as I do towards the man that is trapped underground,' said the spirit of Sarah. 'With or without me you will still end up in the same place.'

'You were a nice human being and a good friend,' whispered Serah.

A chill ran through Serah as the spirit declared that she was no longer in human form and had been amalgamated with her past memories so nothing else mattered as she only wanted love. 'You are my means to get to him.'

'So you sent me on this trip knowing I would end up where he was,' whispered Serah.

'It turned out that way. It was not planned,' said the spirit.

'Why don't you use Lizette?' whispered Serah looking around to make sure that she couldn't be heard. 'And leave me to be with Ricardo.'

The spirit inside was silent for a moment but then explained that Lizette was too strong. Her reptilian trait was far stronger than most and it was difficult for a spirit to enter her body or control her mind.

'Please remember the friendship we once had,' whispered Serah. 'Leave me alone.'

'I need your body,' answered the spirit. 'You have a look about you that reminds me of a girl who my soulmate loved. She is now with someone else and far away. If you save him then he might fall in love with you.'

Serah couldn't believe she was being used and could end up dying for no cause.

'What if he doesn't fall in love with me? Do I then die?' whispered Serah.

'He will, I know it!' screamed the spirit. 'He will fall in love with your body and once your spirit leaves then I will become you. I have the power to take over you!'

'Do you have a magic potion!' screamed Serah drawing attention to herself.

'What potion is that?' asked Akasha, suddenly realising that Serah had a more interesting conversation.

'Sorry,' said Serah turning around to face the others. 'I must have been dreaming.'

'I bet it's the spirit inside you,' said Celeste with authority. 'I think we should get rid of it now.'

'It is better to do it at the right place,' said Francis wondering what would be covered in his insurance if something happened to Serah.

'Just tell it to leave,' stated Leila.

Ricardo interjected stating that he knew of someone who might be able to help at the next stop.

No one had noticed that the bus had taken a different direction, but when Ricardo noticed Serah was talking to herself he had become worried. He had phoned a contact living in the area who had found a place close by for Ricardo to drive to. It was not part of the tour but then having a spirit on board wasn't something he had expected either. As the group seemed to be fascinated with the ordeal then he thought they wouldn't mind the change in plans. He was the driver and could lose his job, but then he didn't care as it was far more important to rid the spirit that was sharing his future wife's body.

twenty one

Saint Leonard was meant to be the next stop but as they entered a town of grey roofs with small windows poking out, they turned down a dirt road that took them deep into a quiet forest.

'Where are we going?' asked Francis curiously.

'Slight detour!' called out Ricardo. 'Don't worry, the group will love it.'

The road became bumpy and after a few jolts in his seat, Francis decided it would be better to have the conversation later. He buckled up his seatbelt as others were jostled in their seats due to the tyres sliding across the gravel. All chatter had stopped, leaving only a few anxious women clinging onto their belts. Lizette thought to tell him to slow down but then she didn't want to distract him.

Ricardo was in a hurry and when a house appeared in the distance, everyone sighed with relief that they had reached their destination.

'Are you Aluk?' asked Ricardo opening the window beside the man who originated from an American Indian tribe.

'I am,' he said lifting his hand to show Ricardo where to park.

With everyone out, Aluk introduced himself and invited the group inside for a cup of tea.

'I think I need something stronger than tea after that ride,' joked Akasha.

Aluk turned with a smile. 'I have that too.'

A fire roared from the wall where chairs formed a semi-circle to face it. With warm drinks in their hands, the women joined Francis to sit and chat while Aluk became familiar with the spirit that didn't want to leave.

'Can you make her go away?' asked Serah with a look of despair.

Aluk took a deep breath in. 'I can try.'

He took hold of Serah's hands as Ricardo watched in silence. Aluk could feel the energy and decided to take his patient to a room where she could lie down.

A room filled with symbols was thick with the smell of myrrh and sage. As Serah made herself comfortable, Aluk grabbed a bowl and ran a piece of wood around it, creating a high-pitched sound that vibrated in the air. A few words in his native tongue joined the ringing sound and after a few minutes the air cooled and Sarah Cupsip appeared before Aluk.

With the spirit removed from the body, Aluk placed his fingers over the host's body for her to sleep through the ordeal. He questioned the spirit as to why she had not moved onto the light and after a conversation which revealed that she wanted to be with her soulmate, he knew that she was no ordinary energy that was hanging around out of confusion. She was conniving and he would have to be the same to make her disappear.

'If I help you connect with your soulmate then will you leave this woman alone?' he asked in a soothing voice.

She promised on her soul that she would, and so with a guarantee of trust between the two of them, he asked for her to enter a space of nothing but peace until the time was right. Sarah Cupsip looked at the bottle he held and played along as she knew that no bottle could hold her.

'I will ask your host and your friend to let you loose under the tree in Nova Scotia. It has a connection to the tree that is in America which was where your soulmate once lived. His energy is connected to the gold that runs through the ground underneath the roots of the trees so you will find him and with your magic you will be able to release him to return to your original home together,' stated Aluk with an aura of confidence.

There was something in his demeanour that she trusted so she allowed herself to go into the bottle which he then shut tight.

Being in the bottle had not been a concern for Sarah Cupsip but what she hadn't realised was that Aluk also had powers that were not of the human realm and was able to seal the object, making it impossible for her to escape. In his native tongue, he had called on Epona who was the Celtic queen of protection. Her job had been to protect horses and he had called on her on many occasions to help the horses he had rescued. Over the years, he had developed a relationship with her and found her powers extended to healing the spines that still held the DNA of the snake. People and horses alike were affected with the reptilian influence that worked its way to the brain.

This case was a little different, but the effects were always negative, and with Epona's powers they were able to work together to surround the body with a positive energy that would keep negativity at bay. While Serah had been asleep, he had asked Epona to help her and once the work was finished, the room returned to being clear of the burning herbs. The woman on the massage table woke feeling free.

'Has she gone?' asked Serah, rubbing her eyes to focus.

Aluk handed her a bottle. 'She is in here. Put it in a safe place and when you get to the tree at your last stop then place it in the hole underneath it.'

Serah looked at the bottle, not believing what she had been through in such a short time. 'Do I have to take the lid off?'

'No,' said Aluk, 'I have requested that the lid come off when she makes contact with her soulmate.'

'So what happens to them then?' asked Serah wondering where two spirits would go to be together.

'There is a realm that they have both lived in and they can either live there or stay under the ground.' Aluk said taking her hand so she could get back to her feet.

Aluk escorted her through the doorway to an anxious Ricardo. 'What happened? Has she gone? Are you alright?'

A hand was put on Ricardo's forehead to calm him down and when Aluk released him, he hugged Serah who then grabbed Aluk to join together in a sense of relief.

An anxious group was also sitting in front of the fire and was not sure how to react when the three people walked into the room.

'Is everything alright?' asked Francis.

'It's over,' said Aluk and with everything being back to normal, Akasha asked about the pictures of the horses on the walls.

Aluk pulled up a chair to join them and explained how he had spent his life looking after horses that had been neglected.

'I don't mean to seem rude,' stated Celeste, 'but isn't that expensive? Where does the money come from to feed and take care of the animals?'

Aluk could understand why she would be wondering where the money came from as the surroundings didn't scream wealth. 'I make money from people who come to me for healing. If I kept the money, I would be able to renovate this house but my home provides me with the accommodation I need so I use the money to bring me happiness instead. It makes me happy to see the horses healed and hopefully I will be rewarded when it's time for me to move on.'

'Do you think that spirits move on?' asked Akasha eager to gain knowledge from the man.

Celeste answered for him. 'You have just witnessed first-hand the effects of a spirit that has not moved on. How can you still question what you know is true?'

'So the spirit has left you?' asked Lizette glad to be rid of the competition that could interfere with her plans.

'She has,' answered Aluk while staring at Lizette. 'So you were going to Saint Leonard to see the caves!'

Francis stood up, taking the cue to leave.

'There is more to my home than a plain house,' said Aluk motioning for them to follow him.

Outside, the trees opened up to fields of green that horses happily chewed on. It was cold, but their coats shone from the few rays of sun and their healthy bodies meant they had been healed. The closer the group walked towards the field, the more aware the animals became and they lifted their heads and neighed and snorted in appreciation to the man who had helped them.

'Are we walking through the fields?' asked Lizette wondering if she should change her shoes.

'No,' said Aluk who took them to a track that went back through the trees.

The cloudy sky disappeared as the treetops merged above the group. With only glimpses of light filtering through the branches it was difficult to see what was ahead, especially when they walked up to a darkness that became solid.

'It's rock,' said Ricardo with a smile on his face.

'Trust you to know,' stated Serah feeling more like herself.

'Oh,' said Leila looking around, 'we're going to meditate here.'

Aluk shook his head and they followed him through a gap that seemed invisible.

Once inside, a light showed the cave that made his house look small in comparison. Feeling inferior, the group huddled together to look around at the giant hole in the rock. Keeping Aluk close by, a discussion commenced as to how it had happened. Was it once a home for someone who belonged to a civilisation that had been forgotten? There were many theories but no one knew for sure. They discussed that it could have been a meeting place with its many ridges for people to stand on as there appeared to be a stage carved into the formation.

The light came from the end of a tunnel and imaginations ran wild as they followed the hallway from the grand room that took them to homes that belonged to people in the past. There were tunnels branching off in different directions but Aluk led them to where they would be most impressed. An opening took them through to where formations dropped from the roof, giving the impression of hanging chandeliers. At any moment, the lights would be switched on when the sun appeared through the clouds, and when it did the reflection in the water took their breath away. A drop fell from above, causing a rippling effect that made the water below appear as silk. Colours changed with the sun's rays, leaving the gobsmacked group to watch in silence.

A smile appeared on Aluk's face as he watched the mesmerised eyes. 'You see, you don't need money to enjoy what is around you,' he said.

Akasha had to make a point. 'You do need money to live or you wouldn't charge for the healings you do.'

'You have a point,' he said, 'but it is used for what is needed and that's all. I don't use the money for anything that is not necessary.'

Akasha agreed that he also had a point and went back to staring at the creation that Mother Nature had provided.

'Personally, I think aliens had something to do with this,' said Celeste taking the attention away from Aluk.

'I agree,' said Aluk as the others looked at him in shock. 'We are all aliens.'

With the change in topic, Francis decided that it was time to head back to the bus.

twenty two

Nackawic came into view in a form of a giant axe.
'What is that all about?' asked Akasha, staring out the window.

Francis went to speak but was interrupted by Celeste. 'It's to keep the aliens away. If they see a weapon of that size from the sky then they will think that humans are huge and will keep going.'

'Really!' said Leila glaring at Celeste. 'Tell me you are joking!'

'I think there is something about giants being here in the past that is real!' called out Ricardo as he drove to find a parking spot.

Serah rolled her eyes but no longer had to fear the unknown as her thoughts were completely her own.

'Come on,' said Celeste rushing to get out. 'There is evidence that there have been giants on this earth.'

She had stirred up emotions that remained on high as they got off the bus to examine the huge structure.

Francis sat near the axe. 'I thought we could meditate here.'

'Here?' questioned Leila, looking around at the other people who were also wondering why there was a giant axe in their view.

'It's on a rock,' answered Francis wondering if he should change his tour schedule as he didn't want to upset his clients.

'Who cares?' said Lizette who joined him to hold hands as they closed their eyes to the stares around them.

A woman passing by asked what they were doing.

'Meditating,' answered Akasha who kept her eyes shut.

'They're probably trying to connect with the aliens,' said Celeste, half-jokingly.

The statement brought on laughter that ended the meditation and included other tourists who were interested in the alien theory.

A woman handed her camera to her husband as she came forward to speak of a trip she had taken where she was sure aliens had once lived. With Celeste having someone to speak to who was on the same page as her, she turned to ask her about that holiday.

'Well,' said the woman as she put her sunglasses into her bag, 'I went to Los Angeles to visit a friend. I went by plane so I brought a book to read to pass the time away. The story told of how there was a tree in America that transports you to other dimensions and realms. It got me thinking so when I got to my friend's house, I used her computer to look up the origins of Los Angeles. I've always been a big believer in things that happen for a reason so I wanted to know what there was for me at my destination.'

'What did you find?' asked Celeste who loved conspiracy theories.

'Well, you know what the internet is like,' she said looking around at her husband who stood behind her with others. 'One thing leads to another. Angeles becomes angels that became aliens.'

'Do you think that angels are aliens?' asked Akasha, shocked that she had received a vision of a man that looked like an angel.

'Well, what do you call beings that came down from the sky?' interrupted Celeste.

Akasha had no answer so the woman continued by stating that she found more information. 'I had no idea there were so many sightings recorded on the internet. Imagine if we didn't have it!'

'What did you find out?' asked Celeste, trying to glean information from her.

'Alien craft were looking over Los Angeles when the Japanese attacked Pearl Harbour. There is a triangle of water on the west side of The States that is a hotspot for sightings. Apparently, people have seen the spaceships coming and going out of the ocean. There have even been people who have used a camera to look under the water and it has recorded domes that are not made naturally. There has to be something inside the domes!'

Leila joined in the conversation with the knowledge she had. 'I think it's gold. Think about it. Los Angeles was originally a gold mining town and the aliens probably need gold and have kept it under the water.'

Serah listened but didn't comment as Leila continued to tell her theory. 'There are alien sightings in Los Angeles, I think because they are watching over their stash. When war broke out, they were probably worried about their gold being found. Wasn't Roosevelt president and didn't he take gold from people?'

'I think you're right,' said Celeste who wanted to know more. 'Where is that gold and where is the gold that was under the twin towers that were destroyed? There always seems to be a war involved when it comes to gold being hidden.'

'Where there is light, there is a shadow,' said the woman who was glad to speak with like-minded people.

'You mean that some in the government work with the aliens,' said Celeste, grabbing the woman's shoulder.

Francis and Lizette stretched to end the conversation that would have continued for hours. Celeste was not happy to leave the woman but there was no alternative, so once ways of contact were established between the two, the husband pulled on his wife to leave.

With the woman gone, Leila stated that the conversation would have continued on to using the pyramids as nuclear driven instruments that would create gold.

Celeste smiled as she put her arm around Leila's shoulders. 'So you do believe!'

Leila shrugged her away. 'I believe in nothing until I see it.'

'Believe in what?' asked Lizette, joining them.

'Nothing,' said Celeste as they walked off to find a restaurant for sustenance.

The spiritual tour was changing. What was supposed to be a quiet week of meditation in the wilderness was turning into a debate over drinks. The restaurant they picked had a bar hidden in the corner and once a drinks menu was placed in front of them, the whisky with maple syrup found its way to the table.

'The accommodation is walking distance ladies,' announced Ricardo who was not going to spend another night listening to silliness while he was sober.

'You're not going to make us walk, are you?' said Akasha as she sat back in her chair.

'If you ladies order another bottle to the table then you are walking,' he said, taking a glass.

With hushed tones and hungry stomachs that grumbled in protest, the women went to order their meals. The specialty was ribs which was requested by most until the waiter turned for the last order from Francis.

'I think I'll have the fish with potato and salad,' he said. 'Oh, and a bottle of whisky.'

Ricardo interrupted, 'You are walking, then!'

'You said that we would walk if one of the ladies ordered,' protested Akasha. 'Francis is no lady!'

Ricardo threw down his glass of alcohol to let them know he was not driving.

Serah had been quiet but with a few glasses of whisky in her stomach, she began to open up. She no longer had to fear visions and the memory of the last drinking session, where the spirit had sat opposite her. It was nothing but a bad dream that was in her bag.

'Are you feeling better?' asked Ricardo as he took her hand.

She nodded. 'I'm actually looking forward to going to Italy with you.'

'You're going to Italy!' interrupted Leila as she slammed her glass onto the table. 'I'm coming with you.'

Akasha waved her hands to gain attention. 'Maybe they want to be alone!'

Glasses were filled by the waiter who hoped that they would give a generous tip at the end of the night. As he leaned over to the left side of Leila, his wish was presented earlier.

'Here's a tip for you,' she said as she put the money into his vest pocket and dragged him over.

'Thanks,' he said as he fell on to Leila's lap.

'Let him go,' demanded Lizette who didn't like what was happening on the tour.

'He fell on me,' said Leila still holding him.

'You pulled him on top of you,' said Akasha who lifted her glass with a smile.

The waiter didn't know what to do as the woman holding him was older than he was. He didn't want to offend anyone as there was the rest of the table that could tip him, so diplomatically he kissed her cheek. As she looked at him in shock, he made his move and got up to fill the rest of the glasses.

Hysterics filled the restaurant with the other diners also witnessing the event and as the night wore on, other patrons interacted with the group. Conversations became intense and were only broken up by a crowd that loved to sing. The owner cringed at the heels digging into the table tops from those who wanted to dance. Once Celeste brought up the conversation about aliens, it was time for the bar to close.

Outside, the cold mist hit their faces but did nothing to dampen their spirits. A thought crossed Ricardo's mind about getting the bus but it wasn't his responsibility to control the women who were walking off in different directions. Dalliances had been formed, which Francis should have put a stop to but he was too intoxicated to take control. With one last glimmer of hope Ricardo yelled out, knowing that everyone could hear him, 'The house is at the end of this street!'

Some turned to see where he was pointing while a couple went off with their new friends.

'I need a horse so I can round them up,' he said to Serah who was balancing on his arm.

'They're old enough to find their way,' she slurred.

He knew that Serah was right and walked her to where everyone else should have been.

It was difficult for him to sleep as he listened for familiar voices to creep down the hallway. He heard Francis talking to himself as he fiddled with the key and waited for the others to follow but it was some time before a cackle of females tried to be quiet as they opened their doors. Being difficult for Ricardo to tell who was amongst the females, he hoped that they were all there and finally fell asleep.

As soon as the sun appeared through the curtains, Ricardo left Serah to sleep as he went to the reception to find out who had taken the keys that were left out for the late arrivals. There were two keys that had not been taken and he wondered who the two were and if they were alright. He had no idea why he felt responsible so went to wake Francis to help him with his search. On his way down the hallway, he turned right to head towards Francis' room when he came across two females sprawled across the floor. Relieved, he hoped that they were the two without the keys. They appeared to be comfortable with their heads on their bags, so he decided to leave them and go back to his own bed which held the body that would support his head for a peaceful sleep.

A knocking on the door made Serah jump and as she looked at

the clock to find they had slept in, she heard the voice of the person trying to get their attention.

'Breakfast is nearly over!' called out Leila. 'I've told them you're coming.'

Ricardo was completely oblivious and curled up into the blankets.

'Get up,' she said, trying to untangle him from the bed.

With a thud, he woke as he hit the floor.

'Sorry,' she said, 'but we have to get up now. We slept in.'

Ricardo massaged his aching head as he watched Serah throw some clothes on.

'Come on,' she grumbled as she tried to dress him at the same time.

It wasn't until they were at the table with the others that Serah found out why Ricardo was so tired. She had no idea how worried he had been and admired him for taking action when he feared the worst. The others listened as he told of his ordeal that got him out of bed too early to look for them and with that knowledge he was given a hug by the women who had managed to get back to the hotel.

'Actually,' said Leila, sipping on her coffee, 'I don't know how I ended up here.'

Ricardo put up his hand. 'I don't want to know.'

twenty three

Salisbury was a stop Serah was going to enjoy. She was no longer the subject of discussion amongst the others as the spirit of her friend was well and truly gone. Although there were only three days left of the tour, they were going to make up for the time that had been lost due to interference. The tour had changed, and so had the group that was participating. No one knew what to expect in Salisbury and that was including the tour guide. Things were out of his control, so instead of telling everyone what they would be doing, he decided to ask the women what they wanted. He expected shopping or to a spa but it was Akasha who spoke up. 'I would like to go for a walk in the woods. I came on this tour to connect with nature and as Salisbury in England is a spiritual place, I presume this one must be as well. I can see plenty of hikers using the paths so they must be good. If anyone doesn't want to connect with anything then they can enjoy the fresh air and exercise.'

Francis looked around to see if there were any objections but there were none. 'Alright Ricardo, pull over where you can and we'll find a path.'

Akasha was first off the bus. 'If you don't mind, I would like to be alone on this walk.'

Francis raised his voice so everyone could hear. 'It's fine if you want to do your own thing but make sure that you're back here in an hour!'

Everyone checked their watches as Akasha took off to be by herself. Lizette caught up with Leila who had casually strolled off at a leisurely pace. The previous night, Lizette had returned to the accommodation alone as she had been confused with her feelings of anxiety. Something was coming up but she wasn't sure if she wanted to follow through with the voice in her head. Her head wanted to end Serah's life there and then, but her heart had wanted to have fun with the others who had taken off with strangers during the night. As Leila seemed to be level headed, she decided to walk with her to discuss the night before. Serah watched the others disperse but wanted to take in the scenery with her own mind so she asked Ricardo if he would leave her alone. He was reluctant, but left her standing alone when Celeste grabbed his and Francis' arms. She took them away, interested to hear what Ricardo had found in his rock studies and how Francis had ended up being a tour guide. Being alone was what Serah needed, but once the others had gone she felt empty. The chatter was gone and the lack of traffic on the road made a beautiful place eerie.

There was only thirty minutes left for her to explore and then she would have to turn around to be back in time. The track everyone had chosen was not the only one that branched out into the woodlands, so to make sure she wouldn't run into anyone else, she chose a different one. It was a path that was well worn with its smooth surface winding through the trunks and bushes. The empty feeling she felt with the loss of her companions was replaced with happiness provided by the songs from the birds. Leaves gave a tiny thud when they landed on the ground and were quickly moved when confronted by creatures that remained out of sight. There was a freedom Serah enjoyed, that she couldn't remember experiencing in the past. Her mind was her own; but she couldn't understand why the chatter in her head had previously always been one that used the word *you* instead of *I*. She walked along thinking that it was nice to be able to say to herself, *I'm enjoying the trip* instead of telling herself, *you must enjoy the trip*. The change with one word made such a difference to her outlook and she loved it. Opening her arms and closing her eyes as she lifted her head to the sky, she took in a deep breath to let go of everything in the past.

She continued to walk in the darkness to picture her life with Ricardo. The vibration of love that filled her, lifted her from the ground. She was at one with the universe and she wondered if Akasha was experiencing the same thing she was. A wet foot brought her back to her other senses. Somehow, she had stepped into a large puddle of water. Everywhere else was dry so she couldn't understand where the water came from. Curiosity got the better of her as she followed a tiny stream the width of her foot to a pond that was surrounded by bushes. A bear that had been eating berries left the bush when it realised that it was not alone. Serah watched it without fear and appreciated the beauty of the animal as it moved away. From the ground came sounds of the creatures that were hidden amongst the fallen foliage, and as her focus changed to take in the life that was lived by others, she noticed something she had only ever read about.

It was a tiny woman, the size of Serah's hand, hanging washing on a line. Serah closed her eyes and then opened them again to focus, but the woman was gone. A hawthorn bush blocked her view and as she tried to push it out of the way, the woman appeared again. 'You can't uproot a hawthorn bush. It is a plant from our world when we once lived below, but its roots are now trapped in the gold.'

Serah went to speak but nothing came out as she bent down.

The chatty faery went on to tell of how she had stayed with her sister who lived in a graveyard in Wales that had a tree that would speak the names of the people who were next to die.

Serah sat on the ground to be closer to her. 'Do you often speak to people?'

The tiny woman shook her head. 'Not many come here. Mind you, I am on holiday.'

'What accent is that you have?' asked Serah trying to comprehend the little person she was conversing with.

'Welsh,' said the woman with a song in her voice. 'And your accent is from where?'

'Australia,' answered Serah who was wondering if the conversation was real. 'Are you a faery?'

'Some call me that,' said the woman. 'My people call me Heather.'

'That's a beautiful name,' said Serah taking in her tiny form with skin as white as snow and hair filled with flowers with a dress to match.

'And your name is?' asked Heather handing her a miniature flower.

'Serah Kohw,' answered Serah as she accepted the flower.

Heather took out a mirror and handed it to the woman with thick blonde hair and dark features.

'Who khares,' said Serah as she read what was written on the mirror. 'I'm saying that a lot lately. Is that how you spell it in Welsh?'

The faery put her hand out for the return of the mirror as she shook her head. 'No, that is your name backwards.'

Heather put her pegs back into the pocket of her dress and bowed reverently.

'Why did you do that?' said Serah surprised with the reaction.

'Because you are royalty. Serah is the name for a princess,' she said, 'except the one that is in the bottle.'

Serah felt for the bottle in her bag. 'How do you know?'

'I might be small but my senses are big,' said Heather, pointing her tiny finger. 'That Sarah was a witch. She took the wrong path in life and she has to pay for it.'

'How do you know about her?' asked an astonished Serah, clinging on to her bag.

'Once she was as my ancestors were,' said Heather in a voice that sang to the air. 'She was a faery that could fly, but she was full of mischief. She should have been a pixie. The goddess of the universe gave her something to do to keep her busy. She was given a job in another realm but she found a branch and remembered that she had magic so she used it for transportation.'

'Is this all real?' interrupted Serah. 'Why haven't I heard about all of this?'

'Because you didn't want to know,' stated Heather. 'There are many who believe in one story but not another.'

'Can you tell me more about Sarah Cupsip?' said Serah, thinking of the friend she once had and really not known.

'She is in love with a man named Gavin Macleod but she has always been in love with a Macleod. The family comes from an island, far north of where I am from, beyond the highlands. They lived there in the fourteenth century and that was where she was truly happy. She had a child but it was taken by the pixies—pixies are troublemakers. But instead of negotiating to get the child back, she used her magic on a shawl that she placed over the baby to keep them away. A princess has to be able to negotiate.'

'So she was punished!' said Serah now starting to wonder about her own past lives.

Heather went back to putting the clothes on the line. 'No, she punished herself. It was the ninth month when the men started to come home with the crops. There was always a grand celebration before the winter months with children being conceived for the summer. Sarah had panicked with the thought of pixies stealing babies. She knew that in her next life she would be given another chance at being a princess and didn't want to risk being taken away in that life. So she gave shawls to the royal family to be talismans of protection. There was a great emphasis on superstition at that time—more than now—and when the nine shawls were given out due to her prediction of being ninth in line for the throne, the number became one of importance. This was to her advantage, of course, but it was pagan times and pagans believed it was three that was the number of significance.'

A thought popped into Serah's mind when she realised that the number nine was from the number three because it was multiplied with itself. 'So did she convince the royalty to keep the nine shawls?' asked Serah, intrigued with her maths.

'She did, but three shawls were given to the three young children at the time and the others were put away never to be seen again. If Sarah Cupsip wants to become a royal then she needs to learn empathy and not think about what is in it for her,' said Heather looking at the bag on the woman's lap.

'Why are you telling me all of this?' asked Serah clutching her bag tighter.

'The Lady of the Lake was here,' said Heather nonchalantly.

The answer didn't make any sense, but then Serah thought about Lamia, the serpent she had met only days ago at the river.

'There is another woman with problems brought on by herself,' muttered Heather before raising her voice to be heard clearly. 'Gwragedd Annwn is a Welsh water faery. She keeps the serpent away and she knows that Lamia spoke with you. But you are not to listen as she was speaking to the witch. She knows the spirit has magic and thinks Sarah Cupsip will be able to break her curse. Gwragedd Annwn has no issues with you, but she feels sorry for Akasha.'

'You know Akasha!' said a surprised Serah.

'I don't, but the water faery does and is willing to take her in as one of our own if she wishes.'

Serah interrupted, 'But then shouldn't you be speaking with her instead of me?'

'Of course,' said Heather. 'But you chose this path, not her. Well, I've told you what I had to so I best be getting on with the packing.'

'Where are you going?' asked Serah, leaning back to stretch her spine.

'It's coming up to Hallows Eve,' said Heather taking the washing off the line.

'Isn't that still wet?' Serah wondered aloud, wanting to reach out and touch the tiny clothes.

'Only takes a second to dry,' explained Heather, 'which is just as well because I have to bake cakes.'

'Halloween,' said Serah fascinated with the information that was held within the small mind.

'You call it that,' Heather replied, folding up the clothes as she placed them into the basket.

'But that is months away,' said Serah.

'It is, but I have a lot to do before I leave here and when I get home,' declared Heather. 'I suppose I could celebrate it here. It might be easier. It's not like we burn bonfires any more,' continued Heather as she produced a suitcase.

'You did?' queried a fascinated Serah.

'Poverty sent the Celts to this land but they kept their customs,' said Heather, starting to pack. 'Things changed slightly. Bonfires were replaced with candles but it is still fire. At the end of the tenth month is when the worlds collide and a soul is allowed to visit the human who lights the fire to show them the way. The eleventh month—written one-one—is the two ones that provide the human with the knowledge that was given by the spirit. The knowledge is to be used for good in the twelfth month because when those numbers are added together, they make three and as I told you, three is magic that is for the good of others. And there's the problem right there with Sarah Cupsip. When she was given the information for magic by the spirit who visited her, she used it for herself. She is no Saint Nicholas, is she?'

Serah agreed as she watched Heather walk into her small house of twigs.

As Serah stood to face the path, she wondered how long she had been there. Her watch indicated only ten minutes, but she didn't believe it and hurried back to the bus where Akasha was sitting on a log. There were things that Serah longed to tell her but after what she had put the others through, she presumed that Akasha would think her visions were back. It surprised her to see Akasha waiting alone as she expected her to be the last one back since she was the one wanting time to connect with nature.

'Did you find what you were looking for?' asked Serah as she drew closer.

Akasha looked up with tears falling from her eyes.

'What happened?' asked Serah putting her arms around her.

Akasha sobbed uncontrollably only allowing a few words to escape at a time. By the end of the sentence confirming that she had not experienced anything, Serah knew what she had to do.

'If I tell you something unreal will you promise not to think I'm possessed again?' asked Serah, bringing a smile to Akasha's face.

'You guys are back already!' called out Celeste who still had the men on her arms.

The others dragged behind and as Serah watched them she knew that the faery story would have to remain with her.

A hand on Serah's arm brought her back to Akasha who desperately wanted information of another life, but she didn't know what to say as they were no longer alone.

'I came back early so I could show all of you what I found,' declared Serah prompting everyone to follow her.

Akasha was by her side but Leila and Lizette were complaining. They had had enough of walking and wanted to sit on the log.

'We'll come,' said Ricardo taking over the role of leading the other two who were intrigued.

Serah took the lead as Akasha questioned her about their destination.

'I was going to tell you, but I think it's better if I take you instead so you can see for yourself.'

Minutes later they were at the turn that took them off the path to where a pond sat.

'Isn't it beautiful here?' said Serah, but it was only Akasha who agreed. She could see the colours in the plants, inhale the fresh air and smell the scents from the flowers. Her teary eyes dried up as she took in the aroma of freshly baked cakes.

'Can you smell that?' asked Akasha but Ricardo, Francis and Celeste were staring at the pile of mud.

'I can smell it,' said Celeste, 'and mud is something that I think only pigs can appreciate.'

'Mud!' questioned Serah. 'What mud?'

'In front of you,' said Ricardo who turned her around to face the way he was looking.

'I see a pond of blue water,' she said trying to see what he was seeing.

'I thought the spirit had left you,' said Ricardo in despair.

'I see it too,' interjected Akasha.

Relieved, Serah pulled back on the hawthorn bush where a tiny door opened to reveal the woman inside.

'This is Heather,' said Serah to an astonished Akasha.

'I wouldn't have believed you,' said Akasha, 'but I'm so glad you brought me here. I really needed to see this.'

'You are Akasha,' said Heather with her voice that sang through the air.

Ricardo, Francis and Celeste watched as the two spoke quietly to each other next to a bush that had died a long time ago. They couldn't see anything of interest at this place and were soon distracted by a small pile of stones Ricardo decided to investigate.

'They can't see,' said Serah to the faery.

'No,' said Heather shaking her head.

'Why can I see?' asked Akasha with a smile from ear to ear.

Serah grinned as Heather explained about the water faery giving Akasha an opportunity to experience another life.

'You mean, I can live with the faeries as a faery?' asked an excited Akasha.

Serah grabbed her arm to turn her towards her. 'She means you can see it not live it.'

'No,' interrupted Heather, 'she can live it.'

'And I want to,' said Akasha with opened eyes.

'But you can't,' said Serah looking back at the others. 'You can't just leave now.'

'Why not?' replied Akasha.

'You have a life at home. There will be people who miss you. You have a job waiting for you,' said Serah remembering that she had made the same statement to Ricardo.

'I have no life,' answered Akasha. 'I have no family. I have lived in foster homes all my life and have no friends. No one will miss me. My job will be given to someone else and so will my home. I have never belonged here. I knew I belonged somewhere else. That's why I came on this trip so I could find it and now I have.'

Serah thought about her own decision being a big one to go to Italy for a week and it surprised her to see Akasha react so promptly. 'How does Akasha get there?' said Serah holding Akasha's hands.

'I'll take her,' said Heather placing new flowers in her hair.

'When?' asked Serah.

'Now,' said Heather opening her front door to allow her guest in.

'How do I explain your disappearance?' questioned Serah holding on to Akasha.

'Improvise,' said Heather. 'Now come in or my cakes will burn.'

Serah let go and watched as Akasha put her finger through the door that shrunk her body to fit inside the house. It had all taken place too soon and when a small face belonging to Akasha smiled up at her through the window, Serah knew that she had to do something or she would be a suspect in a disappearance case.

A scream alerted the others and within seconds they were standing next to her looking at the soft mud on the ground.

'Akasha,' sobbed Serah. 'It happened so fast. I was showing her the gold colour in the bush when she fell into the mud.'

The bush glowed to play along but the others were unconvinced.

'How can she just disappear into the ground?' said Ricardo. 'What really happened? Where is she?'

'I told you,' said Serah with a glare, 'she sank.'

Francis was on the phone calling for help that came in a form of a man with an excavation truck. Statements were taken by the police as the vehicle dug up the ground. Serah cringed, hoping that the faery had taken Akasha away from the demolition as Lizette and Leila watched on in disbelieve that a companion could die such an awful death.

'Why didn't you try to get her out?' the policeman asked Serah.

'I did but she was heavy.'

'So why didn't you call out for help?' he asked.

Ricardo joined the defence stating that Serah did call for help and he did hear her struggle but it had happened too quickly.

'There's no body,' called out one policeman who stood next to the excavation truck. 'If she is in deeper then there is no way that she will be alive.'

'Keep digging,' said another policeman who was gathering information.

'Can't,' said the man with the truck. 'I've hit something hard. Must be rock.'

'So where is she?' asked the policeman who looked over at his force who were wading in the mud. 'Why were you here?'

'Akasha wanted to see something different and I had come across this bush,' said Serah hoping that it still sparkled with gold.

After hours of searching, it became obvious that they were not going to find her and with no one to contact or any information about Akasha to be given, the crime scene was closed.

'I knew they couldn't convict you,' said Ricardo. 'Obviously, you had nothing to do with it. It was a freak accident.'

'Do you honestly believe that?' asked Serah as they walked back to the bus with a silent group.

'I do,' he said squeezing her tightly with his arm around her waist. 'I have to.'

'Are you sure you want to be with me?' she asked Ricardo. 'There seems to be a lot going on with me since I've left home. It's like a can of worms has been opened up.'

'You've come out of your box,' he said. 'Life won't be boring with you around, that's for sure!'

twenty four

Oxford was supposed to divert the attention away from the fact that one of their group was gone, but the shock was difficult to replace. Serah tried to put on a look of sadness but inside she was ecstatic. Someone she knew had gone on to a world that she hadn't been sure existed. She longed to tell them but despite their open mindedness, she looked at them knowing they wouldn't accept what she had to say. It was meant to be a tour to open the mind but she wasn't sure if even Ricardo would accept the truth.

Francis tried to bring back normality by stating that they would stop at a rock to meditate as he had originally planned. The stone he had in mind would also be used for him to say a few words to help with Akasha's departure. It was a nice thing he was doing, but Serah knew it wasn't necessary. He also felt the urge to stop and buy a plant to put into the ground before making his speech. Serah wondered why he hadn't thought of the words and plant at the actual site where Akasha had disappeared, but then she realised he must have been in shock and not able to focus on what to do. Or it might have been due to them only seeing a site of smelly mud and not a place that held beauty.

Quietly they all strolled down to the water's edge and as everyone gathered around to watch Francis dig a hole for the shrub, Serah noticed something moving in the water. With the spirit safely in a bottle, there was no fear of the unknown. She knew her mind was her own, and after experiencing the faery she knew anything was possible. A woman who resembled a mermaid appeared under the water. The woman showed her face and long grey hair when she was sure everyone else was distracted.

'I have information for you,' she said in a hushed tone. 'The Lady in the Well has information from the whales that you once came across. They say there are worlds to share with any woman who wants to be wise.'

Serah wasn't sure what she meant and moved closer to hear.

'People are suffering from panic attacks because they are on the wrong path and cannot accept where they have to go. Unless they let go of the ego that puts fears into the mind, they will not find happiness. Unless they learn to be mindful of the moment, they will not rid the anxiety that rushes them through life. Your group you are with claim that they are open yet could not see the pond. All they saw was ugly mud and when they meditate they don't get any messages.'

'Leila got a message,' said Serah leaning over to whisper to her.

'People need to concentrate on what the lessons were that needed to be learned before coming to the human realm, otherwise they will not go where they are meant to.'

'Why was Akasha allowed to go?' asked Serah.

'She believed and had suffered enough, so she was allowed to see,' said the lady who adjusted what looked like a silver tiara on her head.

'Are there royals amongst your kind?' questioned Serah pointing to the water witch's headpiece.

'I was once part of royalty. Believe it or not, I lived in a fairy-tale castle in Luxembourg. Now I live in water. It was an escape for me. I had magic and at the time it was not accepted and I was condemned to be a witch. The human realm is narrow minded but I don't know why, because we are all the same on the inside. Life under the water is serene and what looks like demolished buildings lying at the bottom of the ocean are palaces beyond belief that accept all races of water creatures. I don't mind living under the water, and if I wish to be on land then there are portals that I can use to take me to other planets.'

'There is a girl here,' said Serah pointing to Celeste. 'See the one with the red hair. She believes in other planets that hold life.'

'She says she does,' said the water witch. 'You have already met a woman who said she believed in aliens, but she didn't see the ones that live under the water and that want to use our home to store their gold.'

'So it's true,' declared Serah. 'They do want the gold for their own use.'

'It has been that way for millions of years,' she said as she slid under the water. 'The stones will tell you.'

'Come on!' called out Ricardo. 'The plant is in.'

Serah moved to hold hands with the others as Francis asked for Akasha to have a peaceful life in the unknown and to be reunited with the family she had lost. He motioned for everyone to sit against the large rock and pass on messages to Akasha through meditation.

'What will you say to her?' asked Ricardo sitting next to Serah.

'Don't know,' replied Serah adjusting herself to be comfortable.

'I'm not going to think of anything and just let whatever there is come through,' he said. 'I've been thinking about you and Akasha seeing a pond when I only saw mud. Maybe there is more I can get from stones if I accept that they do have stories to tell. I often say they do but then I wonder what others think about me. I have an ego I have to let go of.'

Serah looked at him with surprise as she explained that she would try to do the same.

'What are you two muttering about?' asked Celeste who had moved closer to them.

'We are going to try meditation by letting our egos go first,' said Serah. 'Try letting go of yours and maybe you will get answers from the planets.'

Celeste scoffed, 'I don't have any ego.'

'Yes you do,' said Serah, 'otherwise you would get information.'

'Time to close your eyes,' said Francis as a way of telling everyone that he wanted quiet.

Being away from civilisation made it easy to focus on the sounds of nature but Serah was shocked to hear the noise of a flicking tail in the water. She thought the water witch had gone but she hadn't and made herself known by jumping above the river every so often. Thinking it might be a test of distraction, Serah erased the witch from her mind and allowed her brain to go blank. Darkness filled her with a feeling of peace but only for a minute as the splashing soon brought on the chatterbox inside her head that wanted to know who was making the noise. It was a fight but Serah was determined and focused on her breathing as a way to shut out the voice in her head.

The battle with her brain had been long but ended when Francis asked if anyone had made contact with Akasha.

'I made contact with the universe,' said a surprised Ricardo. 'There was a lot of information and I'm not sure if I remember everything. Do you want to know?'

'Of course,' everyone declared in unison.

'Well, we all know matter exists as solid, liquid and gas,' he said before stopping to try to remember everything. 'An energy was telling me that existence of a different state of being lies beyond these three. Psychically attuned observers are able to see the presence of auras. An aura is similar to a magnetic field. It's energy and thoughts and emotions which are on display. Energy acts as a bridge between the physical and psychic states. Beyond the etheric is another state of matter known as the astral plane. Thoughts in the mental body pass through into the astral body and it takes on the form and passes into the physical body. The astral level is a meeting ground for physical and intuitive states of being, guided by cosmic forces. All matter is in a highly receptive state where ideas and images in the plane can be created. Stories are accepted by diverse people and eventually unlock the secrets of the soul. I am attracted to the stones because I sensed they held stories that needed to be unlocked. I feel like now I know I am right.'

'Wow,' said an astonished Francis.

'You got all that?' asked Leila, disgusted that she got nothing.

'Me too,' said Celeste. 'I got information and you were right, Serah, I had been blocking the portals of the planets. They do exist. I went to Saturn and saw where the witch in the water goes.'

'You saw her?' asked Serah looking over to the water.

The others looked as well but couldn't see anything.

'I thought that was a fish splashing around,' said Lizette.

Celeste looked over at the water but it was still. 'I thought it was fish at first but then she took me through the portal and I met the son of Zeus who explained why ancient people believed in gods and why they always relied on the stars to give them information. We are the bodies that move in the same manner as the cosmic forces that drive the universe. We are the reflection of all creation. Our blood moves to the rhythms of the moon. The god's son took me to meet a goddess known as Epona. She is the goddess of the moon and horses. She works with Juno Regina, ruling the universe. They told me of a lady who used to be a goddess and who now lives in Scotland, and if I ever have any doubt as to what they were saying, I can go there and visit her. They told me of beings that have been here but are now in the sky. Their bones are made from the dust of stars as ours are. Our mind and frame embody ancient mythic principles. I was also taken to Venus, which was once a woman who has secrets that are still guarded to this day. We have to understand ourselves to understand the workings of the universe. We strive to understand. Why do you think so many people strive to go to university? It is because we all want the knowledge from the universe that has been forgotten.'

'Wow again,' said Francis. 'I got nothing!'

'Did anyone else get something?' asked Leila looking at Serah. The onlookers shook their heads.

'You need to stop the chatterbox in your head,' demanded Celeste.

'How do you know that he was the son of Zeus?' quizzed Lizette wondering if the whole thing was just Celeste's imagination.

'I know. It was not my imagination,' said Celeste. 'His name is Khrysos and he is married to a woman with hair longer than mine. They live on Saturn and are protected by the rings.'

'Isn't it a ring of rocks?' said Lizette trying to find a flaw in her story.

'The rocks are garnet,' said Celeste who looked down at a ring of gold that enveloped a heart-shaped garnet on her finger. 'Is this proof enough?'

'Where did you get that?' asked an astonished Leila who grabbed her hand.

'From Khrysos,' smiled Celeste studying the object.

'Ridiculous,' stated Lizette staring at the ring.

'Is it possible?' asked Leila staring at the ring.

'It is,' said Ricardo. 'Think about what I was told. A creation from the astral plane formed itself to appear as a solid.'

Lizette stormed off as Serah looked at the ring. There was something about the ring that made her feel safe. She remembered being told in Alaska about buying a ring that had a stone of protection but the garnet had a significance that she couldn't remember. Had it been important to her or was it that it had been important to the part of the spirit that belonged to Sarah Cupsip? The soul that was now in the bottle had left behind a piece of DNA that had lodged itself into Serah Kohw's spine.

twenty five

Nova Scotia was the last stop of the tour and the last day Serah needed to survive. She felt as if there was protection surrounding her but she didn't know from where or whom. She hoped it was Ricardo but she had a feeling she would find out soon.

'We've made it,' said a thankful Francis, glad that the tour was finally coming into its last stop. It had been an ordeal he had never experienced before and he hoped he would never experience again.

'Akasha didn't,' said Leila reminding him of his duty of care.

Lizette interrupted, 'That's the chance you take when you travel. You never know what is going to happen to you.'

Serah wondered if the words were meant as a warning to her and swore to herself that the rest of the time would be spent by Ricardo's side.

Brightly coloured boats matched the houses on the water's edge, lightening the mood of the spectators peering through the windows. A lighthouse stood on some granite that had been smoothed out over the years. It had stories to tell, and so did Francis who resumed the role of being a tour guide. He mentioned that Nova Scotia meant New Scotland and had over three thousand lakes and over a hundred rivers and streams.

Serah looked out at the houses which became more sparse as they drove along the small roads that criss-crossed through green fields with buildings from a different era. Gradually the trees took over to defend the water that poured from the sea, and in amongst a clearing a small property appeared. It was their last accommodation, and everyone eagerly left the bus to explore. Except for Serah who had decided to stay in the bus until Ricardo had finished his duties of emptying the back of all the suitcases.

'Do you not want to leave the bus?' asked a large man with dark hair and glasses to match.

'Day dreaming,' said Serah not knowing what to say.

'I'm Fred, the owner,' he said extending a hand to take her from the vehicle. 'You have come at an exciting time. A well has been found under one of my trees. I was standing beside it a week ago and the ground literally opened up before me. Luckily, I wasn't standing closer or I would have gone straight down to the bottom. I'm not sure how deep it is or what's down there, so I've got professionals looking into it.'

Fred was excited but Serah was not. A hole in the ground was something she didn't want to be near, so she left the owner and went to find Ricardo.

A glowing Celeste ran towards the couple. 'There is a hole under the tree. I wonder if it is a portal. I've been chatting with the guys there and they said their equipment shows there is gold under the ground.'

'Let's help them dig it up,' said Ricardo, eager to move.

'They've been trying,' said Celeste, 'but their drilling rods won't work. They've tried different tools but as soon as they get near the gold, the equipment stops working.'

'Well that means we all need to get shovels,' said Ricardo becoming even more eager.

'Too deep,' said Celeste.

'Good,' interjected Serah who was glad that the hole would be of no interest to anyone if it was untouchable.

A black car turned into the driveway which inspired Celeste to think about the government intervening. But when a woman

stepped out wearing a tartan shawl, Celeste knew she was someone else looking for accommodation. Copper hair highlighted
with gold fell down the back of the woman's green coat as she
fiddled with her shawl to keep out the chill in the air. From the
other side of the car a man appeared with a face that was intimi-
dating. Their affection was obvious as he took her arm, but his
demeanour screamed for everyone to keep away. Celeste stared
in silence that was broken when the woman smiled.

'You are Celeste,' said the woman as she approached.

A shocked Celeste didn't reply.

'I am Aerona; apparently, you have met my brother, Khrysos.'

Celeste was having difficulty speaking. She found it easy to
accept the people in her meditation as they were in her mind.
Celeste had been told she could go to Scotland to meet the woman
who had passed on her job to Epona and it had been a consideration, but now the woman who was once a goddess was standing
in front of her.

'It's a coincidence,' said Aerona trying to calm an overloaded
Celeste. 'I'm here to find out about the hole under the tree.'

Her husband, Derek, was introduced, and he smiled before
escorting Aerona to Fred who seemed overjoyed at the visitors
being attracted to his home.

'Who was that?' asked Serah looking at Derek as if he was Aerona's guardian angel.

'Remember the meditation where I met Zeus,' said Celeste still
staring at Aerona. 'She is his daughter.'

'That's the daughter of Zeus, the god of thunder?' asked Ricardo
sarcastically.

'The god of the universe,' answered Celeste. 'And I think I am
right. I bet you that hole is a portal.'

Serah shuddered. It was one thing to fall into a hole but another
to fall into a portal. She turned towards Ricardo, demanding that

he stay next to her until their feet were safely on the ground in Italy.

Aerona appeared next to Ricardo who turned in surprise to see where she had come from.

'Italy is the place of love,' she said staring into his dark eyes. 'The place where you will find protection. You know that Venus loves that country. Ricardo, you must take Serah to the jewellery shop in Bologna. It is a small town but a place that is connected to the stars.'

'How do you know my name?' asked Ricardo, but Aerona had already left.

A feeling of peace overcame Serah. 'She told you to take me to Bologna which means I am going to Italy. I think she and her husband are here to protect me. Maybe I've nothing to fear.'

'You don't,' said Ricardo pulling her in close.

Francis and the others were standing in front of the tree that stretched out towards the sky. Derek and Aerona joined them as the green leaves shimmered with a glow of gold.

'You see,' said Fred rubbing his hands together. 'Look, that is conformation right there. There is gold under the ground.'

'But we can't seem to get to it,' said one of the men wearing beige coloured overalls.

'There has to be a way,' said Fred who had already formed a list of things he was going to buy with the money.

'You will make enough money,' said Derek in a voice that made everyone look. 'People from around the world will come to look at the tree with the mysterious hole and they will all want to stay at your home.'

Fred went to speak but Aerona cut him off, stating that others had tried to open another well not far away and they had been killed. That was enough of a threat to send the excavators away, and with the prospect of finding the gold coming to an end, everyone went inside to put their suitcases into their rooms.

Fred was a man who enjoyed a feast, and with everyone checked-in he went to work in the kitchen to provide a lunch that would be devoured by his guests. Chickens were placed in the oven and platters were prepared with smoked salmon, crackers and dips. The aroma of the food alerted the attention of the others who soon found themselves sitting around a table that was filled with plates of meats, bowls of fruit and glasses of wine.

'I wasn't hungry,' said Leila sitting down to fill a small plate with quiche and prosciutto.

Glasses were filled as Fred questioned everyone about their lives at home and because all eyes were on Aerona, Derek spoke first. He told of his family which included twenty-seven sisters, a brother who died years ago and a sister-in-law who was a witch. He went on to explain how they all lived close to each other in Scotland where they enjoyed peace. He also told them he had spent most of his life in search of a vampire that had become an alien. During his quest, he had come across Aerona who he had managed to convince to leave her line of work to become his wife.

All eyes were glued to Derek and didn't move when he asked who was going to speak next. Aerona glared at her husband who smiled as he picked up his fork to break the silence. Fred cleared his throat and began to laugh, catching the others off guard. The attention was back now on their host who brought everyone back to reality by laughing off Derek's rendition of home life.

'Alright,' said Fred taking a sip from his wine glass. 'How about you there with the red hair, why don't you tell us about your life at home? And nothing far-fetched please because I don't know if we could all take another story like the one we just heard.'

Derek went to speak but Aerona kicked his leg.

'I'm originally from England but I've been studying pottery in Turkey for the last few years,' said Celeste looking at her shocked companions who were not aware of her artistic side. 'I became interested in planets when another student joined us and I learned he was fascinated with the night sky. He had a telescope and showed me the planets and the stars and when I saw an alien craft one night, I became even more spellbound.'

Fred interrupted hoping that someone could provide a conversation that didn't involve stories of the unknown, but gave up when Aerona prepared to speak.

'Fred, what can you tell us about the area?' said Francis who could see that a change of subject was in order.

'Oh,' answered Fred, happy to speak about reality. 'Nova Scotia was meant to be the new Scotland.'

'Do you know why?' asked Leila hoping for more mystery.

Fred shook his head.

'I think I know,' said Aerona before anyone else could answer. 'It was meant to be a place where a certain woman could live out her life away from the public eye. Her husband had died and her children had taken on her responsibilities. Everyone thought she mourned the death of her husband, but she was depressed because she couldn't be with the Scotsman who she loved. This was a place away from everyone, a place where they could be together.'

'Sounds like us,' said Derek picking up a bread roll.

'Is she here?' asked Leila wanting to meet her.

'No, but she is with him in the old Scotland,' said Aerona.

'Why didn't she come here?' asked Celeste who was mesmerised by Aerona.

'Gold,' said Aerona. 'Gold brought others here even before it was discovered. The metal has been hidden, but there is a force that keeps men searching for it. It's not their fault, it's the Elite that interfered with the DNA of men so they would have slaves to do their dirty work.'

Fred interrupted by stating that the lakes were abundant with fish.

'Hang on Fred,' said Celeste, dampening his enthusiasm as she started putting the pieces together. 'The guy I study with mentioned the Elite. They are the aliens, aren't they?'

Aerona nodded in agreement. 'There was a time, very recently, when a man's greed took him to new heights and his greed for gold took him to wanting the whole world. His wish came true and he is now surrounded by all the gold within the earth.'

'This is fascinating,' said Leila taking some more prosciutto.

Fred gave up and filled his glass with more wine.

'Not all are men,' said Francis in defence. 'Look at Mary Queen of Scots. She was murdered by Elizabeth for the throne.'

'But that's not gold,' said Aerona pointing the knife at him. 'Mary was a Stuart. The King of Stuarts was a mason. Mary's chapel was the lodge for the masons. Sinclair built Rosslyn chapel. The Welsh family were on this land before Chris Columbus and they married into the Sinclair line to keep the secret.'

'I feel like I'm putting a jigsaw puzzle together,' said Ricardo grabbing a piece of chicken to chew on.

'How do you know all of this?' questioned Derek who had never heard his wife speak about the Sinclair family before.

'Brandon Macfarlane told me,' she said in defence. 'He was a mason and helped Henry Sinclair build the chapel. He found out about the secret that came from Solomon's temple in Jerusalem where others think there is treasure. When Brandon came across the scrolls, he knew what he had and used it to his advantage. Brandon was given money and the scrolls were put in a vault that your sisters blew up.'

'My sisters?' asked Derek, thinking back to the time when his life had been mayhem.

'What was written on the scrolls?' said an enthusiastic Leila who didn't want the subject changed.

'Mary Magdalene's bloodline,' stated Aerona to a roomful of

shocked faces. 'You see I can tell you now because people are more open minded. Fred, I am telling you this because I know you want what you think might be treasure under the tree but there isn't any. The Welsh family that originally came here knew this would be a good place to hide the scrolls. This wasn't the only place, of course, but when the Knights' Templars were persecuted for not telling about the treasure they came here and hid the scrolls. Royalty and religious leaders alike thought it was treasure but it was information that only the Elite kept hidden.'

Fred scoffed, 'What a load of rubbish!'

'Have you not seen the marks!' said Aerona glaring at Fred.

'What marks?' interrupted Leila needing to know more.

Aerona turned her attention to her fascinated listener. 'There are signs. You can find an X marked into stones.'

Ricardo threw down his chicken leg. 'I know this,' he said. 'The X on the stones is the sign for a man and woman. It was a decoy so it would not be associated with the Templars who wore the cross as their symbol.'

'The Book of Branches,' said Aerona. 'The book has the answers.'

'How do I get the book?' asked Leila ready to write down the establishment.

'Does anyone know?' asked Aerona waiting for someone else to provide an answer.

Serah put down her cutlery. 'I think I know,' she said in a quiet voice. 'Is it with Venus?'

Aerona smiled as an excited Celeste took over the conversation. 'Khrysos told me about the portal to Venus but I thought he meant the planet.'

'Why do you think the Templars worshipped Venus?' asked Aerona looking over at Serah.

'She was a woman who held the secret to protect Mary's offspring who was a knight,' said Serah not knowing how she knew.

twenty six

'We were meant to meditate around the tree tonight,' said Francis feeling that the conversation needed to come back to the itinerary.

'We should,' said Lizette pushing her chair back to stand up.

The others followed as a reluctant Serah stood next to Ricardo.

'I would really like to do this,' he said. 'Now that I can receive information, I would love to find out what the tree has to say. Sit next to me and if we sit opposite Lizette then she will have no way to get near you before making me aware.'

Serah waited until Lizette was seated on the ground before sitting down. With Ricardo's hand holding hers, she sat nervously and turned to find Derek sitting on her other side. Feeling safer, she agreed to participate and with all eyes closed, she opened hers to watch Lizette. The hole was close to the trunk of the tree and well away from where Serah sat, but she was not taking any chances and instead took in the scent of the white flowers of the myrtle tree. Their evergreen leaves seemed to have healing properties and as she inhaled the sweet perfume, she felt an overwhelming feeling of strength run through her body.

The hand that clung to Ricardo was now fearless, which prompted him to open his eyes.

'Sorry,' she whispered. 'I didn't mean to stop your meditation.'

'Try to relax,' he whispered back.

'I'm okay,' she said wondering if it was possible for anyone to relax in her situation.

Serah closed her eyes to see a vision of a woman with orange hair and golden eyes. She was voluptuous and her curved body moved from side to side as she came closer. She was the goddess Venus who had once been a woman. She had the Book of Branches that kept safe the secret of Serah who was from the bloodline of Mary Magdalene. It was her planet that held the dimension of Dlog where everyone with love in their heart could go once their lessons were learned. The Templars were men who were from her son's bloodline and the mark of the cross that stood for martyrdom was associated with the death of the body, once the soul was released to go home.

With opened eyes the vision disappeared, leaving Serah to sit and listen. Francis provided a guided meditation to bring everyone back but Serah could only hear Venus who reminded her not to be afraid and to tell Aerona that Pyper was well.

'Wow,' said Ricardo as others around him opened their eyes.

'What did you get this time?' asked Francis, frustrated that he still wasn't getting anything.

'I think you might be wrong Aerona,' said Ricardo. 'I received information from a couple of women who you have known.'

'Tell us!' shouted out Leila from the other side of the tree trunk.

'Juliette Miller,' said Ricardo as he looked at Aerona. 'She knows you and she said she had come across a treasure map when she was on board a pirate ship centuries ago. One of the pirates was a man named Kidd. He was a cabin boy when Juliette had come across him but he went on to become well known as the man who captured pirates. Profits being made by the East India Company were being taken, and King William the Third had given Kidd a letter of mark to gain permission to commandeer what was stolen. His crew worked for part of the money that was confiscated but the pirates were gone and with the crews' dream of wealth disappearing, they became pirates themselves. They travelled for two years taking treasure from other ships, making Kidd a wanted man. Gold, silk and jewellery were taken from the Quedagh Merchant who Kidd took to New York to redeem himself. But Indian merchants complained to the British about the theft and wanted Kidd dead. He had buried the treasure and told of one chest but it didn't help him. He was sent to England for trial. He was unable to show that he was doing his job and was hung for murder because he had killed a gunner with a metal bucket due to mutiny.'

'Do you think the treasure is here?' asked an excited Fred.

Ricardo looked over at him. 'There is someone who knows where the treasure is,' said Ricardo looking back at Aerona. 'The spirit of Kidd stayed with his ship. A part of the ship ended up in a museum that Richard Knight visited. Our tour group is well aware of spirits entering other people's bodies. With Kidd inside Richard's mind, he suddenly came across clues that set Richard on the path of being a treasure hunter. He found a piece of furniture with an anchor imprinted on the side. When he pressed too hard, a parchment appeared. It was a basic map but other relics with clues popped up, and when he came into possession of a small chest that had a skull and bones on top of the letter K, he knew that was the last piece of the puzzle. A false bottom revealed a mirror with a removable beading and when the mirror slid aside, it revealed another map. He had difficulty finding the treasure, as the map was old and charts had different meridians in Kidd's time. He thought he found the treasure when the directions led him to an island by the name of Grand Pirate, but it was in Vietnam at the time of communism and impossible to enter. He did try to gain entry but the government would not let him visit, so one night he hired a boat and took a three hundred mile journey to land on the beach that would take him to his treasure. Vietnamese people found him and interrogated him. They would not let him leave his rat-infested cell as they thought he was a spy. It was the spirit of Kidd that kept him alive by talking to him and telling him that he would be freed. Eventually, an anonymous person paid his ransom and he was indeed freed. Kidd looked for another person to take over to help find his treasure since it was not where the mind of Richard thought it was.'

'So is it here?' said Fred, feeling frustrated.

'You said you were visited by a couple of women,' interrupted Leila.

'The other one was Pyper,' said Ricardo with a smile.

Serah took his hand to pull him away from the circle. 'I had a visit from Venus who spoke of Pyper being well.'

'I think we need to speak with Aerona,' said Ricardo who suddenly felt a hand on his shoulder that ushered him and Serah away from earshot.

'What else was there?' asked Aerona once she had them alone.

'Venus said that Pyper is well,' said Serah hoping for an explanation but didn't get one.

Ricardo looked around to make sure Derek was nowhere near. 'Pyper is your daughter and Richard Knight is her father.'

Aerona dropped her hand in defeat. 'Derek doesn't know and doesn't need to know who Pyper's father is. Pyper doesn't even know. As far as she knows, I am her great grandmother, and with what she has been through her father could be a dragon and it wouldn't faze her. Besides, I am only her immortal mother. Pyper was born to another woman in the human realm. I wanted her to experience different lives before taking on the role of a ruler. And I was with Richard well before Derek came into my life. There was turmoil at the time with the human realm that I was dealing with. William Kidd had turned into a pirate and died leaving everyone to think there was a chest of treasure buried somewhere. His wife

Sarah, had strayed from her path and she had to live another life. Venus had intervened and taken the Book of Branches that had been lost during my care. She had lived in Rome and when she found out the scrolls were safe, she left to take care of the planet that held the dimension that I had ruled. Things weren't good for me so Venus saw to it that I would meet Richard Knight, who turned out to be my knight in shining armour until he died and I found myself alone again to deal with the entanglement of people on wrong paths.'

'It's okay,' said Ricardo giving her a hug. 'There is no need for you to explain. Your secret is safe with us.'

'Venus mentioned the Book of Branches,' said Serah hoping for an explanation.

Aerona lifted Ricardo's shirt and turned him around so Serah could see his lower back. 'Do you know why that X is tattooed there?'

Ricardo pulled his jeans back up. 'My mother told me that it was to keep the devil away from my back and away from my brain.'

'Superstition,' stated Serah who was shocked to find out that a mother would tattoo her son.

'What is your family name?' Aerona asked Ricardo.

'Knight,' he answered, 'Ricardo Knight.'

'You are a Templar, a son of Venus,' said a shocked Serah.

'Yes,' said Aerona, 'and you are a daughter of Mary Magdalene and these are more secrets you must keep.'

'So we were meant to be together,' said Ricardo looking at Serah who was staring at him in disbelief.

'I came on this holiday because of Sarah Cupsip,' said Serah shaking her head.

Aerona hugged her. 'I know and that is one sacrifice she has made to redeem herself, but there are more to go before she gets what she wants.'

Derek joined them wondering who wanted what.

'I want to go to bed,' said Aerona who left the couple, knowing that her mission had been accomplished.

Fred took Ricardo away from a gobsmacked Serah. He was interested in the gold that was below his tree, but Ricardo didn't know where Kidd had buried his treasure. Fred didn't believe him and continued to quiz him, hoping to catch him off guard. It was Ricardo's duty to protect Serah but he had left her to walk around in a daze. As she wandered around taking in all the information, she was unaware that the group had split up leaving Lizette to stand by the tree alone.

Feeling tired and wanting to be alone, Serah went to her room and looked through her bag for the bottle that held her friend's spirit. Everything being entwined was difficult for her to comprehend, which made it hard for her to breathe. Suddenly feeling claustrophobic, she left the security of her room to find space and fresh air. Without realising where she was, she peered into the bottle to distract her thoughts of panic. The others had gone back to the feast that still awaited them at the table and Serah, thinking that she was alone, headed for the light from the tree to comfort her from the darkness. Ricardo was her knight in shining armour and she had spent her week with him, living in fear. As she looked down the hole, it dawned on her that being with him had brought out the fears she had kept hidden so she could face them. A sigh of relief came too late as she was pushed by Lizette into the hole, and after feeling the sensation of falling for what seemed like several minutes, she slowly opened her eyes to face a witch that had been released from a smashed bottle.

'Help me,' she heard a frail male voice plead.

'Gavin!' called out Sarah Cupsip. 'Is that you Gavin Macleod?'

'Help me, Sarah!' he cried.

Sarah Cupsip needed a human body to perform her magic and

transferred herself into Serah Kohw who moaned in agony from cuts all over her. The pieces of glass had lodged themselves into her skin, creating such pain it distracted her thinking. She was still trying to comprehend how the fall had not ended her life—and was not even sure it hadn't. The spirit had been a vision in the dark but now she was gone. Serah was about to stand up to call out for help when she saw another vision of her friend, Sarah. It showed the spirit in another life where she had been killed by witches who resembled Derek. Serah Kohw knew they were his sisters and now knew he wasn't joking when he said they were witches. The vision continued to show her former friend as a lost soul with no one to take her to her home in the realm of Sregnach. Serah Kohw watched as the former Sarah Cupsip tried to walk through a tree that was a portal. There seemed to be difficulty which Serah suddenly realised was due to Sarah's spirit needing to reborn as the Sarah Cupsip that became her friend. Sarah's spirit was supposed to redeem herself and Serah suddenly remembered Aerona stating that Sarah Cupsip had a long way to go before transformation could occur to give her the life of the princess she desired—the life that came with love from a prince.

Sarah's vision disappeared and Serah heard the voice of Gavin Macleod. She realised he was in fact not a prince, as he was filled with darkness and needed to stay under the ground.

'Sarah Cupsip,' said Serah with a voice of authority. 'I spoke with Aerona and she said you have to redeem yourself again before living the life you want. You're free so go and live another life and prove to the gods that you are worthy.'

A voice entered Serah's head and it was not her ego nor her chatterbox. 'We are going to get Gavin out of here. His soul maybe trapped but his energy is not. He is like me and only needs a body to take over the brain.'

Serah Kohw placed her hands on the floor of solid gold and spoke a language that she never knew existed.

twenty seven

Lizette laughed as she stood over the hole. It was only a matter of time before her former boyfriend from a different life would emerge from the ground. She waited in anticipation of what he would look like. She hoped the memory she had of his dark hair and features would not have changed.

'Where is Serah?' growled Ricardo as he shook the body of Lizette.

'Gone!' she hissed back at him, but then as she stared at Ricardo's good looks, a thought popped into her head. If Gavin was unable to come back as himself then he could take over the body that belonged to Ricardo. She smiled, and for a moment Ricardo thought he saw her eyes change to that of a lizard.

Pausing for a moment to take in the vision, he considered strangulation but the others had come out after hearing the commotion.

'Who screamed?' demanded Aerona, wrapping herself up in a tartan scarf.

'It's alright!' declared a woman with a golden gown and fur trimmings. 'It was destiny. The soul was trapped but not the energy. You would think that it would go hand in hand but it is its own identity. It is something that has to be finished.'

'Venus,' said Aerona. 'I thought Serah would be safe with a knight.'

'I've been watching over her as well,' said Venus tying her long orange hair into a ponytail, 'but first things first.'

Everyone stared at the woman in amazement. Celeste knew it was the goddess but couldn't believe she was speaking right there in front of them. Their phones had been returned to them, so Celeste grabbed hers from her pocket but it wouldn't work. Others tried to take photos on their phones, also to no avail. With no way of capturing the moment to be reminded later, they stood in awe taking in the sight of the woman who waved her arms, producing a mist which forced almost everyone down to the ground to sleep.

Ricardo looked at his friends on the ground and wondered why he was still awake. 'Lizette isn't asleep!' he called out, still holding on to her.

Derek walked up to him and took hold of the woman who hissed violently. 'Aerona is a goddess, I am a warlock, you are a knight and she is an alien,' said Derek as he produced a small knife of gold which he then drove into her spine.'

Ricardo watched in horror as Lizette fell to the ground. 'You killed her!'

'No,' said Derek, 'only the alien that was inside her. Lizette Leclerk is asleep.'

'But when she wakes up she'll try to kill Serah—that's if she hasn't done so already!' said a Ricardo who was still panicking.

Derek took his shoulder to help calm him. 'The spirit inside Lizette was once in love with the man who is trapped below, but that was a long time ago. She was meant to cross paths with Serah, but Serah was not meant to awaken the alien that wanted to use Sarah Cupsip.'

'What about Serah, do you think Lizette pushed her down this hole or is that too obvious?' said Ricardo trying to see below. 'I have to go down and save her.'

A hand from Venus reached out to stop Ricardo. 'A wolf was once sacrificed when I was in the water. It is time for him to be reborn.'

With both of her hands on the ground, she transformed into

the wolf that the boy sacrificed for a hat of knowledge. The paws bounded passed Ricardo as she leapt into the hole.

'How do we know what's going on?' asked Ricardo looking down the hole only to see darkness.

'I can read her thoughts,' said Aerona. 'She can connect with Serah without the spirit or the energy ever knowing. She is the one to help her.'

'What did she mean about the wolf being pushed into the water when she was there?' he asked trying to make sense of what was happening while still trying to see.

Aerona took him inside, away from the hole and the sleeping bodies. 'Venus came from the water. Originally, she was stardust as we all were. With water, humans evolved slowly through different species, but Venus was a woman of the water and became a human being instantly. She didn't need to evolve. She stayed in the water with the others who fended off the aliens and was there when the serpent asked for a sacrifice. The wolf would have drowned and his soul would have moved on, but he wanted to stay in the human realm so she kept him with her until the time was right. Now with the help of the wolf, Venus will be able to save Serah. She will then set him free to live his life as he chooses.'

'I hope he can save her,' said Ricardo pushing away the plate of food that had been put in front of him for a distraction.

Ricardo smashed his fist on the table. He cursed himself for being distracted but he wasn't going to allow distraction to interfere again so he got to his feet. As he went to take a step forward he felt a rush of energy that pushed him back into his chair.

* * *

A snarling wolf suddenly landed in front of Serah. Startled, she crawled backwards along the smooth surface of the metal that lay underneath her.

'Don't be afraid,' said Venus in a calming tone. 'I am here to help you.'

Serah looked around at the dark space but couldn't see anyone. She wondered if it was the spirit of Sarah or the energy of Gavin that was speaking to her.

'I am Venus and I am in the wolf. Don't speak; just do as I say. Sarah and Gavin can't hear me.'

Glad that her plan was coming to fruition, the spirit of Sarah Cupsip had stayed inside the host's body as she quickly finished her incantations. Despite her preparation not being executed as she intended, she knew her goal was inevitable as she heard Gavin's energy and knew it couldn't wait to be transferred into a human. The spirit had thought of putting him into Ricardo, but knowing that he protected Serah meant Serah would have to remain separated from Ricardo and the others. A growl alerted the spirit to the fact that a wolf was with them. She analysed the spell that she had muttered as it was not one that would produce an animal.

The wolf opened its wide eyes to produce a glow that lit up the gold, providing a light in the tunnel. The spirit of Sarah was pleased to see the path that took her to where she needed to be, but she had no idea that a goddess was manipulating her to head towards the required destination. With a plan coming to an end, the spirit continued her incantations that would control the wolf and allow the energy of Gavin to accompany her. Once she felt the energy of love, she forced her host to stand up. Pain shuddered through the body of Serah, making the sensation known to the spirit and the energy after one step. The spirit forced magic into the host's body to heal the cuts in the skin. Once the body was returned to normal they walked behind the wolf which led them to an opening of ice.

Serah shivered from the cold as Venus explained to her that it was necessary to be where the spirit thought the sleeping dragon was.

'Moan from the cold and she will produce magic that will warm you,' said Venus using telepathy.

Once the wolf pushed Serah Kohw through the opening, she fell to the ground and rolled up into a ball. The spirit was confused since the body had been healed, but when she realised that the host was cold, she spoke an incantation that made her warm. Free from the moaning, the spirit tried to think of where the dragon had gone. While she had been a witch in the realm of Sregnach she had been in control of the dragon that had resided there. She knew the animal had magic far beyond hers and she needed the dragon to help her if she was going to transfer Gavin into a human.

The spirit took in the surroundings of ice as they approached their destination. Glad that she had made it to the end of the tunnel, Sarah Cupsip allowed her host to rest as she waited for the dragon to appear. As the creature protected the gold underneath, she presumed that it would have been there but for some reason, the cavern was empty. The host sat down when she realised there was a delay and as she followed the outline of the dragon, she realised it was the same form as the dragon near the icefields. Being in the tunnel had been a nightmare but it had been quick. Serah Kohw tried to think of the distance between Nova Scotia and the icefield and knew that magic had to be involved to travel such a distance. From the outside world, the lump of ice looked like a dragon and stories had been created. If she could get through the ice, then another story would end up on the internet. But getting through the ice was impossible as it was too thick so she gave up as Sarah Cupsip wondered why the dragon was missing.

Trying to think of past lives while being in the host was difficult but finally the spirit was given confirmation that dragons still lived in the human realm. She looked down at the gold still wondering why the dragon wasn't protecting it then it dawned on her that it must have gone out to find food. Eventually, it would return so she remained inside Serah's body as she listened to Gavin complain.

He was desperate to find a body so the spirit used her energy to find the weakest point. Once a crack was created, she forced her host outside onto the ice field where tourists were walking in the cold. They heard the sound of thunder and watched as a barefooted girl ran from the mouth of the ice dragon. With an astonished look, they stayed motionless as the girl who was wearing a thin jumper and jeans with no shoes, ran up to a man as she screamed for him to get out of the way. He was rugged up in waterproof pants and a jacket and felt sorry for her so when she jumped in his arms, he hugged her but instead of affection he felt a jolt when Gavin transferred his energy into this random young man's body.

Sarah Cupsip screamed with delight that the transformation had been that easy. She thought she would need magic, but it wasn't necessary. With both her and Gavin having bodies, she thought her life was complete—but she was about to find out a shocking revelation. Gavin didn't want Serah Kohw or Sarah Cupsip. He threw her to the ground and took off.

'Gavin come back!' she screamed but there was no response.

Venus stood next to Serah Kohw without any ideas. Her plan had been to somehow seal Gavin's energy in the ice and she had guided the spirit to the ice dragon as a means to gain time to gather her thoughts. With Gavin on the loose she needed to be quick and was about to leave, but first she remembered her duty to the wolf standing by her side. Venus rubbed his ear in gratitude as the wolf bowed and took off to live his life that had been taken away from him. Tourists who were only expecting to see ice were shocked with the otherworldly experience and only looked up when snow appeared, making them drowsy.

Serah felt the snow in her hands and tried to make the spirit within her see reason with the beauty in the world that provided her with the vibration of love. Serah tried to tell the spirit that she didn't need Gavin and there was someone for her to love who would feel the same. Begging with her to go and take on another life to redeem herself made Sarah Cupsip appear before Serah.

With tears in her eyes, the spirit sobbed as she watched the man with Gavin's energy run away.

'I don't want to wait years before finding someone who loves me,' said the spirit that flitted in and out of vision.

'Then go into someone who is going to die,' said Serah Kohw not knowing where the forgiveness was coming from. 'Give them a good life. Maybe that person might be dying because they have lost their path. You can take over and put her on the right track and find happiness.'

The spirit disappeared and with it the spell that kept Serah warm. She screamed at the ice that stuck to her feet. Venus rushed to her aid as Serah explained about being left alone by the spirit. The ordeal was over, and with relief Serah tucked inside Venus' cloak. It was a longer trip back behind the ice but they ventured through the tunnel back to where Ricardo was waiting. Although Serah was feeling a sense of relief, Venus knew there was a job that needed to be done and she couldn't do it alone. Years ago, Aerona had managed to trap the soul of Gavin Macleod, so Venus knew there was a way to trap his energy.

She contemplated as Ricardo felt a release that calmed him while he waited for the return of Serah. It was not a long wait before he heard movement below, but when he saw only Venus, he feared the worse. Her cloak was long and floated like the sea and when she drew it back, a frozen Serah dropped to the ground.

'Where are your shoes?' said Ricardo, rushing to her aid.

Aerona wrapped her shawl around Serah as Derek handed over a pair of sheepskin boots.

'They slipped off when I fell down the hole,' said Serah through chattering teeth.

'It doesn't matter,' said Ricardo taking her into his arms to carry her inside.

Derek looked at Venus hoping that Gavin was still trapped in the gold. Derek's days of hunting men who wanted immortality were over, so he waited with anticipation for the news.

'His soul is still stuck but his energy is with another,' said Venus wrapping the cloak around herself. 'We have to find a way to trap it again.'

Aerona appeared near the tree. 'I really thought he would have stayed below for all eternity.'

'And he would have,' said Derek putting his arm around her. 'What are the odds that a witch would remove his energy?'

Venus faced the tree as the three of them tried to come up with a solution.

'You can't kill an energy,' stated Derek who had had enough of thinking.

The wind picked up, creating a rustle in the branches that drew their attention. As they watched the branches move, a hypnotic sensation overcame Venus. One gust of wind provided a revelation as Venus watched the leaves float like waves to the ground. The image inspired her as it was a reminder of the sea.

'Put his energy in a dolphin,' Venus announced to the dazed couple.

Derek and Aerona's reaction was not what she expected. They laughed, thinking that the statement was made to break the concentration.

'I can't think of anything either,' stated Aerona staring at Venus.

'I'm serious,' declared Venus returning the glare. 'Dolphins are highly intelligent and Gavin would not be able to manipulate one. Other dolphins would protect the one holding the energy that could never be transferred into a human. Being under the deep water would make it impossible for anyone to come in contact with him. Those who belong under the water would help because they know about Gavin Macleod and his association with the aliens. The last thing they want is an alliance with the ones that won't allow them near their gold stored at the bottom of the ocean.'

It seemed probable, and as there was no other choice, Derek and Aerona agreed that Gavin needed to go underwater.

'One thing,' interrupted Derek, 'how do we get Gavin to touch a dolphin?'

twenty eight

Gavin's energy was strong and the man he had infiltrated was no match. A part of the man's mind wanted to respond to the family that was calling to him but Gavin had other plans. Gavin wanted to rule the planet but the body he had chosen was not what he was used to. His former self had been strong enough to match his mind but what he had chosen in haste was not able to display the authority that was needed. Gavin had acted too quickly with the transformation and now he knew he had no other option but to stay in the background until the time was right for him to modify his host.

'Patrick,' said a worried woman. 'Where were you going?'

'Don't know,' he said trying to recall the last few moments that were blank.

'I don't like it here,' said a younger woman. 'Something's not right. One second we're looking at ice and the next we're getting up off the ground with no recollection of what happened.'

'Come on,' said the older woman, 'let's get back to the bus. I think the cold is affecting us. We head back to the heat tomorrow.'

Patrick felt an energy flow through him that was filled with happiness as Gavin knew his time was coming soon. With the news that the family lived in a warmer climate came visions of Gavin forcing Patrick to train and become the athlete that was needed to be fit enough to keep up with the pace. Patrick didn't know it but his thin body that loved to ride skateboards was going to be changed to one that would live in the gym.

The energy that belonged to Gavin planned a schedule and a change of diet. He had anticipated the transformation to take place once Patrick was home but was pleasantly shocked to find his influence already taking effect when his host denied a bar of chocolate. His mother was a little suspicious as it wasn't like her son not to accept junk food, but then she put it down to the ordeal at the icefield. Others on the bus had complained about memory loss which the tour guide passed off as a freak of nature. The only conclusion the group could come up with was that an intense gust of wind must have frozen them. Glasses of whisky with maple syrup were handed out along with bars of chocolate, but that didn't appease some of the tourists. Not wanting to miss out on a tip, the guide decided to make up for the bad incident by providing an experience that tourists rarely participated in.

'Now, keep this to yourselves!' called out the tour guide. 'This doesn't normally happen, but to compensate for the circumstances beyond our control, the tour company has organised something special. You are all going to a place where you can feed wild fish and if you are lucky you will see other wildlife. The water comes in from the ocean and it is said that the fish come inland to be eaten when it is time for their souls to move on. Believe what you want, but it is an amazing sight!'

Excitement grew amongst the group with different expectations being formed; most thought of bears catching the flying fish. However, Patrick could not muster any interest in it and instead had a strong urge to go home. His enthusiastic mother might have let him off with the chocolate, but she was not going to allow him to miss out on an opportunity that most didn't get to cherish.

'Come on Patrick,' said his sister as they followed everyone else to disembark the bus.

'Do you think we should get off the vehicle that provides us with safety against wild animals?' said Patrick feeling miserable that they weren't going to the gym at the hotel.

'Big words,' said his sister sarcastically as she was used to him providing grunts instead of sentences.

'Come on,' said his mother giving him a push.

Loaves of bread were handed around as they walked on a path that led them through the dense trees. The family wondered where the water was until they heard the sound of others up ahead who called out at the incredible sight. They had expected to see small fish but were elated to find dolphins were also at the water's edge with their mouths open to receive food.

'So the dolphins come here to die?' asked an elderly gentleman putting his hand in the bag of bread.

'I'm as dumbfounded as you are,' said the tour guide. 'I wasn't expecting dolphins to be here. You are definitely lucky today.'

Patrick's sister took out a handful of bread and knelt down next to one. She didn't know if it would swim away or not but was glad when it didn't move. After a few slices, she wondered if she should be handing out bread as the mammal was meant to eat fish. It worried her and she sat back trying to think of what she had learned at school, but her education had not covered dolphins and their eating habits.

'What is it?' asked Patrick. 'Why have you stopped feeding them? We won't get to leave until all the bread is gone.'

She turned to him to ask if he recalled being taught about animals and what they ate.

'That's what you're thinking about,' he said snatching the bag out of her hand. 'Who cares!'

He took the rest of the bread and shoved it into the wide mouth of the dolphin that was closest to him. Breaths were held as they witnessed the surge of the creature that seemed larger out of the water. With one swoop, the dolphin grabbed the food and whacked his tail against Patrick who fell to the ground.

'We're not going to fall again, are we?' screamed a tourist recalling the icefield incident.

'Patrick!' screamed his mother who ran to assist her son.

The others didn't know where to look. They were fascinated with the wildlife but their curiosity about Patrick's wellbeing had them watching as his mother and sister lifted him back to his feet. Once reassured that he was alright, the others turned their attention back to the water, but it had now become still.

'Whisky and chocolate anyone!' called out the tour guide once he heard the murmurs of the disgruntled tourists.

Patrick took a bar of chocolate as he headed for his seat. The tail had caught him off guard and he had lost his balance. It had happened too quickly, but when a boy sat next to him with a phone that had captured the moment, his focused changed with the extraordinary event. He watched the footage over and over trying to make sense of it all but one thing he knew for certain, was he had evidence of his incredible holiday tale.

* * *

While Derek and Aerona had contemplated their moves, Venus had left her physical body to contact a dolphin that lived in the deep. She had heard his thoughts of curiosity with the world above, so offered him the opportunity to feed his fascination. Having an energy that belonged to someone else was not going to hinder him so the dolphin agreed and left with a pod of others to explore the Earth from a different angle. Telepathically, the dolphin invaded the thoughts of the tour guide and with a bit of persuasion was able to convince him to go to where the dolphin needed Patrick to be. The mammal knew what he had to do, but didn't know how he was going to persuade Patrick to the water's edge when the young man already had someone else influencing him. It had been a chain of events that had provided an opportunity for the dolphin and the scene witnessed by the pod was enough to keep them underwater for a lifetime.

To humans, the surroundings had been surreal, but between the trees were energies of negativity. They were held at bay but the true beauty was masked. The dolphins could see beyond the bad food that was being fed to them, the infected water and the polluted sky. They knew that the humans were seeing a flow of water from the sea and a forest of green but they knew it was actually red. The interpretation of the human's brain was different and they understood why humans would never be able to see what was under the water. They returned to their home where they lived with water people who had created a world that benefited everyone and everything. The aliens that stored their gold had tested their tolerance but they had managed a mutually beneficial agreement. It was a harmonious life that would not be interfered with and one that Gavin's energy would have to get used to.

Aerona, unaware of what had just occurred, was still laughing at the thought of sending the energy of Gavin to Sea World.

'What's so funny?' asked Derek crossing his arms in defence.

'I have an idea,' said Aerona uncrossing his arms.

Venus jolted from her solid state. 'It's taken care of.'

The couple stared at her as she explained about the dolphin that had taken Gavin to his new home.

Derek sighed with relief at the thought of going back to his home in Scotland and would have left immediately if it hadn't been for Aerona wanting to check on Serah Kohw first.

With Venus in tow they went inside to see a defrosted Serah

wrapped up in blankets. The sight brought a smile to their faces as they pulled up chairs to explain about what had taken place.

'So I'm free,' said Serah holding a giant mug of cocoa.

'Yes you are,' said Venus stretching the body that had been rigid.

'We are also free,' said Derek raising his eyebrows at Aerona. 'Free to go home.'

'Free to go to Italy,' stated Ricardo with a large grin.

'I go there sometimes,' said Venus. 'I might see you there.' Her cloak swayed as she marched out the door to release the others who were still asleep on the ground.

Sounds from outside alerted Aerona to the waking group who would have questions she didn't know how to answer, so she kissed Serah on the forehead before leaving.

'Deny everything,' said Derek as he left to follow Aerona through the back door.

Francis was the first to stumble inside, thankful that his bus driver and Serah were well. With a memory that was fading in and out, he turned around to look outside to count heads.

'Akasha is missing,' he said, turning to Ricardo.

'Remember to deny,' whispered Serah.

'Who?' asked Ricardo, trying to look perplexed.

'Akasha,' said Francis, going outside.

Leila, Lizette and Celeste yawned wearily as Francis asked about Akasha.

The humming in Fred's eardrums stopped as he listened to Francis. 'There was no Akasha here last night—or was it yesterday,' he said feeling confused.

'I remember Akasha,' said Celeste getting to her feet. 'She fell into the mud.'

Lizette rubbed her head. 'Everything seems hazy to me. I'm having trouble remembering anything.'

'I'm the same,' said Leila stretching out her arms. 'What did you give us Fred?'

'Nothing,' he answered trying to get his balance.

'Where's Serah?' asked Lizette, suddenly realising that she might have pushed her down a hole.

'She's inside with Ricardo,' said Francis looking bewildered. 'You know what I think?'

'What?' said Celeste ruffling her red hair.

'I think that we have experienced something out of this world,' said Francis feeling enlightened. 'We meditated to connect and I think we did.'

'So now you believe in aliens!' said Celeste sarcastically.

The statement brought back the humour and with laughter being heard outside, Ricardo asked if Serah would accompany him to Italy.

'I know I said I would,' she said with a sigh, 'but after what I've been through I really think I need normality in my life.'

'After what we have been through,' he said, 'I think that normality will never be in our lives again. It's all over and we both survived so let me take you on a holiday that most tourists have.'

'I don't know what to do,' she said with tears in her eyes.

Ricardo hugged her as he took the mug away. 'Let me decide for you and I promise there will be no otherworldly stuff. I won't even touch a rock.'

A smile on her face brought hope to Ricardo who pulled his phone from his pocket to make the calls that would allow Serah to be with him for the next week.

'Isn't it hot in Italy this time of year?' she said, starting to warm up. 'I only have winter clothes with me.'

'You're going to Italy,' said Ricardo as he laughed, 'the home of fashion. We fly into Rome and I will take you straight to the shops so you can pick out some clothes. Isn't that every woman's dream?'

Her head fell back onto the seat. 'I give up,' she said peeling the layers of blankets away.

Before she could change her mind, Ricardo pulled her to her feet to usher her to her room to pack her bag. The flight wasn't for another five hours but he wouldn't feel safe until she was on the plane. Things had been too unpredictable for him and as soon as Serah was ready, he bid everyone farewell and pushed away the women who wanted to converse with Serah. A taxi was already waiting which provided a perfect excuse and once they were strapped in, Ricardo relaxed with the knowledge that they were on their way to their destination.

twenty nine

The flight from Australia to Canada had been long, so Serah knew what to expect. She hoped being with Ricardo would help pass the time. Feeling excited about going to a different country helped to ease her mind, but the previous events still haunted her. Serah had hoped to sleep on the plane but even in the taxi, every time she closed her eyes, the visions of the events appeared. She needed a distraction to vault the memories away which was provided when it came time to change planes.

As she was a novice when it came to travel, the trip to Canada had been an adventure, but she was becoming accustomed to airports and was surprised when she realised all airports were the same. The hustle and bustle amused her as she dodged her way through the other passengers. But as she had no idea where she was, Serah had to focus on Ricardo to get to her destination.

After such a long flight the last thing she wanted was to sit down, but when Ricardo took her to a café she knew that there was time to kill. Expecting to leisurely find a comfortable seat, she was shocked to be left at the nearest table. Chuckling to herself, she presumed that he was desperate for coffee as he was Italian, but he had not behaved that way on the tour. Wondering what was going on, she sat to wait for his return while listening to the woman next to her make conversation with another stranger. Serah was not used to other languages and inexperienced with seeing the world. As she watched other tourists try to find their transfers and gate numbers for their departures, it dawned on her how small her world was at home. If she had not been given the ticket to travel then she would still be none the wiser. It had only been a few weeks but she had experienced so much and as she looked at others, she wondered if they had endured a similar adventure.

Ricardo came back with a hot drink. 'Deep in thought?' he questioned.

She smiled before taking a sip. 'I was just thinking about what I've been through and if anyone here has had a similar experience.'

'Probably not,' said Ricardo taking her hand, 'but then maybe.'

Ricardo checked his watch. 'Last call for the plane,' he said taking out his boarding pass to check on the gate number.

Serah followed and once strapped into their seatbelts, Ricardo closed his eyes, relieved that he had managed to get his soulmate to the plane that would take him home. His hand took hers and as he felt her soft skin against his, he relaxed and fell asleep.

The tight grip that held Serah loosened and as she watched him sleep, her mind went into overdrive. Anxiety settled in and she needed a distraction, so she turned to the woman next to her and hoped she understood English.

The middle-aged passenger smiled, diminishing the fear that was building up inside Serah. In a moment of calm, she smiled back at the woman wearing a suit. 'Do you understand English?' asked Serah, glad of the diversion.

'I do,' she answered with a Canadian accent.

Serah laughed, 'Of course you do.'

'I know what you mean,' said the woman as she undid her buttons. 'I've done it myself. I start chatting with someone and when they speak back in another language, I have to remind myself that I'm not surrounded by Canadians any longer.'

'Some Canadians speak French, don't they?' asked Serah.

'They do but not where I come from,' said the woman as she took some hand cream from her bag.

Serah studied the woman's nails that were polished to highlight the rings on her fingers. She wondered what she did and what she was headed for. Because the woman had on a suit, Serah thought she might be some sort of business woman and going to Rome to make a deal.

'You have an unusual accent,' said the woman breaking the silence.

'I'm from Australia,' she answered. 'I went on a cruise through Alaska and then onto a bus tour through Canada.'

The woman looked over at a sleeping Ricardo.

'He was the bus driver who has talked me into going with him to Italy,' stated Serah, looking at his peaceful face.

'Lucky you,' said the woman looking away from him to stare at Serah.

After a moment of awkwardness, Serah spoke up to take the focus away from herself. 'What is that you do?'

'I'm a school teacher,' the woman replied, waiting for the reaction.

'I wouldn't have thought that was your occupation,' said Serah.

The woman giggled. 'Most think that, but I take my job very seriously. I have a responsibility as a teacher to guide children into adulthood. There are choices to be made in life and I hope I give them the guidance required to make the right decisions. I know I look conservative, but I'm out there with my teachings. There are too many kids on computers and they have lost empathy with playing those killing games. I try to teach empathy through animals.'

'How do you do that?' enquired Serah, admiring her companion.

'Small things,' she said. 'Speech is one. You hear the phrase, man's best friend and you think of someone who has a dog but when someone says, I was treated like a dog then you think the person was mistreated rather than cared for. I do think we can go too far with being politically correct.'

'I understand,' interjected Serah. 'In Australia, the phrase "king hit" got changed to "coward punch" to try to stop the violence glorified in the news.'

'Exactly,' she said. 'A few years ago, I came across a woman who rescued a horse. She asked for advice from others regarding his healing and was shocked at the lack of knowledge. People who advertised themselves as being able to rehabilitate animals were lacking in communication skills. She told me to go on Facebook and see how many people are out there, rescuing animals. There should be no need for animal rescue. I asked my students what their thoughts were regarding the animals. The result was upsetting to the point that I felt the need to do something about it. I introduced a class at school, once a week, to educate children of the importance of animals. Really, some of the school lessons are outdated and it would be better for society if children realised that animals feel the same way we do. With older students, I think it would be beneficial if they came in contact with neglected animals. If they can learn empathy towards animals then apply it to the rest of their lives, the empathy will be passed on to other people, hopefully resulting in a kinder civilisation.'

'You are so right,' said Serah, impressed with the woman's passion.

'I get carried away,' the woman said, squeezing Serah's hand while giggling.

'I think it's good you have a mission and it sounds like one that needs to be implemented,' Serah stated. 'I do nothing. I have no passion to change the world and I do nothing that gives me joy. But I do know there is something I am supposed to be doing.'

'I was like you,' said the teacher. 'I was living a nothing life until my son was born—then I changed. I didn't want him to grow up in a world of worry. There's no trust and you definitely can't judge a book by its cover.'

Serah smirked, 'I know what you mean. I trusted a woman on the trip and she ended up pushing me down a hole.'

The woman waited for an explanation but Serah had regretted mentioning the event. She had wanted to forget the trip but with one sentence she had unlocked what she wanted hidden.

'I think I know what you mean,' the woman said, taking the statement to be a metaphor. 'People assume that I'm in a position of power due to the way I dress but the suits are for my own pleasure. I wear them almost all the time, except for when I'm really doing one thing I really love. Then suits are out of the question!'

The statement intrigued Serah. 'What is it that you enjoy?'

'You would never guess,' she said with a giggle, 'but I love hearing stories from stones.'

Serah couldn't believe what she was hearing. She was surrounded and hoped that Ricardo would sleep through the entire journey as she wouldn't be able to bear listening to the two of them speak about rocks.

'That's why I'm going to Italy,' the woman said with an enormous smile. 'There are myths that come from there about giants. Graves have been found of humans who were twelve feet tall. They think they were the Anunnaki.'

The passenger was losing credibility, yet Serah couldn't help herself but pass on information she had acquired whilst being with Ricardo. She told of the man who had feet that were twelve inches long.

'That's right,' the woman replied, glad that someone shared her interest. 'That is why twelve inches is called a foot. He was very influential.'

Serah listened to the woman but couldn't understand how she had remembered the information about the man. Ricardo had opened her mind with his tales from stones but then a lot had happened to open her brain. She hoped that maybe she had heard it on the television but she wasn't sure. The conversation had now changed and it was one that she didn't want to have, so she yawned as a way out and put her head onto Ricardo to join him in sleep.

thirty

An announcement to put the seat back to its original position meant the plane was soon going to land. Ricardo woke with a start, alerting Serah to the situation. As they adjusted their clothes and moved the pillows and blankets to one side, Serah turned to look at the woman next to her who had also woken with a start.

'I'm sorry,' said Serah, 'I didn't mean to startle you.'

'I'm fine,' she responded putting herself back into position.

'And I didn't introduce myself. I'm Serah Kohw.'

'I'm Ricardo,' he said, leaning over to take the lady's hand.

'Nicaule,' she answered, 'Nicaule David.'

'Interesting,' said Ricardo, looking at the ring on her finger. 'May I look at it? I'm interested in stones and inscriptions of the past.'

'So am I,' she answered, handing over the ring. 'The ring was given to me by my father. Apparently, it has been handed down over the generations!'

Ricardo studied it in detail but said nothing as he gave it back to Nicaule.

The plane was descending and within minutes they were landing on the runway.

'We made it!' said Ricardo, eager to take the bags from the overhead locker.

With their suitcases in tow, they left the airport to enter a land that was far hotter than the one they came from.

'Why didn't you comment on the ring?' Serah asked Ricardo once they were alone. 'I thought it was unique but your face went blank. Why?'

'I think that was the ring of Solomon,' he said to a blank-looking Serah. 'Don't you know anything about history?'

She continued to stare at him without expression.

Feeling cross with himself, he changed his tone. 'Apparently, the ring had powers.'

'What, and you think that is the real ring?' asked Serah, still pulling on her suitcase.

'It had the inscription on it,' he said. 'The name of god.'

'It was a replica,' said Serah unable to believe he could be so gullible. 'If it had powers then she would be achieving her goals.'

'Her name is Nicaule David,' he said. 'Solomon was the son of David.'

'I think the heat is getting to you,' she said, 'which reminds me, you promised me summer clothes.'

Ricardo had gone through a lot to get Serah to Italy, so to avoid further distraction he found a taxi that would take them to a hotel where they could leave their luggage and head out into the mayhem of Rome.

'Shouldn't we get out of the city?' suggested Serah looking at the very expensive shops.

'It's too hot for you to be in jeans and boots,' he said. 'We'll buy you a dress and shoes for starters and then you can buy other things along the way.'

The stores were interesting but the crowds were crazy. Cars beeped and people yelled out in frustration. Large tourist groups followed flags, and people tripped over uneven pathways. The stench of rubbish thrown to the side of the roads sent Serah towards a store to buy a bottle of perfume, and with a bottle of water in her hand they dodged the locals to find a boutique. The city was too busy for her liking but her prayers were answered when she found a floral dress and flat sandals.

'Can we leave now?' she asked in desperation.

A taxi took them back to the hotel where they were greeted by a man at the door. His accent was not Italian and his sense of humour was unbearable as he refused to let them in. He had not performed when they had first arrived, but then they had not noticed him when they had come from the airport.

'You've finished shopping already,' he said, still standing in front of the door. 'I think you need to go out again. You have not been away for long enough. The temptation of the bed is too great and if you lay down then you will go to sleep and upset your body clock.'

'Thanks for the information,' said Ricardo, giving him a tip so he would move out of the way. 'He has a point, I suppose,' said Ricardo. 'Maybe we should do a tour of the city.'

'Or we could soak in the spa tub,' said Serah pointing to the lift that had a picture of the spa area next to the doors.

She thought he would follow her but instead he headed for the concierge who booked them on a dinner tour. It made sense to stay awake but the thought of walking in the heat wasn't enticing.

'You can sit in an air-conditioned bus to view the city and then we can enjoy an authentic Italian dinner,' said a persuading Ricardo. 'Besides, you should see Rome since you are here.'

The comfortable chairs in the lobby helped relax Serah's body and by the time the tour guide came in, she was half asleep. She didn't want to leave the chair and would have quite happily sank into it for the rest of the afternoon, but Ricardo pulled at her arms so there was no choice but to follow the others onto the bus.

It was a different view of Rome but it was a city the same as she had witnessed in Vancouver with its homeless people. She thought about Nicaule and how she wanted to change the world. If there was money to send rockets to outer space then there was enough money to look after those in need. It infuriated Serah, but she kept her thoughts to herself as she looked out the window. Others commented on the remarkable buildings that the Romans had put together and between the walls of graffiti Serah could see the ruins that had lasted for thousands of years. Stones steeped with history were everywhere and she could see where Ricardo's interest came from as the crumbling structures were a testament to an ancient civilisation.

The tour guide raised the sound on his microphone to inform everyone about the city that was built on top of another city. The comical man explained about the government that tried to change the structure of the streets, but at each attempt they came across remnants of a ruined city that once existed below. Archaeologists claimed the new discoveries as their sites, and so to stop the disruption of traffic it was decided to leave the roads as they were.

It was a slow drive through the traffic with many close calls as drivers tried to fit into small gaps between others. The cobblestoned roads were narrow with not much option for parking. Smart cars were everywhere with the tiny automobiles being able to fit into much smaller spaces, but its popularity meant that there was a great deal more on the road. Chaos was inevitable but the Italians had created their own road rules which seemed to work, according to the tour guide. Their crash rate was low, which amazed Serah who looked out as drivers manoeuvred their way through streets that would normally be considered a single lane. The smaller cars created two and sometimes three lanes, and when the bus came to a standstill, Serah watched the dance that was being performed by moped riders and pedestrians who were waiting for the moment to make their move. Music was provided in the form of beeping horns and police sirens that seemed to be used in excess when a Diplomat needed to get through. The markings for parking spots for one car had also been ignored to allow others to squeeze in. The original driver who parked had only one chance to get out of a blocked parking spot, and that was to hope the other drivers had abandoned their cars without putting on the handbrake so they could be moved aside.

Drivers had provided the start of an entertaining night which continued on when Serah and Ricardo arrived at the restaurant. Cheerful waiters and a couple of men played music and sang songs to sing along to. The atmosphere brought everyone together with laughter that continued on through the night. Serah was glad she had left the lobby behind to indulge in the cuisine. First course consisted of fruit and bruschetta which was then followed by the singers and more antics from the waiters. Next course was ravioli served by a waiter who had his own style of providing parmesan cheese by dropping it from above people's heads. Next course was rigatoni followed by a sing along where they discovered that one of the group could actually sing. Next dish was a choice of fish or meat followed by everyone receiving roses as was the tradition to celebrate different festivities for certain people.

The waiter referred to Serah as Juliette and she found out why when Romeo gave her a large bunch of roses with her gelato. Ricardo was not impressed, but calmed down when the larrikins continued to hand out smaller bunches of roses to every female on their way out. Hilarity was in the air and continued on the bus ride back to the hotel where Ricardo had to listen to everyone comment on the size of the bunch of flowers that Serah was given. It had been a good idea to go on the tour and with exhausted bodies, Ricardo and Serah fell asleep immediately. However, it didn't last as they woke up several times during the early hours of the next morning.

thirty one

'Curse that man,' said Serah. 'I really thought that I would sleep through the night.'

No longer being part of a tour group meant that, after tossing and turning through the night, they could sleep in. When they finally made it to the dining room, all that was left were pastries and strong coffee. Serah had only drunk dandelion tea at home but was becoming accustomed to the strong substance with the caffeine kick. Over breakfast they decided on another tour that would take them to the Vatican.

Tourists lined the wall to enter, but the tour guide ignored them as she walked passed. 'The property, which is over one hundred acres and surrounded by a wall, is its own country,' she announced as she pushed everyone through the entrance.

Once inside, they were told to follow the tour guide and not to lose her as she might not find them amongst the thousands of others. To help identify her, she carried a pink flag for them to follow, but it was difficult as most of the time everyone looked up to take in the paintings on the ceilings. Somehow they all managed to stay with her despite having to deal with other tourists bumping into them, guards changing instructions with directions when they felt like it and professional pick-pocketers. Gypsies intending to steal money from tourists would dress up to blend in, but on one occasion some who were dressed up as nuns were caught out. The tour guide told how she had witnessed the event and wasn't sure what was going on when she saw the nuns being arrested by the brightly coloured Swiss guards.

It all seemed very hypocritical to Serah who listened through the earpiece about the money that was involved with creating the Vatican. The buildings were created from stone and filled with marble, gold and copper. Every turn they took revealed more paintings, tapestries and carvings. Lavish surroundings that would be priceless stood in a place where they took donations, yet they didn't pay any tax. She found some of the stories interesting but questionable. It was still hard to believe that people believed in science fiction when they lived in an age of science, but then what she had experienced over the last week would have been considered fiction, although she knew it was fact.

The touching fingers in Michelangelo's huge painting of The Creation of Adam fascinated Serah. The interpretation was of a human connecting with God, but Serah's eyes focussed on what she saw, as people inside a brain-shaped structure, reminding her of an alien ship filled with beings that were connecting with a human. She shared her interpretation with Ricardo who reminded Serah that the earpieces were supplied by the Vatican and were rumoured to be bugged.

'Do you really think that they are interested in what I have to say?' Serah questioned too loudly.

'You would be a code red,' said a man standing next to her from the group. 'Besides, there are many theories out there other than the gods giving information from above.'

Ricardo listened as the man explained about the Egyptian artefacts that were on display. 'Some believe that Osiris, the Egyptian god of the underworld, brought intelligence to our civilisation.'

'I wouldn't mind going to Egypt,' stated Ricardo.

'Oh no! I said I would come here but that's it,' Serah said, taking off to look at the souvenirs for sale. Serah was not religious but was attracted to the image of those fingers touching each other. A small tin with rosary beads inside had a picture of the fingers on the lid and as she picked it up, she felt an energy beside her.

'Are you going to buy that?' asked a quietly spoken Venus.

A shocked Serah stared at the goddess as vivid memories of what she had been through flashed through her mind.

'Sorry,' said Venus, 'I didn't mean to startle you, but no one else is going to tell you why you are so fascinated with the picture.'

'Are you watching me?' asked Serah looking around to see who else was about.

'You are always watched and I am a watcher,' she said changing her golden cloak to a fitted jacket. 'Buy the box. The beads make a nice necklace and the tin will hold your pills.'

Serah laughed at her sense of humour. 'I don't know why the picture of the fingers touching each other intrigues me so much.'

'It annoys you,' said Venus, 'because you know that it is the middle finger that is used for healing and not the index fingers as portrayed in that painting. Take a look and you will see that when a blessing occurs, both the middle and index fingers are used together. They don't want people to know about healing because there is money to be made in the pharmaceutical industry.'

'Who is "they"?' asked Serah looking at the picture on her purchase as she handed over money to pay for it.

There was no response. Serah was left with a mystery to solve. She had seen the movie, The Da Vinci Code, and she had no intention of embarking on a similar mission looking for clues. Recalling the moment she had hired the movie brought back the memory of her feeling ill. It had been a strange sensation that no tests suggested by her doctor could explain. Venus had appeared for a reason and that was to jolt her memory of the news that she was from the bloodline of Mary Magdalene. She had tried to lock it away as she wanted to be a normal tourist but when she noticed the snakes that were painted and carved into the building, she was glad to have her protector with her. She needed to leave immediately and walked through the exit where she found people selling cheap souvenirs and begging for money.

It was a sight that she could not bear so they headed for a street that once would have homed Romans. A small café beside the road provided them with food, drink and a distraction that came in a form of a couple from Australia who sat on the table next to them and were more than happy to chat.

Ricardo listened in on the conversation about Australia, and when Serah began to discuss the weather and clothes, the men turned their attention away from the females.

'Are you interested in the Vatican,' asked the other male, 'or is it just us tourists?'

Ricardo laughed. 'To be honest, I've never been in there before.'

'So what are your interests?' the man asked, not wanting to listen to the women's chatter.

'Stones,' replied Ricardo.

'I know a lot about stones,' said the man with a body covered with tattoos. 'I'm originally from England. Do you know about the ring hidden in the Vatican?'

Ricardo shook his head.

The man was grateful to have someone he could share his knowledge with. 'There was a stone that the Celts wanted. It was supposed to contain energy that would help you communicate with the gods or aliens; whatever you want to call them. The stone was powerful and too much for any mere mortal to deal with. Apparently, if you had it then you could use it to influence others.'

'I've never heard of that story,' said Ricardo wondering if the man was making it up in jest.

'I did a tour in England years ago before I met my wife,' he said. 'It was interesting. We were taken to different standing stones and told of stories. Some seemed far-fetched but others made me think there could be some truth to the stories.'

'Why do you believe in the story of the ring in the Vatican?' asked Ricardo.

The man looked around before speaking. 'Well, when a spirit enters a body and won't leave, it is always a catholic priest who is called to get rid of it.'

Ricardo sipped on his coffee pondering over the information.

'What are you thinking about?' asked Serah, taking in bits of their conversation and not liking what she was hearing.

'I'm thinking about going to the Colosseum,' he lied.

Serah knew that he wasn't telling the truth but she didn't care as she needed him to avoid any influence that would send them away from normality.

It was crowded at the Colosseum but worth the wait to enter as it was a magnificent structure. But it was hard for Serah to understand why such a building had been built to provide entertainment. The Roman citizens lived from day to day in conditions of hardship and the Colosseum was meant to provide a way for them to forget about their unhappiness. It took nine years to build and many men to travel to Africa to return with wild animals. Gladiators risked their lives fighting against the animals, many of them volunteering as it was a way to die with a chance of experiencing fame. All victors received cheers from a crowd of sixty thousand people, and that was something they were unlikely to have experienced elsewhere. Death was imminent so they had nothing to lose; entertainment had taken over and had become their goal in life. They had been distracted from reality, and that had a huge effect, not only on them but the loss of animals that were being slaughtered for amusement. If the Roman Empire had not ended, there would not have been any wildlife and not have been the flow in nature that was needed to continue the life of the planet.

Serah felt every word that was spoken by the guide, but she had to admit the building was a remarkable achievement considering the technology of the time. Everything had been taken into account from the rooms being created for warriors underneath the stadium to the materials used to cover the roof to provide shade. It was a mammoth undertaking and one that changed the way of life for everyone, which Serah noticed when they walked past a stand selling magazines filled with gossip from people wanting to be movie stars.

Something struck a chord with the realisation of the unhappiness being with people who wanted to go back to the stars in the sky. She hadn't realised it before, but being influenced by a goddess was starting to put everything into perspective. The uneven ground made walking tricky, but a raised stone turned her towards a man selling his paintings on the side of the road. They were different from the others who generally copied the paintings onto good paper to make them look real. Serah was taken by one painting that showed an historic background and featured a girl in a pink dress, representing fashion. It was a statement confirming her thoughts that people no longer helped one another, living in isolation, and one that she had to buy to put up on her wall at home to remind her where civilisation had gone wrong. Maybe she could become passionate about something and help to change the world. She wished she had taken Nicaule's email address and hoped she could find her on Facebook.

'We need to move,' said Ricardo dragging her away to avoid a tour group that was dispersing.

Ricardo hailed a taxi and they went to a place that looked interesting but where they still really needed to watch their step. Strolling the Spanish steps and throwing coins into fountains made for a better walk. They found themselves behind another tour group, so instead of trying to pass them, they decided to join in to hear some information about the history of the city. But there was too much to absorb so they veered away when they entered a square surrounded by restaurants. They chose a small café where musicians were playing, which made the atmosphere enjoyable. Once the ensemble was over, the musicians asked for donations from the patrons before leaving. A woman from another table laughed at the request as she put money into the guitarist's hat. She was Australian and Serah listened to her as she spoke of the cruise that she had been on which had sailed through the Greek islands.

Serah was fascinated with the table of people from different nationalities who had travelled through Europe. She wanted to join them but Ricardo wanted to be alone. The table grew louder with each bottle of wine that was emptied and when the conversation changed to energy, it was Ricardo who decided to move his chair closer to them.

Serah couldn't believe that he could be influenced so easily but joined him as he listened to a woman named Sabela who had been to Machu Picchu and spoke of gateways. She mentioned to a stunned table of tourists about what she had experienced, including an incident where she had touched a rock that had buzzed through the air.

Ricardo prompted her as she began to steer away from the topic of the unknown due to the chatter that had changed theme.

'Do you want to know what I was told?' asked Sabela as she looked around for acknowledgements.

The others weren't sure; Serah didn't want to know but Ricardo did and blurted out for her to continue.

'Okay,' she said, 'I wasn't the only one who experienced this, but when I touched the rock I saw white people coming up through the ground. They said they lived under the sea. I don't know which sea but it has strong currents and there is one area that is calm and has an abandoned ship. I think the name of the vessel is Roselie. They showed a vision of a triangle filled with debris and an object that flew out of it using matter to move. It was like a warning because I think the energy is negative.'

'What type of object was it?' asked a woman, suddenly intrigued.

Sabela tried to recall the vision and stated that it was a bell shape.

'Oh,' said the excited woman, 'I know about that. I was in Germany and Hitler had captured scientists who had created a flying machine that looked like a bell.'

'Really?' asked another tourist. 'I want to go to Germany.'

'So do I,' said another, 'but I am interested in different types of stories.'

'What stories?' said Ricardo wanting to find out more.

'The Grimm brothers' stories.'

Laughter returned to the table with the change in conversation as more wine was brought out by the waiters.

'I think it's time to go,' whispered Ricardo to Serah.

She couldn't believe that he was only interested in other worldly stories but she didn't say anything as her eyelids were growing heavy and bed seemed to be the perfect solution.

thirty two

It was an early start the next day with a surprise announcement from Ricardo that they were to join a tour that would take them through another part of Italy. He had planned on taking her to his home to get his car but he wanted Serah to experience a normal holiday. Furthermore, as she still had her heart set on returning to her life in Australia, he didn't want to frighten her with a commitment that she might expect if she were to meet his family. There was something else he wanted her to see, and this tour would to take them there.

Tuscany was in the direction the tour would take. Leaving on time was important as there were eighteen other tour buses headed the same way. Traffic was chaotic but the bus managed to squeeze through the cars parked illegally on the sides of the road to head out into the countryside. The open road provided a calmer view with villas dotted on the hills sloped with green. Now and again the scenery would change when a wall would appear on top of a hill. Small towns crammed inside boundaries that had stood for centuries with only cracks to allow sight of what was within. In ancient times, communities had lived together in fear of invasion and only broke free to live separate lives a few hundred years ago.

Siena was the next stop. It was one of the walled towns from medieval times. The tour group left the comfort of their bus to view buildings from the thirteen hundreds that were turned into homes, crammed into the small place with narrow cobbled streets.

In this town cars were bigger and everyone had to scatter quite a few times to let them through. Other buildings held shops and cafés and one was so small it could only hold one table inside it. The narrow streets were not what Serah was used to but the large wooden doors that hid garages or open courtyards intrigued her.

They walked along, mesmerised with the old town, and tried to imagine what it would have been like to live there. It was a romantic notion, but because it was a place that kept people packed together, it allowed disease to spread easily. It would have been a difficult life without modern conveniences, and as Serah looked around she wondered what type of life Ricardo had lived. A sound in the distance of revving cars brought them back to the present, and with a curious group in tow they made their way to the square where more cars had gathered. It was a rally with vintage cars stopping at the square to be checked off before moving on. As it was a sight that no one expected, many sat at a café and watched.

The square was surrounded by restaurants and eateries filled with onlookers, creating an extra workload for the staff who were only used to being busy in July when the cobblestones were covered with dirt for a bareback horse race.

'You'd think they would be used to the crowds in the summer,' said one of the group, ordering a sandwich filled with salami and cheese.

'I suppose people get caught off guard,' said Ricardo defensively.

'You're Italian,' noticed the woman.

'I'm showing my girlfriend Italy through the eyes of a tourist,' he said with a sly look.

'Aren't you lucky,' said the woman with a smirk on her face.

'You've never called me your girlfriend before,' said Serah, surprised at the statement.

Ricardo took her hand. 'I would like to call you my wife but I'm not going to push it.'

The woman interrupted them. 'You should marry now. Don't put it off. Who knows what the future holds.'

Others joined in on the conversation, stating that they were taking the opportunity to do things while they could, like travelling.

'I have known too many people who have waited to travel later and then haven't been able to due to poor health,' said a Dutch woman.

Her husband nodded in agreement. 'Look around you. We are in a place that has survived for ages, but who is to say that it will be here in years to come? When we get to Venice, I'm taking as many photos as I can because it might sink, never to be seen again.'

An English man who sat next to him agreed. 'Look at Atlantis. That is a place none of us will get to see. When the world was flooded, it didn't survive.'

'People didn't survive,' said someone from another table.

'Some did,' said Ricardo. 'The ones who used the wormholes to take them to other planets.'

Everyone was taken aback by the statement which instantly split up the group.

Some chairs moved to surround the table of people discussing travel ideas and countries to see, while others moved to another spot to speak about ancient aliens. Serah didn't know where to sit. She wanted to listen to tourist spots but then she wanted to stay with Ricardo who was sitting with the people who were interested in planets. Her coffee and cake arrived so she stayed put and listened to the information being given to her about the people from thousands of years ago who were taller with larger heads. As she took a bite of her cake filled with cream, she saw the vision of the water rising. The beings from another planet had needed gold but they didn't want to dig for it themselves. They had interbred with humans to provide them with slaves who were tall and muscular. They became comfortable here, not having to do any work themselves and reaping the benefits. Their ruler had become displeased with his own people who decided they wanted to stay, so in order to make them return to their own planet, he flooded the earth. Some couldn't bear to leave their loved ones behind so they provided knowledge of the wormholes that would take them to a safe place while they waited for the water to subside.

Serah tried to block the information and was glad when the tour guide turned up to take everyone back to the bus.

'Firenze is our next stop!' called out the guide which brought on a change of topic.

The women spoke of the leather bags that were made in Florence and were excited to be going to a factory where the bags were made.

'Why is that you have you always bring up other worldly information when a discussion starts?' said Serah as Ricardo sat next to her.

'Sorry,' he said. 'I can't help myself but I will try to stop.'

With the chatter on the bus being about leather and the guide making jokes about cows, Serah sat back, glad that there would be nothing extraordinary for Ricardo to remark on.

Florence was the capital city but it was not as busy as Rome. It was easy to stroll along the streets that were broken up with small market squares. Stalls provided bags in every shape and colour, distracting a group of women. They seemed to know something, so Serah followed them to find out. She looked at her own handbag which was years old, giving her an excuse to buy another one, so she stayed close to them as they broke away from the group to enter a shop that had been making leather bags since nineteen forty-eight. The smell of the leather was intoxicating, and as Serah looked around the shop she took in the workmanship. The owner was happy to discuss the quality with the group of women and when he brought out his latest design that was about to hit the market, Serah made a purchase without hesitation.

Ricardo had waited outside with the other husbands who worried about the prices, but when he saw the smile on Serah's face, he didn't care about how much his future wife had spent. Instead, he took her hand and walked along while listening to the husbands who complained about the budget. It was a balmy afternoon, but that was being ignored with the banter from the guide, so as Ricardo knew where the hotel was, he pulled Serah back from the crowd to take in the beauty of the sun falling behind the hills.

As they stood in the shadows from the buildings, Ricardo motioned to the guide that they would stay back and catch up in a while. It was a moment he wanted to share with her as he was sure she would see the beauty nature was providing. He stood behind her, pushing her face up to see the changing sky, and as he placed his arms around her front, he closed his eyes and placed his face in her hair. He loved her, but there were things she needed to accept before she could truly allow herself to love him back. For now, he wanted her to let go of her senses and take in what was around her.

She looked at the buildings that had stories to tell but could only hear the breath of Ricardo next to her ear. He made her heart beat faster, confusing her senses. Her soul wanted to take her down the alleyways but her body could only feel Ricardo against it. Despite the shade, the weather was hot and she needed to cool down, so she turned to him to ask if there was a pool at the hotel.

'There is,' he answered with a grin on his face, 'but you can't use it.'

'Why not?' she asked with disappointment.

'Because we meet for dinner in half an hour,' he said taking her hand to show her the way.

'But I would rather go in the pool,' she answered making him stop.

'I wanted you to enjoy the moment,' he stated glaring at her.

'What moment?' she queried.

'Exactly!' he said putting his hands up in the air. 'I wanted you to experience the sunset.'

She took back his hand. 'I did.'

He paused in the middle of the alleyway and kissed her before heading off to meet the others.

Dinner started out well with the entertainment being provided by a couple who were still disputing the price of the leather bag. Bruschetta appeared on the table with a bottle of wine, but when Serah's salmon panini turned out to be a salami roll, the table knew that there were going to be problems.

'I'll tell them,' said Ricardo about to move.

Serah stopped him. 'I'm so hungry I'll eat it.'

Pasta appeared along with leftovers which were devoured with laughter due to everyone trying to stop Ricardo exploding. An American couple pacified everyone with their stories of their life on a farm which included a fostered donkey. And another American couple who originated from the Ukraine had everyone in stitches with the food that was thrown at them because the waiters didn't understand that they couldn't eat gluten. It was a comedy of errors which was helped by the large consumption of alcohol, and it would be spoken about for days to come.

thirty three

Many tourists appeared for breakfast with sore heads. For some it was so bad that they decided to stay at the hotel instead of visiting the museum of Michelangelo's David. The queue was long and as they waited in line Serah chatted with two Canadian women. Sellers of genuine reproduction paintings tried to block them as they lined up at the entrance and in an attempt to move them, Serah explained that they weren't interested. Everyone expected them to step aside but instead they yelled out profanities, taking everyone by surprise. The two Canadian women were horrified when Serah swore back at them but when Ricardo sprang into action, everyone cheered him on. For the first time Serah saw the Templar that was inside Ricardo who ran off after them demanding they come back with the cartel leader to apologise for the abusive language.

Luckily the line had moved and the guide appeared with tickets for them to move inside as Ricardo received pats on his back. Comments continued and the chatter didn't stop until information was given from the guide who mentioned that the statue was of the boy from the David and Goliath story. Serah rolled her eyes thinking that Ricardo would have a story to tell about the stone, but as she looked closer at the sculpture she took in the detail of Michelangelo's work. The block of marble had been carved five hundred years ago and still the facial expressions changed in the light. It was a piece that was meant to stand the test of time to remind people of the past.

The museum was a school of art in the town where Michelangelo and Leonardo da Vinci both lived. She tried to imagine what it would have been like, but was fascinated more with the reason why Michelangelo would want to sculpt David. Hearts of love were carved into David's eyes which took her back to the image that she had seen in Siena. David had been the one who had fought the Anunnaki. He had rebelled against the offspring who were the giants. He was the one who stopped the slavery and sent the aliens away. Michelangelo had known and left an image behind. The story was in the eyes as it always was. David had fought for love and she looked at Ricardo who had displayed the same passion. There was no need for her to fear anything as he would die for her but then was it because his DNA made him protect the line of Mary Magdalene. She needed air and walked outside to the streets of Florence followed by a bewildered Ricardo.

'Where are you going?' he called out to her.

'We're allowed free time so I'm taking it,' she said wanting to be alone.

Footsteps became louder as he got closer. 'I'll show you around and I promise no stories about aliens.'

He put his arm in hers and stopped at points of interest to explain about history that was taught from school books. Statues were everywhere with the most interesting being those around the square where the Medici family had lived. A detailed statue of a horse with the first Medici member on his back dominated. A large stone building at the corner of the square was where the family lived, but greed of power stopped the Medici family from marrying outside their own family and three hundred years later, they had vanished.

A café provided a good view of the square and, to play it safe, she let Ricardo order her lunch in Italian. Bruschetta, minestrone soup and a potato fritter appeared before her and it was the best she had ever tasted. Whatever Ricardo had said had worked and she sat up in her seat to enjoy the flavours.

As her stomach filled, she watched the tourists admiring the statues. 'I wonder if they know what they are looking at.'

Ricardo put money on the table. 'We have to head back.'

He took her through streets that were out of the way and quiet. The back streets were not normally explored by visitors, but should have been as they provided an aroma that opened Serah's senses. The smell of sandalwood, tomato leaves and apple spread out to the street and called for her to enter the premises. The old shop with magnificent furniture of carved wood displayed fragrances that were too irresistible. Serah took a bottle and sprayed her clothes but should have asked Ricardo to interpret the label first as it turned out to be air freshener. There wasn't any concern as the spray was naturally made, but it did make her blush. With a few purchases, she was redeemed and they headed off to meet the others who were impressed with the aroma.

The Italian tour was different to the one Serah had experienced in Canada. With a sense of normality she joined the other women who were not a threat to her, to look at a tower that took everyone's breath away with its size and slope. They had arrived at Pisa and were anxious to see the structure up close. It looked as if it would fall over at any moment so they were all keen to investigate, but their guide was in a mad panic to get them into the church.

'Oh no,' said a worried Serah, 'you haven't . . .'

'What?' asked Ricardo trying to figure out what was wrong, but then laughed. 'No, I haven't organised anything.'

'No,' interrupted a frazzled tour guide, 'but the niece of the priest has. She wants to renew her vows and the church is about to close.'

Normally the guides were paranoid about losing tourists and always carried a flag and stopped for a head count, but that wasn't the case this time as the door was held open by a man who tried to score a cigarette while waiting.

'I guess the cigarette companies are glad that Europeans smoke,' said Serah explaining about the rules in Australia that would send the companies out of business.

The guide managed to smoke a cigarette before closing the door behind him. He explained about the building adjacent being the one where you had to be baptised before entry and how you had to be true to god before admiring the church which had been built with stolen spoils from previous wars. Normally the guide would ask the question as to who was baptised, but he was in a rush and quickly spoke of the columns made from solid granite. Everyone agreed that they were impressive but were surprised to hear they had been taken from a mosque centuries before, as it was usually the other way around. There were flaws in the stories which didn't concern Serah as she was glad to hear a story from history that didn't involve the supernatural.

Once out of the building, the guide complained about Florence interfering with Pisa, which Serah found quite comical. He also explained about the tower leaning but said that if it was fixed then no one would visit. He had a point, and after a gelato, which was mandatory once a day, they all left to have dinner at an olive farm.

Several bottles of wine that were produced in the area awaited guests who sat at long tables covered with chequered cloth. Comments were made about the olive oil on sale as food continually appeared, appeasing the hunger that had built up over the day. The feast took place at an olive farm that made more sales as the night wore on. A dessert was handed out which consisted of a sweet wine for dunking biscuits followed by a glass of grappa. Music played as sales went through the roof and waitresses were called to deal with the money. Then guests were left alone to work off some calories by dancing on the concrete that would have been the driveway.

Ricardo joined in with the circle of women as Serah spied a two-month-old, Newfoundland puppy running around in the kitchen. Not being able to help herself, she went in search and found the large face that looked up at her. There was no choice other than to pick him up and carry him back to the table and once they were comfortable, his eight-month-old brother joined him to be cuddled and lap up the attention.

'You left me with those drunken women,' said Ricardo in a fluster.

Serah continued to cuddle the puppies.

'Why can't you cuddle me like that?' he asked patting one that jumped up at him.

'You're not as cuddly,' she said sarcastically.

'I can put on weight,' he replied, rubbing his stomach.

Serah went to answer but the dancers were back and dragged him to the dance floor where he couldn't escape. The women were in high spirits and bonded in a sing-a-long that included Ricardo who could not hide. The frivolity continued in the bus, to the delight of the bus driver.

thirty four

Bologna sparked interest within the group. Everyday there was a game of musical chairs on the bus with everyone having to move two seats down for a different view. Serah thought it was a good way of meeting others from the group, but when a man sat opposite Ricardo and started to speak about the day being Friday and the thirteenth day of the month, she knew Ricardo would not be able to help himself; it was the day the Templars were prosecuted for heresy because they wouldn't provide the names that were kept secret. She listened as they spoke of Venus who helped fight against the Anunnaki and provided protection for those who were not interbred. Venus had offered her planet as a safe haven and the men had let the females go first. Those who were left behind were unaware they would be caught in a flood.

Serah needed a disruption and looked out at the mountains with tunnels and large aqueducts for bridges. But it was of no use, she couldn't block out what she didn't want to hear and continued to listen to the man speak of a spaceship that had rescued some of the men and taken them to Mars. The last conversation she had had with the man had been about farming so she had presumed him to be a farmer. She had laughed at his jokes, but now he was telling Ricardo he had spent some time at NASA and knew that Mars once held life. His voice lowered but Serah could still hear him as he continued on about a sphinx on Mars that had knowledge under its paw and of how meteorites that had crashed into planets, left behind stones that held secrets.

Her elbow nudged at Ricardo but he was too engrossed.

'Don't you think it's more than a coincidence that Cairo means place of Mars?' said the man. 'Xenon 129 was found on Mars after the explosion.'

Ricardo didn't know what xenon 129 was, but Serah knew it was a conspiracy and didn't like where the conversation was heading. Ricardo, on the other hand, was fascinated and urged his companion to continue.

'NASA sent a machine to the Ares Vallis region. They know Mars was destroyed by a comet which was described by the ancient people as a feathered serpent,' he said fuelled with excitement that someone understood him. 'There are feathered serpents on the pyramids in Mexico. If you ever travel through South America and the surrounding countries, you will see evidence of tunnels with orbs that flicker with gold. There is even a cavern made from clay that has gold fleck in it. The feathered serpent was the god from Mars. When their planet was destroyed, they moved to earth millions of years ago.'

'Wait,' said Ricardo, 'if that was millions of years ago then the timelines are out.'

'They were,' the man replied. 'Time was out of alignment and has only recently been put right.'

Ricardo looked confused but knew the man was right. He didn't know how he knew, but something inside him said that things had changed and it was only a few who were aware. There had been mention of things being distorted and as he pictured the people with knowledge, he looked over at the man's hand and noticed the stone in his ring. He knew many people wore rings of protection but only now realised that the protection was of the knowledge and not the person. Ricardo was meant to protect Serah and whether she wanted to or not, he was going to give her an engagement ring because it was not a sign of ownership but a sign of belonging. There was safety in numbers and once someone was identified as being in that group then protection was provided. With a mission in mind he turned his attention to Serah who had closed her eyes once their conversation had ended.

With the bus parked, the tour guide went into action to wake up those who were sleeping off a hangover. It was a slow group that staggered from the bus last who hadn't noticed the change that had taken place. At first glance, the town seemed like any other medieval town, except the cars were larger and more expensive. The smart cars were replaced by Ferrari, Maserati and Mercedes. The driving and touch parking was the same with every gap being taken over by pushy Italians, but the atmosphere was different. There was a respect for the community in the form of clean pathways and stone walls that were not covered with graffiti. The guide took them through tiny streets and explained about the history of the buildings and the previous occupants.

The most interesting was a church that had been designed by an astronomer whose name was being used for the shuttle to Saturn. Serah cringed at the fact and dragged Ricardo away from the American farmer. She would have taken him outside, but a two centimetre hole in the roof kept her still. A light shone through to hit a line created on the floor to tell the time as well as the month. The building was designed to cover many aspects of astrology and had been very popular with the people throughout the ages. It would have been the largest church in its day but when the Pope at the time heard about it, he stopped the construction of the sides which would have formed the shape of a cross from above. To make sure the building would not be finished, the Pope built other buildings on each side of the church. The group listened on in disbelief as they were also told that the Pope stopped the marble and statues from making their way to finish the project.

The information prompted the farmer who was back in Ricardo's ear. 'Amazing story, isn't it, for a man who runs a religion of redemption.'

Serah went to drag Ricardo away again but was distracted by the guide who explained about the artist who had painted on the wall his depiction of life.

Six hundred years ago, he believed that God, Jesus and Mary were up above in heaven, so he painted them and put other people in the middle and in hell down below. He painted a monster named Lucifer who was eating Judas and punishing Caesar for their crimes. He painted other religious leaders who were depicted in hell also. Threats had been made over the years concerning the display, and at one stage an army had been posted around the building to protect it. Eventually they caught those who were responsible for the threats but there were still undercover guards.

A group of women escorted Serah away from Ricardo who had to escape to find a jewellery store. He knew the farmer had provided him with a sign that it was Bologna that held the stone of protection, so in order to get the ring, he had asked the women for help. Happy to oblige, they took Serah to a delicatessen selling food that was fresh and free from preservatives.

'They eat well here,' said one of the Canadian women.

'Why isn't this food anywhere else?' asked the Dutch woman. 'Mind you, we do have good pastries in Holland.'

'I thought Amsterdam would be full of food considering the amount of people who have the munchies from those coffee shops there,' said the Canadian woman in jest.

The group laughed as they ate slices of meat and fruit full of flavour. Wine was brought out for the group to wash down the meal and that was when the guide turned up to escort everyone back to the church.

'Why are we going back there?' asked Serah who was happy to sit with a glass of alcohol.

'Go in and see,' he said ushering her though the door.

Ricardo stood under the ray of light with his knee on the line that had been placed on the floor years before.

'What are you doing?' she whispered as she looked around to see the whole tour group enter with interest.

'I need you in my life and I need you to wear this ring,' he said aloud.

She looked up through the tiny hole in the roof and saw the gold leaves that floated through the air. They fell at her feet and she knew she had no choice. It was destiny and she should be grateful it was Ricardo who was her protector.

'I will accept the ring but I need time to think about the commitment,' she said putting her hand in his.

A gold ring with a stone of garnet was placed on her finger as a group of people cheered. The noise exploded through the building, sending sounds through the openings and suspicious looks from security. The explanation was left up to the guide who managed to get the group away from Bologna without any charges and back on the bus to head for Venice.

As they arrived at the city surrounded by water, Serah expected to see a city centre with canals instead of streets, but Venice was a lot larger than she thought. What she had seen on television was nothing in comparison with what lay outside the square. Gondolas took them along the canals as they saw first-hand the destruction to the buildings by the invading water. The islands were man-made and were designed as a fortress for the fishing community, but the population had expanded and become wealthy, bringing in more riches with more extravagant buildings being built. The island had become too heavy and started to sink into the water table below the islands. This water table had been their source of drinking water. The buildings would have been beautiful in their day but now they were crumbling. Large chunks had fallen off and the structures were on the move. A mass of tourists stared at the surroundings, thinking the city wouldn't exist at all in the future. The guide explained about the government extorting as much money as possible to help towards the situation, but what wasn't expected were the fines handed out to tourists if they purchased illegal reproductions from sellers who swore everything was genuine. The police roamed around but had not been able to stop the gypsies who were spread out throughout the country and who made their living by pick-pocketing. Venice was ripe with thieves, so Ricardo took Serah's bag to hold it close. He also took his coins from his pocket and placed them in the bag after hearing the guide state that everything found in a pocket was considered a donation.

The romance had gone from the city on the water but the hotel still held its charm. As they sat down to dinner, Serah listened to the different points of view provided by everyone who sat around an enormous table. Wine helped to encourage speech and it was a pastor who complained when fruit was presented as dessert. The tour guide tried to appease him but Ricardo stepped in and a few minutes later rum cake was brought out to finish off the night.

thirty five

It was an early start to explore Venice, beginning with a factory where glass objects were made. A talented man created a seahorse with ease so everyone could appreciate the workmanship involved before being left to explore the creations. Vibrant colours caught everyone's attention as they perused the shelves filled with items, but once Serah caught a glimpse of the prices, she quickly headed outside followed by a few others. They saw an old gondola sitting out the front of the building and went for a closer look. The workmanship was intricate, far surpassing the standard vessels that were passed on from father to son.

A trip on the water took them to the islands of Venice that were connected together by bridges. A market square connected streets that became alleyways holding shops with the most beautiful clothes Serah had ever seen. The prices were astronomical, so walking past and looking in the windows was enough for Serah, though most tourists moved in and out of the stores. However, Ricardo was interested in the Ferrari shop that was used to house Michael Schumacher's car so a group went in search of the car. Unfortunately, when they arrived at the shop they learned the car had already been moved to Milan. Despite the disappointment, everyone squeezed through the tiny walkways without much thought until one of the group mentioned it would have been interesting to watch them move the race car through the narrow alleys. Another of the group took out a map to find larger streets but there weren't any, which intrigued others who wanted to know how anything at all could be brought into the city centre. It sparked a conversation, but in the end the map was put away as it was impossible to decipher what was a street or a bridge to cross the water or a dead end.

The buildings were on the lean and some were abandoned. One was sold to Hilton hotels for one Euro but it cost them hundreds of millions to fix it up. Everything for sale was expensive because part of the cost went to pay for the upkeep of the islands. It looked like a losing battle that was not worth the effort. Living on the water seemed very frustrating and taking goods from the boats to the shops, restaurants and homes was a mission. They watched one such man working at a café as he tried to manoeuvre supplies whilst cursing under his breath. He was entertaining, and Serah would have liked to linger on to see how he managed, but she was on a mission. She had decided to buy a mask. The Carnivale masks were everywhere but after six hours of walking, eating and drinking, she gave up trying to decide on which one.

The Carnivale occurred once a year and was a celebration to end the fasting from meat. The masks came into play because the aristocracy at the time wanted to join in on the fun but didn't want to be noticed. Traditional stories being elaborated over the years made Serah wonder what the Carnivale would be like in centuries to come. With half an hour to spare, they walked along other streets with overpriced glass objects and eventually found a vase that took her liking. Ricardo made a cash deal with the seller, but she went out the back to wrap the vase out of view of Serah and Ricardo. The glass was covered and they weren't able to see inside.

'I have a feeling that when I get home that there will be a plastic bottle inside all the wrapping,' said Serah putting the small purchase into her bag.

'So you are still determined to go back to Australia,' said Ricardo who had hoped the different surroundings might have opened her eyes to a new lifestyle.

A few of the group passed them, reminding them that there was a bus waiting to take them to Verona.

It was another medieval town holding history from stones that Serah wasn't sure she wanted to hear. She looked at her stone in the ring and wondered if she was making the right decision to leave Ricardo. A part of her wanted to go home as she knew she wouldn't miss the conspiracies and stories, but when they got to Verona and she realised it was the home of Romeo and Juliette, she knew some stories were inspiring. It was a story of love that hurt the heart of so many women and she didn't want a heart that ached.

Many tourist buses were parked around the market square so everyone could visit the house that had once belonged to Juliette. Although it was centuries old, the house was still magnificent. The solid stone structure was ornate and still held the tiny balcony where Juliette used to stand. The story by William Shakespeare was slightly exaggerated but that was to be expected.

The tour guide explained that Juliette's family had benefited when the Roman Empire ended and amalgamated with Christianity. The Pope tried to gain control which found the two main families in conflict over religion. Juliette's family was wealthy despite her father being illiterate. He signed with an x, as is sometimes still in use today. He was a large man who had a foot that was twelve inches.

'Twelve inches is a foot,' said Serah to herself, remembering her previous conversation with Nicaule on the plane.

'He was a giant so you know why he had power,' said the farmer, standing behind her.

'Romeo's family followed the catholic side, who were poor,' continued the tour guide.

'You see that wall,' said Ricardo pointing to the smooth wall that held the balcony. 'Romeo used to climb that wall to see Juliette.'

'Shshhh,' said the Canadian woman who was taking in the love story.

'They weren't allowed to be together but they ended up marrying and lived happily ever after,' said the guide. 'Shakespeare needed more drama so he changed the ending.'

'You see,' said the farmer following Ricardo, 'there is always truth to a story.'

Serah grabbed Ricardo before he could get caught up in the subject.

A large mountain appeared before them growing in size the closer they got. To get to the other side they had to drive through the rock via a tunnel that was seventeen kilometres long. Once on the other side, they were in Switzerland. The scenery changed to large mountains with farms perched on top for the cows to graze in the summer. At the bottom, barns sat in preparation for the winter months for the cows who preferred to hibernate from the cold. Not only had the language changed but so had the attitude. In Italy, it was total chaos with nothing organised but Switzerland was organised right down to the chopped wood that had to be stacked neatly near the houses.

Serah was surprised at the change. 'I didn't know we were going to other countries,' she said. 'I feel as if I've gone through a portal.'

'It's the same land,' said Ricardo. 'I thought that meeting my family would be too much for you. I didn't want to put any pressure on you because I think you've been through enough. I wanted you to experience a normal holiday and open your eyes to other lands.'

'So where do we end up?' asked Serah looking around at the houses that consisted of wooden boxes with ornate balconies.

'We end up in Britain,' he said not wanting to reveal the true final destination. 'Look outside!'

She went back to viewing the scenery of rocks but knew Ricardo was up to something. It worried her that they were so close to the mountains. Who knew what was under them and who knew what would emerge? She wanted to think about something else and listened as the guide pointed out the cows that provided the best milk for the Swiss chocolate.

It was a long drive but they finally got to their hotel in Lucerne. A large lake lay flat in front of a grander version of a Swiss chalet. The rooms were alpine and filled with antiques. Green and gold furnishings complemented floral tapestry materials and a large window beside the bed overlooked the mass of clean water that fell from the mountains to envelope them. A picture stood before them as they sat and looked out the open window, and it only changed when the sun set behind the rocks. It was a serene way to end the day and it helped to ease Serah's mind as she was having difficulty trying to erase the memories of the past weeks.

thirty six

Ricardo took off early to ride a cable car to the top of an alpine mountain. The peak was six thousand feet up with a lookout that stood beyond the edge. The cable car also had an observation deck on the roof which reminded Serah of the gondola in Whitby, Canada. Before leaving Australia, she had tried to conquer her fear of heights by attending a class with a hypnotherapist but she thought climbing to the top of a mountain was pushing it to too far.

There would be a report of the view from Ricardo and the others and it would surely make her envious, but she didn't know if she could stop herself from wanting to jump off the edge. Ricardo had pleaded with her to go but she had faced enough fears. After farewelling the group, she looked outside at the view of an inviting-looking village. With the drop of temperature in the air, she rugged up to take a walk along the side of the lake; that was sure to take up the morning. It wouldn't provide the view from the top of the mountain but it would be an experience.

Fresh mountain air filled her lungs and tightened her face as she admired the neat homes, oddly decorated with everything from garden bed ornaments to a tiger head on the porch. Huge amounts of water fell from the mountains, providing fresh water into the lake. Serah peered into the water that seemed to be too clean to support fish. People darted in and out of the local store and women dropped off children at school. Everyone stopped to say, 'Guten Morgen,' and even the brown cows with long eyelashes looked her way. Their bells rang as they moved from their food to the barns. She smiled as she walked passed them, remembering the guide telling them that all other cows were imposters. For the moment, she was the imposter, the alien to the town. The sound of the pouring water alerted her to the rocks making the pathway to the lake. Following the flow, she ended up at the edge and stood to take in her reflection. As it began to change, she felt herself leave her body but she was not meant to go. With a jolt, she was back and recalling the voice that belonged to the Lady of the Lake. Serah listened to the rationale that reminded her she had good reason to fear heights and falling from the edge; her fear had been real. She knew she was going to fall and she had. Lizette had pushed her into a hole, so the fear of falling should have been over. She had to let go of the fear and accept that she was safe with Ricardo. A feeling of empowerment took over her as she looked at the garnet stone in her ring. It glowed as if to confirm that she had faced her fear and it was over. As she looked up to the mountains that peaked into the clouds, she knew she actually could stand on the edge and wished she had listened to Ricardo, but it was too late. Instead, she thanked the voice in her head and thanked the lake that provided her with her own experience. As she strolled back to the hotel, she spied the bus that had returned with excited passengers. The group were still in the car park chatting about their adventure so she braced herself to listen about the view that she had missed out on. It was possible for her to change the subject if she chose to mention the encounter, but that was something that she didn't want to share.

The town of Lucerne was the next stop with the first point of interest being a lion that had been carved into the rock. He was lifelike with an emotional face of anguish and a paw on a shield that belonged to the Swiss. He was there to represent the Swiss Guard who died while protecting Marie Antoinette. Their motto was to die with honour and never surrender, and that was why they guarded the Pope. A smile came to Ricardo's face when he felt how impressed the others were. He wanted to show them his X on his back to confirm that he was a Templar but thought better of it and remained silent as the guide spoke of the lion that was in a cave. Because the sculptor thought he wouldn't get paid, he started to carve the cave into a shape of a pig, so they paid him before he could put on a tail.

Another landmark was an ancient bridge where painters had produced priceless works of art. Someone had burnt the bridges at some point, destroying most of the paintings, but as they walked along looking at the remaining artwork that resembled death, Serah thought there might have been a reason for the destruction. The town was old and from the Gothic era with large buildings that held turrets and housed overpriced fashions. A green, silky top with long sleeves appealed to Serah who walked in leaving, Ricardo to wait outside.

'I like the Italian way,' said Serah to a surprised Ricardo as she walked out. 'I think I'm too used to the Italians with their disorganised ways because I'm not coping with the Swiss who seem to be too organised.'

'What happened in there?' asked Ricardo looking through the windows.

'I tried on a top but I wasn't sure if I wanted to spend so much money so I thought of putting it back,' said Serah in a fluster. 'I don't know if I want it or not but the shop assistant was standing over me, hanging it up while I was looking at it. It's silly. I'm being silly. Let's go.'

Ricardo took her hand and dragged her back into the shop to see the saleswoman roll her eyes at an indecisive customer. 'Take the top,' he said to Serah as he put the money on the counter, 'and if there's anything else you want then I'll pay for that as well.'

It was happening too fast and before Serah could comprehend what had happened she looked inside the plastic bag to find her top with a hat and scarf.

'Did I pick out the other items?' she asked Ricardo but he didn't answer.

She looked at the soft woollen hat and scarf and then looked at the price tags. They were a waste of money as they would never be worn. There wasn't a need for such clothing living in a warm climate. It occurred to her Ricardo was taking her to somewhere cold and it worried her, but the questions would have to wait as their tour guide was waiting for them.

A boat was waiting to take them on a lake surrounded by a forest. The calm water rippled but Serah was too scared to look into the water. Instead she listened as the guide, who was drinking too much, exaggerated his stories. By the end of the trip he had invited everyone to join him at the bar outside the hotel for a free drink. With the falling sun came the drop in temperature, leaving many of the group wanting to stay inside to eat dinner. A few ventured outside to accept the drink and as Ricardo produced the new hat and scarf, Serah was glad he had bought them to keep her warm for the nightcap outside. Happy to be warm, she rugged herself up and went outside to accept a cocktail. It took a few sips before she realised that Ricardo had no way of knowing they would be outside later in the evening and in need of warmth, which meant there was more in store. She opened her mouth to question him but was too tired, so instead she placed her lips around the straw and drank, thankful that someone was looking out for her.

The next day they were on the road again. Signs changed and so did the landscape. Mountains reaching into the clouds were replaced by flat ground used for farming. Small villages built centuries ago popped up here and there. And every now and again a chateau would appear showing the beauty of old France. Serah wondered why the stop had been brief in Switzerland but there was a deadline to the tour and it was getting closer. So much had happened in such a short period of time. A cruise of a life time had changed her life and an impromptu tour had forced her to face her destiny. Her will was her own, so if she chose to return to Australia then it would be her decision. Serah was not going to let anyone influence her any more. Going to Italy had seemed a smart move with something to take her mind off otherworldly experiences. If she had gone home she might have ended up insane but at the moment her head was numb from an adventure which made it possible to deal with. Quietly she prayed that there would be no further experiences for her other than the experiences shared by all tourists on holiday.

The coach was comfortable and when it veered from the motorway to make a pit stop she decided to stay put. They were on their way to Burgundy for lunch, but due to traffic the meal would have to be a takeaway from the restaurant at the petrol station. Some complained, but beating the traffic had been the correct decision which became apparent when they finally got to Paris.

It was mayhem driving alongside the maniacs. Locals created lanes that didn't exist, pushed in front of each other and abandoned their cars wherever they could, without any consideration to others. The group was told of one roundabout that had an accident every fifteen minutes and the insurance companies had come to an arrangement to pay fifty percent of the damage regardless of who was at fault. They drove through the city taking in the beautiful buildings with their carvings and gold leaf. Padlocked bridges sparkled in the sunlight but it was at night when the city really shone.

From what Serah could gather, European cities were not the cleanest. She presumed that people were distracted from the rubbish by the allure of the architecture. For some reason, she seemed to be the only one who noticed it, but when the darkness set in she saw the city as everyone else did. Lanterns shone on the bridges, enhancing the workmanship from medieval times. Many of the roads and buildings were changed during the time of Napoleon as he didn't like the narrow streets. He wanted wide, straight streets so he could see if the enemy were coming. At the end of the street that now housed overpriced shops, he designed an arch to honour himself. One of the carvings was of him being crowned emperor. The picture depicted an angry looking Pope who stood next to him, and as Napoleon didn't think anyone was above him, the statement was clear that he had grabbed the crown from the Pope and made himself the ruler. Serah laughed at his sense of humour but others thought him arrogant. Either way, he didn't get to see the finished Arc de Triomphe as he was poisoned to death by the British when he went into exile. It seemed strange that people would pay tribute to a man who they had exiled. There were many stories in the history of France, so to see Paris from a different perspective, the tour guide took them on a river cruise.

People were awed when the Eiffel tower sparkled in the dark and lit up the night sky. But most didn't know about the man who constructed it to show the world that iron was a strong material that could be used to construct tall buildings. The tower was put together like a Meccano set and mountain climbers were used to set the pieces in place. Once the point was made about the iron being able to reach great heights, the French wanted it taken down. They thought it was ugly. But telecommunications were being created and there was a need for an aerial to be placed somewhere high. At the time, the tower was the tallest structure around and so was allowed to remain.

There were many conflicts of interest with the French. They were passionate about their heritage and wanted everyone to speak French, but then they threw rubbish everywhere instead of putting it in the bin.

The boat ride could not hide the homeless people who ironically lived under the bridges that people came to see. And as the buses squeezed their way back to the hotels, the tourists glanced at streets filled with shops where vast amounts of money had been used to create labels. There was awe amongst everyone with the elaborate displays, but the advertising was diminished with the sight of the homeless who huddled together in the entrances to keep warm and beg for food.

thirty seven

The next morning Serah hoped for a different outlook when the bus appeared to pick them up for a sightseeing tour of Paris in the daylight. Paris had always been something romantic and out of reach and now she was standing in it and didn't want to be disappointed. With high hopes, she took in the architecture of the buildings and ignored the rubbish remaining from the traffic that had disappeared for the weekend. They drove through the tunnel where Princess Diana had died in a car accident and on the top of the spot of her death was a flame of gold. The statue had been put there before the event and an explanation would have been given but Serah blocked the spirit from her mind.

It was an intensive tour as their guide had a vast knowledge of history. The group learned that Maxims earned its right to be called an exclusive restaurant because it had created an idea during the war. After the animals from the zoo were eaten, there was nothing else to sell but the small shop came up with an idea and produced macaroons. There was much to learn as most buildings had stories to tell.

Notre Dame stood out the most with its massive structure displaying different eras. It had taken hundreds of years to create and by the time of completion the Gothic period was in fashion. Eyes looked up to the gargoyles that were placed on the walls to ward off evil spirits and to direct the water through their mouths to divert it from the brickwork. The sound of the running water sounded like, 'gargoyle' so that was how the statues got their name. Also, it was the same sound that was created when water was gargled in the mouth. The building had the most beautiful artwork which was only restored due to the interest after the movie, The Hunchback of Notre Dame.

There was a lot to see and they continued on to where several obelisks and the like had been stolen to be placed around Napoleon. But there was one obelisk still remaining that was given by the Egyptians as a message of thanks to the Frenchman who broke the code with deciphering the hieroglyphics. There seemed to be a continual circle of stealing and claiming, and Serah wondered what the last stop had to offer. A large glass pyramid stood in a courtyard of old buildings which held endless amounts of artwork. They could have spent the day looking inside the museum, but instead Ricardo headed for the Mona Lisa which he believed was a fake because it was a lot bigger than he thought it would be. Serah covered her ears as a hint that she did not want any information from other sources and once Ricardo realised what was going on he led her to the exit.

'I'm taking you to somewhere fun,' he said as he pushed and shoved his way to create a path for Serah to walk to the train station. Signs being in French made it difficult to find the correct line but with a picture of Mickey Mouse on the board, they knew they were heading for the right direction.

Disney appeared through the window and they got off to walk the manicured paths that took them to the entrance. Boys with cheap tickets intercepted them as they lined up. Neither understood French but soon understood when security took the boys away.

'It's a bad omen,' said Serah. 'Maybe we should go back to Paris and go with the group to watch the Moulin Rouge!'

'Definitely not,' said Ricardo. 'I went to Disneyworld in Florida when I was younger and I've always wanted to go back. All the Disney parks are the same so I know you will love it.'

Ricardo reminisced about the haunted mansion that had been decorated for Halloween. He remembered the plants that flourished and the tomb stones and effects that were life-like. Every detail had been taken into consideration. However, when they lined up for the ride, all they could see were weeds. Hoping that the lack of flowers was part of the theme, they went inside where Ricardo complained about the park being a cheap and nasty version. Serah had no expectations so didn't know any different as she thought that the stopping and starting was part of the ride. It wasn't until they got to the big thunder mountain ride that she realised things weren't right. After an hour's wait they were told the ride wasn't working so they proceeded to leave when a fast pass was handed out for them to return at a later time. It was a comfort to know they didn't have to line up again, but Ricardo wanted his memories to be confirmed. He had experienced fun with the rides but had also enjoyed the taste of the chocolate ice-cream he had eaten when he visited the EPCOT centre. The EPCOT centre was divided into groups with one half displaying life of other countries. As a child, he had walked through the French part and been given an ice-cream that tasted unlike any other. He wanted Serah to taste the French chocolate ice-cream but there were none for sale. Feeling disappointed, he looked for a place for dinner that would fill their stomachs as they watched the sun set.

Twilight brought on a different perspective and atmosphere, filling the park with energy. Fireworks lit the sky and brought the castle to life, bringing a smile to Ricardo's face. Memories that seemed so long ago returned to his mind. His life with his family had been good and he wanted Serah to know that her life could be filled with good memories if she allowed it. The lights that flashed in the sky sparkled in her eyes and with a smile on her face, he knew he had achieved his goal of showing her a life that was better than the one she would go back to.

Time was running out for him to convince Serah, so when they left the train station in the middle of the night, he was determined not to show his concern at being lost. He had been given directions from the guide on how to return to the hotel, but in the dark the directions didn't make sense. Being in a commercial area meant everything was closed so they kept walking until they were saved by a taxi who five minutes later dropped them off at the hotel.

Despite the disappointment of the park not living up to his expectations, his past memory was replaced with a new one that included Serah. As long as he had her in his life then he was happy. After a sound sleep, he woke up the next morning to say 'au revoir' to France as they drove to Calais to catch the ferry. Serah, on the other hand, was still tired from the late night traipsing, so she slept most of the way and remained delirious once on the boat. It was her stomach that finally woke her from the daze as she glanced at the open water. She wondered what England would be like but when the food changed from pastries to a chicken and salad sandwich on wholemeal bread, she knew she would be happy. The French lifestyle wasn't for her. The French sticks had been fresh and the croissants that were dunked into the coffee were divine but not the diet she was used to. She wondered why the French ate croissants, as according to the guide it was the Austrians who had created the pastry. He had explained that the Turks had wanted to invade Austria but needed to get through a wall. They had decided to dig a tunnel underneath but it was early in the morning when they made their move, which disturbed the bakers. The bakeries were busy in the mornings and when they heard the noise, they warned the guards who defended the wall and frightened away the Turkish army. In their flight, they left behind coffee beans and flour which the bakers used to commemorate the occasion.

They created a pastry with the discarded flour and shaped it into a crescent as that was the symbol the Turks used.

It was an interesting story but she didn't want another pastry again for a long time, so she made sure by heading towards an old English pub once they were settled into their hotel.

At the lobby, goodbyes were said, addresses handed out, hugs were given and a happy tour guide left with his tips. A mention was made to meet at the restaurant for dinner, but Ricardo didn't object to the decision of being alone with Serah at the local pub. So with another round of farewells, Ricardo gladly followed Serah towards an establishment that was only a short walk away.

The tiny room filled with tables, chairs and paraphernalia from a bygone era was inviting, and as they studied the menus Serah smiled with the selections that were on offer.

'I hope the food is as good as the menu,' she said looking at other plates being served.

'Food looks good,' said Ricardo thinking about the roast that had just been placed in front of a patron.

'Fish and chips for me,' said Serah, 'and a shandy.'

Ricardo laughed but waited until she had finished her drink and meal before telling her that he had made further plans.

With a full stomach and empty plate Serah sat back in her chair taking in the atmosphere of the room. It was summer but there was a cosy feeling that kept her in the seat. Normally in the warmer weather, she was keen to go outside and stare at the stars but in England she was happy to stay indoors. There was a part of her that didn't need to look elsewhere as she believed she had seen enough.

'What are you thinking about?' asked Ricardo taking her hand.

'I have a strange feeling,' she said. 'I feel like I'm at home.'

'I'm glad you feel that way,' he said quickly, 'because Aerona has asked for us to join her.'

The relaxation immediately left Serah and she tensed at the statement. 'I'm going home.'

Ricardo interrupted, 'You said you feel at home here.'

'Yes,' she stated, 'but I'm not at home, am I? You said you would come with me to Australia if I went with you to Italy.'

Her lowered voice grew louder alerting others to their conversation, and eyes around the room kept returning to the couple.

'Aren't you glad you went on that trip?' he said staring intensely into her eyes. 'Please Serah, I beg you,' he added, rubbing his finger over the stone in her ring.

'I'm not giving you an answer now,' she said taking her hand away.

'Fine,' he said leaning back in his chair. 'Make a decision in the morning.'

'I meant about the marriage proposal,' she said looking at her ring.

He realised that she had decided. He had picked the wrong time to tell her about their next destination. Cursing to himself, he wished he could rewind time to change the sequence of events. He closed his eyes to plan his morning to change her mind. She was set to be his wife and with one statement he had blown it. Opening his eyes to beg for forgiveness, he stopped short at the sight of Serah still eating her fish and chips.

He took in his surroundings where people were unaware of the couple and their conversation. The plate before him still contained food that had not yet been eaten. A second ago he had a clean plate. He shut his eyes again to rid the hallucination. With one eye open, he looked down expecting to see the food gone but it was still there. He had wished for a reversal in time and had been given a second chance. How it had happened, he had no idea, but didn't care. Carefully he chose what to say and when she sat back with a satisfied stomach he got down on his knee to ask for her answer.

She looked at him as he smiled knowing what her decision was and as he rubbed the stone he realised how his wish had come true.

'Yes,' she said with the excitement of taking him back to her home.

Not sure of his next plan of action to get her to Scotland, he kept quiet and escorted her back to the hotel while thinking about sleeping tablets that would keep her quiet until they were at the destination.

'You're back,' said one of the group who had been speaking with a concierge. 'And where are you two off to next?'

Serah was about to say Australia but was cut off when a lady appeared wearing a tartan scarf. 'They are visiting me in Scotland.'

Aerona beckoned for them to get their luggage as she smiled at a dazed Serah.

'What's going on?' she asked Ricardo as they waited for the lift.

'Don't know,' he said turning away from her.

'You do know,' she said grabbing his cheek. 'I bet you planned this.'

He looked at her with a grin. 'I presume it's because we're officially engaged. She probably wants to give us an engagement present.'

'Rubbish,' she said defensively.

With bags in tow they bid farewell to the remaining tourists who were going their separate ways. Out of curiosity the American farmer asked where they were staying, as Scotland was too far to travel during the night. Their accommodation in London was already included, so he wondered why they didn't wait until the morning but Aerona put an end to his intrigue by telling him they were staying with her before moving on. A baffled group waved goodbye and with the cover of darkness Aerona took off her cloak to cover them as they disappeared to be teleported to Scotland.

thirty eight

Traffic that had passed them moments ago had disappeared and the concrete ground had been replaced with carpet.

'Where are we?' asked Serah looking at the glimmer in the dark.

'My home,' Aerona said as she pointed at a flame from a candle that grew to light up her room.

'Why am I here?' asked Serah wondering why Aerona lived in such a small cottage.

'You are here because I have to tell you something,' said Aerona. 'And my home is small because we don't need much and neither do the others who live in this community.'

Serah looked around trying to picture a place filled with cottages. 'How did you know what I was thinking and why couldn't you tell me in London?'

Ricardo didn't know how to respond to Serah's anger that was slowly growing.

'I have to tell you about Sarah Cupsip,' said Aerona motioning for her visitor to sit in front of the fire that had decided to light itself.

Serah fumed as she paced the room. 'I was in London. I could have spent one day looking around! One day to do something normal.'

'What's to see?' said Aerona, dismissing the idea. 'A big clock and an old building. Do you really need to see that?'

'Yes, I would have liked to see Big Ben and the palace!' declared Serah still pacing.

Aerona interrupted, 'Things aren't what they seem. I thought you would know that by now.'

'But I want them to be,' said Serah. 'I don't want to know what is behind the scenes.'

'You want to go back to your life of longing?' asked Aerona sitting down.

'I longed for nothing,' Serah said, turning away to face a stone wall painted white.

'Really,' said Aerona. 'Are you sure you didn't long for the life that Sarah Cupsip had?'

Serah's eyes welled as she remembered the wish she had made to be like Sarah Cupsip and travel the world. 'I might have wanted to explore but I didn't want her life. She spent her life looking for her soulmate. I don't need to do that, do I, because I have found him.'

Ricardo smiled with the announcement but couldn't interfere so kept by the fire.

'Well, then,' said Aerona in a calmer tone, 'it makes no difference where you go.'

'Why?' asked a concerned Ricardo.

'Your destiny is to help Sarah Cupsip,' said Aerona. 'She has gone into a body of a woman who was about to die in an accident. She has befriended a woman who is happy and will make a great ruler as she has only love in her heart. My concern is that Sarah Cupsip will direct her on a path of unhappiness that will end with this friend being killed in a car accident.'

'Who is she?' asked Serah not wanting anyone to experience her turmoil.

'You know that there is a lot to a name,' said Aerona. 'This woman is Dyana Happy. She has to continue on the path of happiness to help others. She must die happy in her sleep.'

Serah thought of the golden flame that had been installed above the tunnel where Princess Diana had been killed. She had blocked a message. Could she prevent the event from ever happening? A lot had taken place over the last few weeks so she knew anything was possible—but then she shook her head.

'You don't believe,' said Aerona, 'but you stand here before me knowing that I know magic and you stand in a house that is surrounded by witches. And you are about to marry a Templar.'

Serah shook her head again. 'My head feels numb and I don't know if I can take any more. This is too much for me. Put me back in time? Put me back with Sarah Cupsip before she got sick?'

A thought entered her mind. If she went back in time then she would be her old self, living her old life. She could refuse the tickets from Sarah Cupsip and not go on the trip. She looked at Ricardo and thought of a life without him, then collapsed in a heap on a chair.

'Time has gone backwards anyway,' said Aerona looking at Ricardo who stared at her.

'But I'm still here,' said Serah starting to sob.

'Time went back when Sarah Cupsip entered the dying woman,' said Aerona. 'You two have to go and befriend Sarah Cupsip and make her see that she can have the life she desires once she rids herself of the ego that wants to destroy the happiness of others.'

'I want to go home,' said Serah taking the tissues that Ricardo provided.

'You said you wanted to go to London,' said Aerona, 'and so you shall—and your home now is in England.'

A gust of wind expelled the flame leaving them in the dark. A hand grabbed at Serah who screamed and only stopped when Ricardo appeared before her in a room lit by electricity.

'Are you alright?' enquired a soft voice from the other side of the door. 'I heard a scream.'

'We're fine,' said Ricardo opening the door to a kind woman with shoulder length, blonde hair and fluffy pyjamas.

'You're the new tenants,' she said extending a hand.

'Yes,' said Ricardo, 'I'm Ricardo Knight and this is Serah Kohw.'

'Another Sarah in my life,' she said. 'I'm Dyana but please call me Dy.'

'I would rather call her Ana,' whispered Serah. 'Honestly are we to call her Dy Happy to remind us that she has to?'

'Just call her Dy,' whispered Ricardo, squeezing her arm.

'I should leave you two alone,' said Dy. 'I can sense confrontation and I'm not one who is good in that situation.'

Serah went to stop her but she had already shut the door.

'There is an aggressive streak coming out in you,' he said still holding her arm.

She released herself from his grip. 'Don't be ridiculous. Besides I have a right to be angry.'

The flat was on the second floor and plainly decorated in beige. Hollow doors matched paper thin walls allowing in the sounds of the television turned on next door. A small kitchen incorporated a lounge dining room that displayed two doors being for the bedroom and bathroom. Serah laughed at the building that housed royalty and wondered how Sarah Cupsip would ever accept her surroundings when she longed for grandeur.

They sat on the lounge that filled the room, trying to think of how to persuade Sarah Cupsip to be kind. They couldn't, and ended up falling asleep to wake moments later to the sound of cars and people passing by.

'How do I change Sarah Cupsip?' wondered Serah hopelessly as she got up to look outside.

'We'll have to play it by ear,' Ricardo replied, running his hands through his hair, hoping for help from others.

'Why is it our responsibility anyway?' demanded Serah closing the curtains.

He stood up to hold her hand but she wanted to go back to sleep.

Keen to end the task they had been given, he decided to stay awake and went to the kitchen to look at an empty fridge. He knew his next move, so quickly got changed to find a food shop. With quick movements, he was out the door and bumped into a stranger who held the spirit of Sarah Cupsip.

'Oh, sorry,' he said immediately recognising within this woman the energy that gave him grief. 'I'm Ricardo Knight.'

'I'm Serita Tazzasorso,' she answered taking in his dark features.

The fair woman in front of him had a stronger Italian accent than he did and for a moment he forgot that she was Sarah Cupsip.

'How long have you lived in England?' asked Ricardo as he escorted her down the stairs.

'Many years,' said Serita exposing the pink highlights in her hair as she moved in the light. 'What about you?'

'Not long,' he answered holding the door. 'Do you know where the local shop is? There is no food in the fridge.'

Serita laughed, mesmerising Ricardo. He couldn't think straight and listened as she spoke with a voice that sang like an angel. 'I was heading that way myself so I will take you there.'

He stayed by her side as they walked the path to the local shops, stopping occasionally to watch as passers-by stared at her.

'Keep up,' she said turning around to look at his strangely familiar features. There was something about him that was appealing but she didn't know what it was. He was handsome but there was a connection that pulled on her heart strings and went beyond appearance.

A man called out from a jewellery store. He recognised Serita, as he had saved her when she had been close to death.

'How was your trip?' he asked coming out of the store to hug his friend.

Serita put her arm through Ricardo's and clung to him as she told the shopkeeper of her visit to Italy. She had gone to see her former home to recuperate and had spent time with family she had not seen in many years. Many nights had been spent eating and drinking. Ricardo was struck by her hypnotic voice. Serita had come back to England a different woman and had found herself taking singing lessons with the hope of joining the opera.

The shopkeeper held her again as he forced Ricardo away with a glare. He wanted to know about her health, so Ricardo took the hint to leave. Turning around, he left behind the embracing pair and nearly bumped into another woman. With a start he was about to speak but stopped when he noticed the crystals in her purple hair. She seemed solid so he didn't know how to react when her feet left the ground. With squinted eyes, he watched as she floated beside him.

'Don't get distracted,' she threatened as she walked past him.

He turned back to Serita who smiled.

'I have to go,' he said leaving the two to catch up.

Ricardo continued to walk along the path wondering who else he would bump into, but when he noticed a small shop selling food he soon let his hunger take over from his head.

The store had only been a block away so with a box filled with food, he headed back to Serah. Thinking about what to make for breakfast was a distraction from what was around him and as he extended his hand to open the front door to the building, another hand took the handle. Her pink nails matched her hair and with the aroma of perfume coming from behind him, he knew that Serita was trouble.

'Didn't get what you wanted?' he asked staring at her empty hands.

'No, I'll have to go elsewhere,' she said prompting him to go inside.

Once through the door, Ricardo edged away from her to go up the stairs first. Not wanting to converse, he didn't look back and bid her farewell as he rushed to his door.

'What is it?' asked Serah as she watched Ricardo stand against the door taking a deep breath.

'I met Sarah Cupsip, but now her name is Serita Tazzasorso,' he said without taking a breath. 'She is definitely trouble.'

'Why?' asked Serah as Ricardo put down the box and walked over to hug her.

'She's hypnotising and I think she likes me,' he said. 'You will have to be the one who talks her into changing her path.'

Serah thought about her former friend and wondered what her own life would be like if she could stop Serita from influencing Dy. She hadn't thought about it when she had been with Aerona but maybe there was a reward for her action. Maybe she could go back to her home in Australia. Something had to be done so she showered and changed as quickly as she could to knock on Serita's door.

'I'm Serah Kohw,' she announced as Serita answered. 'I'm Ricardo's fiancée.'

Serita looked her competition up and down, wondering how to win over Ricardo.

'Hello,' said Dy who was just leaving her flat, 'I'm glad you two have met.'

They both stared at her as she hummed down the stairs.

Serah knew that Dy would end up being a princess and that Serita would spend years using her friendship to influence Dy's unhappiness. The spirit within Serita had always wanted to be a princess but had never been able to stay within that being. Her jealousy had always got the better of her. The spirit thought it was because she needed to be loved and couldn't see that to feel love, she first had to give it. It was going to be difficult to change a wheel that had gone in circles for centuries but there was no other choice. In order for Serah to be free she had to get Serita away from Dy.

'I suppose I should invite you in,' said Serita, stepping aside.

thirty nine

They sat over a cup of tea while Serah listened to Serita explain about her life of hardship. She had struggled over the years, bouncing from one job to the next. Dy had been her salvation, getting her a job with children, but it wasn't what she wanted. There was something else. A car accident had proved to be a blessing in disguise as she believed she had found what she was looking for while recuperating in Italy. The trip struck a chord and brought up a discussion regarding the land of love. Serah was able to get her to open up about her love life that was non-existent. There had been many dates but none that had won her over. Ricardo came up in the conversation but that was ended very quickly by Serah.

A knock on the door halted the chatter as Ricardo put his head through the doorway. 'Just checking up on my fiancée,' he said. 'I thought I'd come and join you.'

Serita grabbed another mug while Serah wondered what he was up to.

'I was thinking,' he said holding the back of a chair. 'We're so close to Ireland and we have nothing to do for the weekend so why don't we go over for a drive. You know, have a look around.'

'Sounds like a good idea,' said Serita wanting to spend as much time as possible with Ricardo.

He took the mug and filled it with tea from a pot. 'I'm glad you agree because I'm ready. You go and get ready,' he said to Serah with smouldering eyes.

'Why do you want to go there?' Serah demanded.

He glared at her for not playing along. 'Because you know how I love rocks and there are so many there to see.'

'Yes,' said Serita, 'there are some fascinating stones in Ireland with many stories.'

'Come on,' said Ricardo taking Serah from the room. 'Grab your things, Serita, and we'll meet you outside in half an hour.'

'Take your tea,' she said. 'You can give me the mug back later.'

He lifted the beverage in appreciation and escorted Serah back to their flat before lowering his tone. 'I have an idea,' he said. 'There is a wishing chair in Ireland and I'm going to put her on it.'

Serah rolled her eyes. 'Really, you think that will solve the problem,' she said turning away from him with raised hands.

He grabbed her to face him. 'After what we have been through, don't you think that anything is possible?'

'So we take her there and get her to make a wish to become a princess,' said Serah. 'Even if the wish came true she would end up in the same situation. She needs to learn empathy.'

Ricardo could hear the frustration in her voice but his answers always came from stones. He took Serah's hand and rubbed on the garnet not knowing what to do.

The door burst open and an excited Serita entered as she knocked. 'I just got a phone call. I don't believe it. I'm going to be in a musical. I'm so happy. It's a big production that's going to take me around the country. Can you believe it?'

Serita being happy lifted the spirits in the room. There was a reaction and a chance for Serah to convince Serita of her path to happiness.

'I can't go to Ireland,' she stated, 'but let's go out for lunch to celebrate.'

The energy changed when she left the room, leaving the couple wondering what to do.

'I have a feeling this is the opportunity but I don't know how to take advantage of it,' said Serah.

'I suggested playing it by ear earlier,' he said, 'so let's do that.'

An anxious Serah hugged him. 'I feel so close to the answer.'

With the food put away and the lounge straightened out they went downstairs to find Serita chatting with Dy.

'Let's go,' said an excited Serita.

'I don't know why I feel so anxious,' said Dy as she walked with Serah.

'I've been anxious as well,' said Serah as Serita dragged Ricardo off towards the café in the distance.

Dy took Serah's arm as she explained about the effort she had gone to get Serita a job. She felt disappointed to be losing a friend who had been an enormous influence in her life. Serita had mentioned trying to get Dy into the musical but she was feeling too depressed to be involved in anything other than work. Serah listened in silence as Dy spoke of her feelings that had become foreign to her. Her life had been filled with happiness, but lately she had stepped back and watched her friend blossom while the feeling of being alone was growing.

'Maybe it was intuition that I would be alone,' said Dy. 'I always thought I would be an influence for the greater good but now I think it's Serita who is destined to make a change.'

Serah hugged Dy's arm trying to sort out the mess in her mind, but as she listened to Dy speak of a prince who had contacted her, she knew that Serita had been given the opportunity to be in a musical to separate her from Dy's life.

A filled café bustled with laughter as patrons sipped on coffee. Dy knew of another café but Serita refused to go elsewhere. As they waited for a table, the chatter dropped to listen as Serita announced that she was going to be in a musical. Moments later a table appeared with four chairs.

'How did you do that?' said an astonished Dy who followed Serita.

'Positive power,' said Serita handing out menus.

All eyes were upon Serita as she spoke to Ricardo but Serah didn't mind as it gave her time to think. She looked around the establishment to see a board filled with notices. A polo match was taking place that afternoon and it included a prince playing for charity, but it was a sign that Dy was not interested in. Serita had too much influence so to keep her at bay, Serah instructed Ricardo to stay with her as she dragged Dy to the match.

It was meant to be, and as Serah kissed her ring for luck, she watched as an enchanted prince brought Dy back to happiness. The darkness that had drained her disappeared. Serah watched as others asked where her clothes came from. Being modest, Dy told them the designs were something she had picked up at a charity shop but Serah knew the garments had been sewn by Dy. There was a change in the air so Serah left Dy and rushed back to find Serita still speaking to Ricardo.

'What will you do with the fame and fortune?' asked Serah as she joined them.

Serita was caught off guard but wanted to impress her audience so she told them that she would donate her spare time to stopping animal cruelty. Looking at the admiring eyes, she continued on about being empathetic and taking responsibility for the animals that were neglected and in need of help. There was a look of shock on Serita's face and an uncertainty in her voice. Still she kept an eye on her audience until she could find a change of subject. 'Where's Dy gone?'

'Oh,' said Serah, 'she met up with someone at the polo match.'

'The prince,' said Serita angrily as she stood up to the confused faces of other diners.

'Let Dy go,' said Serah. 'You don't need her life. You have your own. If you can show your empathy through animals then you can have the love that you so desire.'

'Love from animals isn't the same,' said Serita, still with an angry tone in her voice. 'Love is what you get when you are rescued by the prince.'

'Your prince was the prince of darkness,' whispered Serah. 'Stop the cycle. It has brought you nothing but heartache. Find love through the animals and they will lead you to your knight in shining armour.'

The statement took Serita by surprise and with a new outlook she released the arm of Ricardo who then escorted his fiancée home.

'What now?' asked Serah glad to be out of the café.

'Don't know,' he said. 'Do you think we've managed to change Serita?'

'What do you mean by we?' she said giving him a nudge. 'I was the one who did all the work.'

He laughed and as they walked along the street of parked cars, they noticed a change in the air. Buildings of stone transformed to modern structures that incorporated units and included Serah's home. Ricardo stopped, taking in the change of climate.

'I'm home,' said Serah, 'so we must have made things right with Serita. I had a feeling I would be rewarded.'

Ricardo stared at her in amazement. 'You can accept such a quick change? Well, I'm having trouble. That was too fast.'

'I don't care how fast it was,' she said smiling. 'I'm home, I'm back in Australia.'

'Of course,' he said putting his hands in the air.

forty

Australia seemed to be the answer to Serah's prayers. But what she hoped for was not going to happen. Technically she had been a tourist for five weeks and should be returning back to a life of normality. She unlocked her door to the apartment she rented knowing there would be no one to greet her. What she wanted was to be welcomed by a family and friends. She wanted to share her adventures, but instead she stared at an empty stale home. The holiday she had experienced was like no other she had heard of and she had survived it with the prospect of coming home to a normal life.

A plain apartment with no pictures had been her life, so with teary eyes she faced the fact that her life at home was not really living.

Turning around to face Ricardo she realised she had not given his home life a chance. He had a family, and being part of one would be another experience. It was possible for her to create her own family and being with Ricardo would be a distraction from her routine, but the reality was nothing in her life was going to change unless she changed it.

'You think far too much,' he said taking her into his arms.

'I know,' she sobbed, 'but look at what I've been through.'

'And you survived,' he said inhaling the scent of her hair. 'It's over and maybe it was meant to be. Your life would have stayed the same if you hadn't left this box.'

Ricardo lifted her from the floor to take her into her home. 'The next time I carry you into a house it will be our home.'

She stared at him, feeling confused as she was already in her home.

'This is not a home,' he said placing her on the couch. 'This place has no soul, so unless you have an enormous social life or a job that you live through, I suggest that you leave.'

Serah took in his words, thinking there was a possibility for a fresh start. 'We don't have to live in this apartment. We could move away from the city.'

'Do you have money to move?' he asked. 'Because I don't.'

Her office job barely covered the rent and expenses. 'We could move to the country. The further out we go, the cheaper it will be.'

He sat closer to her as he put his arm around her shoulders. 'I work with rocks, so what will I do for an income? There is no history here.'

'Yes there is,' she declared. 'There is a different history here and as for rocks we have an enormous one in the middle of the country.'

He sighed as he sat back. Australia had never been a place of interest for him. All he knew was that the country was far away from the history he knew. When Serah had spoken of Australia, he had pictured a large desert filled with kangaroos and dangerous animals and what he had seen advertised on the television had shown beaches, so it had been a disappointment to arrive inside a concrete city.

'Alright,' he said. 'Show me a life outside of the city. I want to see the real Australia.'

'We could work our way around Australia but you would need to apply for a visa first,' said Serah drying her eyes at a thought of a new goal. 'Oh no!'

'What is it?' he asked wondering why she didn't like the idea.

'We don't exist here,' she said taking his hand. 'We appeared here. We didn't come through an airport. Who knows where our luggage is and who knows where our passports are.'

Ricardo smiled. 'Then I don't need to worry about a visa.'

'But one day you will,' she said sitting back into the couch, 'and how do I explain being here when I didn't arrive!'

'Don't worry, I will ask my family for money and we can take a tour around Australia while we work it out,' he said getting to his feet.

Serah laughed at the statement.

'What now?' he demanded.

'You can't take a tour bus around the country. It's too big.'

'So what do you suggest?' he asked folding his arms.

'Let's go out for a coffee.' Serah took hold of him to leave behind the empty apartment.

There was a place that would seem familiar to him so they took a tram ride to a street where Italians congregated. The hustle and bustle of the tram trying to squeeze through cars made him feel at home but when he saw the cafés lined up, his eyes opened wide.

'I thought you would like it here,' she said as she pulled him from the tram to cross the road.

Impatient drivers beeped and Ricardo yelled at them in his native tongue. Laughter was back in their lives and Serah sat outside a café listening to Ricardo chat with the owner. A weight was lifted from her shoulders and as she took on the mood of her surroundings, she knew she could live in Italy.

A coffee appeared before her, delivered by a glowing fiancé.

'What were you chatting about?' she asked taking a sip.

'I can get a job here,' he said. 'The owner likes me so I have it all sorted out.'

'It's okay—'

Ricardo interrupted, 'No, you took a trip through Italy for me so I will work here. This is like being in Italy anyway for me. And the giant rock you talk about, I can study that on my days off.'

A smile widened across Serah's face as she continued to feel his energy lighten. Spending a few minutes with another Italian had helped bring out the Ricardo she loved. There was a passion within him that she wished she had. Her life had been work and home with nothing in between. Although she knew Ricardo would not be able to see the rock on his days off, she knew once he learned its distance, he would find rocks she wasn't aware of. Was it going to be a case that where they were was irrelevant as Ricardo would find the stories in the stones anyway? Serah didn't know what to think and stopped when the owner returned to join them.

'Buongiorno,' said the man wearing a large gold chain, 'Come sta?'

'She doesn't speak Italian,' said Ricardo.

'A si, yes,' nodded the owner. 'I am Roberto.'

'This is Serah,' said Ricardo. 'She will be my wife soon.'

Serah rubbed her eyebrow as she looked away.

'Good,' declared the owner shaking Ricardo's hand. 'Is it a big wedding? You can have your guests come here for drinks after the reception. I love weddings!'

Cars beeped beside them, taking the romance away from the idea. Drivers were heading in different directions. All of them had destinations; some good, some bad. A small car weaved through the other cars in a hurry. Serah noticed the sticker on the back window warning that a baby was on board. As she watched the car come uncomfortably close to another one, Serah wondered if the mother and child would get to their destination. A long, loud beep made her realise the woman's path was coming to an end which would mean a short life for her child. The scene played on Serah's mind as she didn't want her life to end without friends or family. Ricardo was determined to be married. If they married in Australia, then they would be alone, but if they married in Italy, it would be the large wedding that the Italians expected.

The smell of the coffee took her away from the fumes of the cars and as she looked at Ricardo speaking to his new friend, she wished she had friends. The language had changed to English but she wasn't listening to them. All she could hear was the chatterbox in her head that kept telling her she would be in a box for a long time and even longer if she didn't break out of the familiar surroundings.

Out of curiosity, other men joined the conversation. The strong accent reminded them of their former home and they wanted to know why there was a blonde woman with the newcomer. To sit and chat, they needed a coffee, so the owner took them inside to place an order. It was a break that Serah needed, so with the interference gone Serah took Ricardo's hand to explain about her decision.

'We can get married in Italy,' she whispered.

Ricardo dropped his cup down into the saucer. 'Really, you mean it? Do you mean go to Italy for the wedding and then come back here or go to Italy to live?'

'Live,' answered Serah.

Standing up, he pulled her into his arms to the cheers of the men inside.

'You are a very lucky man!' called out one of the men.

'I am,' whispered Ricardo with a smile.

'I am too,' whispered Serah as he placed his forehead on hers.

'I hope not,' he continued to whisper.

'Hope not?' questioned Serah.

'Hope you are not a man,' he said with a smile that revealed his perfect mouth.

Her demeanour softened leaving no doubt she was not a man.

'Are you sure you want to marry me?' she asked hoping he would be serious.

'Of course,' he said taking her shoulders and staring at her face. 'I'm your protector so I can't live without you.'

'I want to marry someone who loves me,' she said looking at the paved ground.

He placed his fingers under her chin so she could see into his eyes. 'Believe me when I tell you that I fell in love with you the moment I laid eyes on you.'

She hoped that it was the right decision they were making but there was one thing she knew — she would be the sensible one in the relationship. Ricardo had taken off to speak to his new friends about his return to Italy without any regard as to how they were going to get there. As she stood shaking her head, she was surprised when he suddenly re-appeared before her.

'Why are you shaking your head?' he asked. 'Have you changed your mind?'

Serah laughed. 'No but you haven't thought things through.'

He shrugged his shoulders.

'How do we get to Italy without passports and how do we leave here when we technically haven't arrived?'

With a glare, he took her hand and rubbed the garnet in her ring.

'Really,' she said sarcastically. 'You think—'

forty one

Serah blinked at the change of scenery. A second ago she had been standing in a busy street in Victoria and now she was in front of a small restaurant on a quiet road. The beeping cars were gone. Curious people had been replaced with a robust woman who stared out through a window.

'Ricardo!' she said knocking on the glass. 'Ricardo, entra!'

They entered as the woman took off her apron to run towards them. At first Serah wondered who she was but worked it out when a man appeared from the back, speaking in Italian with obvious excitement and arms open wide. Both he and the woman hugged Ricardo tightly, so glad to see their son home.

'Chi è questa donna con te?' said an over excited mother, wanting to know immediately who Serah was.

'My fiancée,' he announced as three sisters appeared from behind the back of the restaurant. 'Serah is from Australia. She speaks English.'

Adona, Donata and Coco eyed off their prospective sister-in-law before running up to her.

Serah didn't know what to do so she froze as they stopped in front of her.

'Give her some space,' said his mother, Genevre, taking the hint to switch language so Serah could understand.

His father, John, knew it wouldn't be long before the shrills would escalate from his daughters so he headed back to the food preparation, knowing that Ricardo would follow him.

'I'm sorry about my sisters,' said Ricardo. 'I should have warned you, but I wasn't expecting to be here so soon.'

Serah smiled as she looked at the women similar in age who wore dresses that complemented their curvaceous bodies.

The women were no longer teenagers so they tried to contain themselves to make their introductions.

'I'm Adona,' said a woman in her early twenties with a soft smile.

'I'm Donata,' announced a woman with long, wavy hair and lashes that matched.

'Coco,' declared the other sister who leapt forward to hug an overwhelmed Serah. 'Your hair smells nice.'

Genevre moved her daughters aside to hold Serah by the shoulders. 'You need fattening up,' she announced taking in the skinny stature of the fair woman with a mop of blonde hair.

'Don't listen to her,' interrupted Adona. 'You're beautiful.'

Coco changed the subject by asking about the wedding.

'We thought we would marry here,' said Serah looking around for Ricardo who had managed to disappear with his father.

'When?' asked Donata hoping to be a bridesmaid.

'Soon!' called out a voice from the behind the door.

Donata wanted a date in order to prepare, so Ricardo returned to brave his sisters. 'How about tomorrow?'

All eyes were upon him with the statement but it was his mother that broke the silence. 'I need a week to organise everything.'

'We need to organise dresses,' said Donata.

'Food and flowers,' announced Coco.

'Invitations,' declared Adona. 'We have such a huge family and we have to send out invitations to your family as well, Serah.'

'Yes,' interrupted John who had been speaking with his son and knew about Serah not having any family. 'It would be nice to have a large wedding, but it is Ricardo and Serah's wedding and not yours.'

His wife and daughters glared at him.

'We want a small wedding,' said Ricardo.

'Can we at least get dresses?' pleaded Donata.

Serah smiled as she stated she would love to have flowers and dresses for her sisters-in-law, so with excitement back in the air, the women stole Serah to go shopping.

The local village was small with only a few dress shops, so Coco started up the small smart car as they all squeezed in. Once Serah was buckled up, she looked at the others who were not. For a moment she forgot she wasn't in Australia but kept her belt on as she clung on for her life. The tour Serah had taken through Italy had been in a coach so the erratic driving of others had been entertaining. Now she was part of the dance that took place to get to their destination, it wasn't as funny. She closed her eyes.

'Are you tired?' asked Coco turning around to look at Serah.

Serah gasped, 'Shouldn't you be watching the road?'

'Yes,' said Donata giving her sister a nudge.

Adona turned towards Serah. 'I'm so sorry, I was so excited by the news, I didn't think about how you must be feeling. You're Australian so I presume you have just arrived from a long flight.'

'Of course she's tired,' said Coco. 'You're always putting clothes first, Donata.'

'I am not!' shouted Donata as Coco turned the car around.

Serah hung on to the seat in front of her as her vision swirled. 'No, it's okay, let's get the dresses.'

Coco turned again and after forty minutes the car stopped to let out a staggering Serah.

The women had spoken too quickly in the car and with broken English, Serah had no idea what they had organised.

'The shop is over here,' called out Donata who was already a few shops ahead.

Old buildings with large windows displayed designs Serah had never seen before. The main street bustled and horns beeped from expensive cars. She laughed at the similarity to the street that she had been on only hours before. Again, things had changed too quickly and Serah wondered if there would be a time when she would wake up to find it had all been a dream.

'Come on,' said Donata impatiently as she opened the door.

'Sorry,' said Adona. 'My sister is excited. This is the first wedding in our family.'

'You're not married?' asked Serah surprised they were all single.

Adona shook her head. 'Our father is protective. Besides, I think that he wants his sons to be married first.'

Serah stopped as she asked about Ricardo's brothers.

'Including Ricardo, we have four brothers,' stated Coco joining in on the conversation.

'I think with your family alone, there will be enough of us to celebrate the wedding,' said Serah feeling nervous about meeting his brothers.

'You don't have a large family?' asked Adona.

Serah shook her head as she looked at the uneven pavers. 'I don't have any family.'

'So that is why you don't want a big wedding,' said Coco motioning for Donata to enter the shop.

'That's fine,' said Adona putting her arm around Serah to manoeuvre her to catch up with her sister.

The heat from the outdoors disappeared as they entered an air-conditioned shop, filled with wedding dresses. Racks around the room held designs that varied from plain to fairy-tale. As it was going to be a small family affair, Serah searched through the plain rack despite Donata's insistence on the more extravagant garments she dragged out. A few dresses were picked by Serah so the sisters looked through the colourful bridesmaid dresses to try on with her. It was an experience that should have been enjoyable, but as Serah looked in the mirror and saw the reflection of herself in a wedding dress, the emotions took over.

Chatter from the others provided distraction but hearing the laughter from the sisters only reminded her of the family life she had missed out on. It was going to be her wedding day but it was also going to be Ricardo's. He should have been allowed a big wedding with his extended family. Cursing her life, she wondered if she was making the right choice for Ricardo. Because of her, there would be no mother or sisters of the bride to share in the fuss. There would be no father to give her away. She didn't even belong to a religion, which she presumed Ricardo's family would. Could she be a part of a ceremony in a church? She felt the sobs deepen within her and went to take off the dress.

'What are you doing in there?' screamed Donata as she knocked on the door.

'Come out,' said Coco. 'Don't be shy with us. We are your new sisters.'

The statement helped to ease the pain, so with rubbed eyes she stepped outside to gasps of joy.

'We have a beautiful sister,' said Coco, 'who will give us bella bambinos to play with.'

'She doesn't speak Italian,' announced Adona, walking up to Serah with a tissue. 'I know they are tears of joy but you can't cry on the day.'

'What do you think of our dresses?' asked Donata, parading around the dressing room in a ruby coloured dress that was tight fitting. 'I thought we should match the ring Ricardo gave you.'

Serah looked at the garnet and agreed.

'Okay, let's get the dresses in the car,' said Adona.

Paying for the dresses had not been a consideration but as Serah looked at the price tag, she knew she couldn't afford it. 'Maybe we should look around some more first.'

Donata glared at her with her dark eyes. 'This is the best shop.'

Serah had no other choice but to explain, but was cut off by Donata who announced she had already been given money by her father.

'Go pay,' said Coco heading back to the change room.

'Then we can go and get a drink,' announced Adona.

'I think I need something stronger than a coffee,' said Serah still looking at the price tag.

'Of course,' said Coco from her room. 'Vino!'

Apart from being on the tours, Serah had not experienced a life with other women. When Sarah Cupsip had been her friend, it had been only the two of them who had gone out and it had been to restaurants to hear about the travels that Serah envied. At work, the females were just acquaintances as she had never been able to fit in with their lunch time pub meals. There had always been a sense of not belonging, but it changed when she sat at a table with her new family to enjoy a glass of wine.

forty two

Ricardo had explained to his father about the reality of his fiancée not having a family and as John could see the love that his son felt, there was no hesitation in passing the money onto his daughter, Donata, to pay for the dresses. Genevre had caught up on the story of the surprise wedding while their daughters were shopping, so quickly organised the food before their return. Things were chaotic at the restaurant with John calling on his sons to help with the cooking while Genevre decorated and placed a sign on the door to notify others that the restaurant would be closed for the night.

Three scruffy young men walked in to find an ecstatic brother they couldn't remember ever being so happy.

Enzo was the first to hug him as he asked what was going on. At first, Enzo had thought it was a welcome home party but when he realised that they were in need of suits, he knew Ricardo had done something big.

Domenico and Angelo laughed at Enzo who was about to congratulate Ricardo on getting a job as a geologist.

Genevre wasn't in the mood for games as she had flowers to collect so she decided she should be the one to tell her sons about the wedding.

'Why so soon?' asked Angelo.

Domenico interrupted, 'She's pregnant.'

Genevre glared at Ricardo but he shook his head.

'I love her,' said Ricardo as three brothers rolled their eyes, 'and I have to go and get a suit and we all need to be ready before she comes back.'

'We haven't met her yet,' said Enzo, also wondering what the rush was about.

'You will,' said Ricardo trying to push his brothers out the door. 'I want to surprise her. She doesn't know the wedding is tonight.'

'Alright, alright,' said Domenico taking the car keys from his pocket.

The drive was longer than expected as the local shops in the village didn't have a suit that would fit Ricardo, so a phone call was made to Coco to stall Serah for a few hours. Not knowing that his sisters had taken Serah to the expensive part of town, he thought he would be safe to walk around and look for his clothes, but when he passed a restaurant and saw his sisters with a tipsy Serah on the dance floor, he forgot about his plans.

'Is that her?' guessed Enzo as he watched Serah move around his sisters.

'She can dance,' said Domenico waving his hands in the air to sway his body.

Angelo laughed but soon got a clip on the back of the head by Ricardo who fumed at his family. The men on guitars stopped playing when they heard the sound of a very angry man entering the premises.

'I asked you to look after her!' yelled Ricardo as he walked over to Serah.

His fiancée was only interested in dancing and continued to sway as she fell onto him.

'You call this looking after her!' screamed Ricardo.

'She was having a good time,' retaliated Coco.

'Why are you here anyway?' demanded Adona folding her arms.

'I was getting my suit,' he said before lifting Serah into his arms to take her home.

'I think we're going,' whispered Enzo to Domenico who declared he would drive.

'I'll go home with the girls,' said Angelo who motioned for his sisters to leave.

Once outside, the reality of Ricardo's anger became clear. A surprise had been ruined, so to make amends Angelo and his sisters went in search for a suit for Ricardo.

'Everything will work out,' said Domenico as he drove through gaps in the traffic.

'I don't know,' said Ricardo who looked at his fiancée passed out on the back seat.

'We'll take her home and she can sleep it off,' suggested Enzo as he conferred with Domenico who agreed.

A plan was in place and Ricardo hoped it would work out. Domenico had further suggestions but once he caught the glare from his brother in the mirror, he decided to keep quiet. So in silence it was a quick trip back to the family home where Serah slept on Ricardo's bed.

Downstairs, a discussion took place around a wooden table. Ricardo was having second thoughts about the surprise but his brothers didn't want him to be disappointed so they went to their rooms to get dressed and leave Ricardo with his thoughts. As he sat on the wooden stool, he looked around his home which was crammed with pictures and other signs of life. It was a contrast to where Serah had lived and he hoped she would be able to cope with the madness of his family. Until he had a job, they would have to live with his parents and work in the restaurant. His life had always been interactive and he wondered if his fascination with stones was due to a need for solitude. What it was he wasn't sure, but his spirits lifted when his clean shaven brothers came down wearing black suits.

'What am I supposed to wear?' said Ricardo laughing at his brothers posing as they stepped down the last step.

'This,' announced Angelo as he walked inside followed by three quiet sisters. 'Put this on. The restaurant is all set and mum and dad are ready.'

Coco interrupted, 'We'll get Serah ready.'

Adona held up a hanger and cover that concealed a dress.

Ricardo pushed the stool away as he stood up. 'Alright, I suppose she has to get used to us anyway.'

'Of course she does,' said Donata who carried the other dresses.

A tap on the door stirred Serah who had been in a deep sleep. She looked around at the room she didn't know. Had it all been a dream? She tried to remember how she had ended up in the room but couldn't. Then she noticed the stones on the shelf and knew it had to be Ricardo's room. Somehow, she had ended up in his room and she presumed that whoever was tapping on the door would want an explanation.

'I'm coming,' said Serah taking a deep breath.

'It's Donata,' said a quiet voice as Serah opened the door.

'Oh, I'm glad it's you,' said Serah as the other sisters joined them. 'This is Ricardo's room, isn't it?'

'Si,' said Coco. 'I mean, yes.'

'Is your mother here?' asked Serah.

'No, why?' responded Donata taking the dresses out of their covers.

'I didn't know if she would be happy with me being in his room,' whispered Serah.

The sisters laughed as they grabbed their dresses.

'Get dressed,' said Coco, 'and drink this.'

Serah looked at the clear substance wondering what it was.

'Water,' said Adona. 'Please drink lots of water.'

With there being no cause for alarm, Serah put on her dress, and once the sisters were ready they went to work on the new family member.

'I was thinking about leaving my hair down,' said Serah as they tied her hair back to put on more make-up.

Coco rummaged through her lipsticks until she found one that matched the ring.

'You need red lips,' said Adona. 'You need colour.'

Donata played with Serah's hair, ignoring the request to keep it down. The sisters stood back for a moment, gazing in awe at the vision of beauty in front of them, only being snapped back to the urgency of the situation by a knocking at the door. 'Are you ready?' Enzo was calling out.

'Ready for what?' asked Serah wondering why the women were in such a rush.

'We have to get to the restaurant,' said Adona.

'But I'm dressed for a wedding,' stated Serah thinking about removing the make-up.

'It's a rehearsal,' intervened, Donata. 'It's an Italian thing.'

Not knowing what was going on, Serah followed the women to squeeze back into the smart car.

'Lucky you didn't buy the big Cinderella dress,' said Coco speeding down the street.

'I thought I would go to the church in a limousine,' stated Serah trying to keep her dress in place as she slipped in her seat at every corner. 'Lucky it's just a rehearsal.'

Donata stared at Adona not knowing what to say so they kept quiet, and when they arrived at the restaurant they walked inside to find Ricardo and his brothers standing at the end of an aisle that had been created. Serah wondered why the rehearsal was at the restaurant but she didn't have time to think as she was whisked to the side by Ricardo's father.

As John asked to accompany her, his daughters threw petals

on the floor. Slow Italian music that seemed familiar played in the background. Not knowing what to do, Serah took John's arm and let him guide her to a smiling Ricardo. He was not meant to see her dress before the wedding and she wondered why they had gone to so much trouble for a rehearsal. Despite her confusion, Serah smiled sweetly at the family that lovingly admired her in her wedding dress as Ricardo took her hand to steady her. A man stood in front of them spoke in Italian and before she could ask for a translation, Ricardo asked her to say 'I do', before slipping a gold ring on her finger. She stared at Ricardo in confusion as he whispered that she was finally his wife.

'This was real,' whispered Serah staring at his grinning face.

He nodded as he kissed her hand. 'You are part of this family now.'

She didn't know how to react as she was happy and angry at the same time. A part of her wanted to explode but then the music changed pace and with the smiles of her new family came a sense of gratitude. It was an occasion she wanted to share, so with a nod, the customers who had been warned not to come were allowed inside.

A feast had been prepared and with Serah's permission, the customers were allowed to join them to share in the chicken, pasta, potatoes, grilled vegetables and salads. Glowing candles led the couple to their table decorated with fresh flowers which fragranced the air. The moment they sat their glasses were filled with wine and once the glass was empty it was filled again. Plates with food continued to be brought in by the waiters for the night and as soon as the first set of food had disappeared, meats, olives and pizza appeared in its place.

'I don't know if I can eat any more,' said Serah pulling on her dress for it to expand.

Enzo walked passed her and offered a hand. 'That's why we have music. We dance away the food.'

As Serah stood, she looked around the room and felt all the stares directed towards her. Someone clapped to coax her to dance but Enzo was not allowed to be the one to partner her. Ricardo was by her side and with a brother pushed away, she was led by her husband to dance in front of everyone. Not being one for attention, she stared at the sisters who she now belonged to and they quickly came to her rescue. It wasn't long before the seats were pushed to the wall and even the waiters joined in. How drinks were passed around, Serah wasn't sure, but her hand was never empty.

Eventually, feeling the pain in her feet from the high shoes that Donata had provided, she gladly sat, and once everyone realised the bride was no longer standing they joined her to eat dessert. Clanging noises from spoons tapped on glasses rang through the establishment with people wanting to speak. Ricardo rose to the occasion and declared his love for his wife. A blushing Serah smiled as she thanked everyone. She would have continued with the speech but was it cut short for her to run to the bathroom.

Whispers went around the room as a shocked Ricardo looked at his glaring mother. With a shrug, he shook his head but his sisters were already running behind her. The thought of having a child in the family excited them but it was short lived as Serah appeared from the bathroom and declared she was not pregnant. Ricardo smiled with the knowledge but was concerned as to why she vomited.

'Are you alright?' he asked when they were alone at their table.

Serah drank her water. 'I'm not used to drinking wine and this is the second time in one day I've had too much to drink.'

'I did worry that the surprise might have been too much,' said Ricardo holding her hand.

A face glowing from the light of the candle faced him as she stated that initially she had been upset but her emotions had changed as the night was one to remember.

Ricardo looked intently into her eyes, sparking a memory of their time spent together in Canada.

'Are you going on a honeymoon?' asked Coco who was suddenly joined by her sisters.

'We've done things back to front, haven't we?' said Ricardo staring at Serah.

Serah laughed. 'We've done things I don't think others would believe.'

'What have you done?' asked Angelo.

The couple turned to face one another as Ricardo stated that they had experienced another life.

'I suppose Canada would be different,' said Donata wondering what it would be like to live in other countries.

Ricardo laughed and carried his wife outside to the small car that would take them home.

The bed Serah had slept on during the day was now covered with petals. She presumed his sisters had something to do with it but was surprised to find that it had been Ricardo's idea. Champagne sat in an ice bucket but Serah couldn't face another drink. Candles provided little lights that caused various colours to flicker from his crystals.

'You really love stones don't you,' said Serah taking off his jacket.

'I love you more,' he said looking for the zip on her dress.

She laughed as he continued to search. 'There isn't one.'

He pushed her onto the bed out of frustration and listened to her laugh uncontrollably.

'What am I going to do with you?' he said, lying next to her.

'What are we going to do?' she said turning to him.

'Do you mean now?' he asked as he faced her.

As she stared at his dark features, she contemplated how her luck had changed and with his eyes upon her, she undid his buttons to remove his shirt. Being with Ricardo was like being in a dream and as she started to remove her dress she noticed the sign on his back.

'I forgot about your tattoo,' she said running her fingers over it. 'No matter what we do, you will always be a Templar who has a connection with stones. It is obviously your destiny to seek the story and being with me shouldn't stop that. Maybe I am part of that story, if I believe I am a descendent of Mary Magdalene, but none of that matters to me anymore. I have a family now so I'm quite happy to leave my past in the past. But if you want to know why you have a mark that your brothers don't, then I understand.'

With flickering lights and scented petals, Ricardo held his wife as they sunk into the mattress of peace and tranquillity to wake up in a room that was not his own.

forty three

Trying to recall the events of the night before, Ricardo lay under the blankets looking at the fireplace. Golden flames played on his mind and then he remembered the amber crystal he had played with as Serah slept. She had accepted his urge to continue on with his search for his story. At the time of the discussion, he had mentioned that the search could take them elsewhere but as long as she was with him then she was safe. The sounds of her sleepy voice played in his head. He had not been able to sleep and taken hold of the crystal to help him think.

Pulling another blanket over Serah he watched her sleep and when he realised the crystal was still in his hand, the visions of the past presented themselves. So in order to see what he was meant to be shown, he placed his head on the pillow to look at the ceiling. A deep breath helped him to focus on the times he had touched stones and received stories. From a young age he had been interested, and now he saw flashbacks to the teasing he received from his brothers who didn't share his passion. Another vision appeared before him of an incident at school when he had questioned the teacher about history only to be told not to interrupt. Then he was shown his time studying geology at university and being shown evidence of giants that once lived on the earth. He had needed a part time job and found an advertisement in the paper for a bus driver for a tour that would take him to where the Templars once were. Celeste appeared with her flaming red hair showing him the planets and then through Serah he had not only found love but found out about goddesses.

He sat up looking at the piece of amber, focussing his thoughts on where he was now. The last vision showed him at home in bed asking to find an answer to his quest. Aerona had been the person he presumed would help, so that meant they had to be in Scotland.

A groaning sound alerted him to his wife who was slowly waking from a drunken sleep.

'Why is it so cold?' asked Serah turning to face Ricardo for an explanation.

Then she noticed her surroundings.

'Well—' he started but Serah interrupted. 'Where are we?'

'Scotland.' He waited for a reaction but didn't get one.

'Do you think there are clothes for us in the wardrobe,' she asked sarcastically, 'because I am not going outside in my wedding dress.'

He laughed, grateful for her sense of humour and got out of bed to check for clothes.

'You're not going to believe this,' he said still laughing, 'but someone else has a sense of humour too.'

'Why?' asked Serah sitting up, then she got a good look at the tartan outfits.

'I bet this is Aerona's doing,' he said taking hold of a blue tartan jumper. 'It has to be her, because before we met her we used to use a plane.'

'Okay,' said Serah getting out of bed, 'let's get this over and done with.'

Ricardo noticed the rips in the dress where he had found it difficult to remove and decided that the quest could wait.

'What are you doing?' she yelled as he jumped over and fell on the bed.

'Enjoying my honeymoon,' he declared as he ripped the rest of the material.

Serah punched him. 'Look at my wedding dress. It's ruined!'

'Doesn't matter,' he said throwing it on the floor. 'You're not getting married again.'

Trying to be angry with him was impossible so she gave in to let him wrap himself around her. She felt his warm body and closed her eyes as she told him she had waited a long time for love.

'Good things come to those who wait,' whispered Ricardo with a serious look.

For a moment, they stared into each other's soul and knew they were meant to be together. They had been together in a past life; even his scent of metal was familiar.

He massaged the back of her neck but that made her sleepy so to avoid her drifting away, he squeezed her tightly.

'You're suffocating me,' she said punching him again.

He held her arms. 'I know what my quest is,' he said as she struggled, 'and that is to tame you.'

'What quest are you on about now?' she asked giving up.

'I was thinking about my quest and we ended up here,' he said still holding her arms and kissing her before she could ask another question.

Their bodies kept them warm, but as the fire went out the question arose as to where the room was. Ricardo was the first to move towards the wardrobe where he gladly put on the warm jumper and found a pair of jeans that fit perfectly.

'I'll have the same clothes,' said Serah motioning for him to throw a jumper her way.

With clothes on, they opened the curtains to see frost on the ground.

'I think we need jackets and boots,' said Serah going back to the wardrobe.

'Funny, isn't it,' said Ricardo, 'that everything is provided for us. Do you think we are in Aerona's house?'

Serah shrugged her shoulders. 'There's only one way to find out.'

A hand held Serah's arm as Ricardo made his way through the opened door first. Acting on instinct, he took vigilant action to make sure his wife was safe and only let down his guard when he entered a kitchen where Aerona sat with Derek.

'Come sit,' said Aerona producing a hearty breakfast of bacon, eggs and baked beans.

'I'm starved,' said Serah taking a seat.

'I see you are now used to magic,' said Aerona placing toast in front of Serah. 'Well, it isn't magic really. Only a manipulation of energy that humans have forgotten.'

Ricardo's ears pricked for information but Serah was oblivious and poured herself a cup of tea.

'Why are we here?' asked Ricardo. 'I feel I'm so close I could touch the answer.'

'Eat,' said Derek. 'Trust me when I tell you to just go with it. You will find your answer.'

Ricardo watched his wife eat and decided to do the same. Once his stomach was filled, Aerona asked him to go outside where he would find others in need of help.

Feeling full herself, Serah eagerly stood up to leave. 'I need to walk off this food, so I'll go with him.'

Ricardo followed to help her with her jacket before braving the bitterness of the outside world but was surprised when he opened the door to a mild climate.

'It doesn't get cold here,' said Derek joining them to admire the view of the cottages that surrounded them. 'I also have a large family and we are all close by here.'

They remembered their discussions around the dinner table in Canada where others had thought it was a joke that Derek had twenty-eight sisters.

'But be warned, when you leave the gate, rug up,' said Aerona who glowed with gold.

Following the path through the community of witches was peaceful. There was a sense of protection and Serah savoured the sounds of the animals living in the trees that sheltered the track. Clean air filled her lungs and as she focused on the refreshing breeze she was taken aback when Ricardo opened the gate.

Gusts of wind whistled past their ears and for a second Serah contemplated going back, but Ricardo had been told to help, so with woollen hats that appeared in their pockets, they warmed up to venture on.

'I wonder who I have to help,' asked Ricardo as he took the gloved hand of Serah.

The wind died but the chill remained as they came across some rocks on the outskirts of a village. Most tourists would have headed to the pub but Ricardo was drawn to the stones, so with his wife in tow they climbed a path to find another couple kissing.

'Maybe we should leave them,' said Serah turning around.

'Too late,' said Ricardo giving a wave. 'I think we've disturbed them.'

'Hello!' called out a voice with an unusual accent. 'Do you understand English?'

Ricardo laughed, 'I can speak English.'

'I can as well,' said Serah wondering where the couple were from.

'Where are you from?' asked the woman, wrapped up in a scarf.

'I'm from Australia,' said Serah who moved closer to introduce herself.

'I'm from Italy,' stated Ricardo who was intrigued to know where the man with similar features to his own was from.

A hand appeared to shake with Ricardo. 'I am Aidan and I'm from Turkey.'

Aidan's partner untied her scarf which covered most of her face and spoke, 'I am—'

'Dy!' said an astonished Serah. 'What are you doing here?'

'You know them?' asked Aidan.

The women hugged as Ricardo explained about the time when they had lived in England.

Leaving the men to chat, Serah took Dy to one side to ask about the prince.

'It wasn't meant to be. I was meant to go to Turkey and meet Aidan,' said Dy giving Serah another hug. 'We have a lot to talk about.'

'We do,' responded Serah, wondering about the length of time they had been apart, but their conversation would have to wait as they were being called back to join a discussion.

Ricardo looked at Serah as he asked Aidan to repeat his question.

Aidan couldn't help feeling something odd was going on, but shrugged his shoulders to ask again where they were.

'I know it sounds strange,' interrupted Dy, 'but we have no idea where we are.'

'What do we tell them?' whispered Ricardo as he turned his back on the couple.

'You are standing amongst sacred stones,' declared Serah spinning around.

Aidan and Dy looked around with confused expressions.

'What country?' asked Dy, wondering what her friends would think.

'This is the Isle of Skye,' said Serah nonchalantly. 'Out of curiosity, how do you not know where you are?'

'I can't explain really,' said Dy, trying to comprehend the madness.

Ricardo put up his hand. 'We understand so you don't need to explain. Were you transported here without any knowledge?'

'How did you know that?' asked Aidan surprised that others shared in his experience.

Dy intervened, 'I fell through a wall.'

'What we've come to realise is that everything is for a reason,' said Serah taking hold of Ricardo's arm. 'And to help you to understand the situation, I think you need to speak with Aerona, a good witch.'

'Where is this Aerona?' asked Aidan who followed the couple wondering what method of transport would be used.

Ricardo turned to face him. 'Here in Scotland.'

So with zipped up coats and scarves to cover their necks, Dy and Aidan followed the couple to what looked like a commune. A gate opened and Dy gazed in awe at the field of flowers beyond the trees as Aidan took off his scarf. Paths led in different directions but one in particular snaked through the trees and led to a small home with a thatched roof. Dy gasped again at her surroundings as she waited for the white witch to respond to the knock on the door. A bright light appeared but it wasn't white but gold.

'Aerona,' said Serah, 'this is—'

'Dyana and Aidan,' continued Aerona who welcomed them inside.

Aidan held Dy back. 'You know us!'

Dy wondered if the woman really was a witch.

'Come in,' Aerona beckoned standing aside so everyone could enter.

Serah hesitated. 'Do you mind if Ricardo and I leave? I don't really want to get involved with their story.'

'Very well,' said Aerona. Before closing the door, she mentioned to them, 'Your destiny is in the town of Scone.'

forty four

There was a feeling within Serah that she would meet Dy again, but for the moment they had different destinies. Not knowing where Scone was, she asked Ricardo for his phone but he had already checked the destination which was five hours away by car.

'We don't have a car,' said Serah wondering how they were going to get there.

Ricardo typed into the phone to look up train services as Serah asked where the money would come from.

'What are we going to do?' asked Ricardo looking up to the sky.

'Ask Aerona,' said Serah looking back at the house as she opened the gate.

Feeling frustrated, Ricardo checked his phone again to find that they were already in Scone.

'Really!' said Serah turning around to look at a ruined castle.

'It's magnificent,' said Ricardo looking at the palace that dominated the hill.

'It would have been in its day,' said Serah trying to picture what the building would have been like before years of disintegration.

Ricardo looked confused. 'Can't you see the beauty of what's in front of you?'

'I do have an imagination,' she snapped back.

'You don't need one,' said Ricardo walking towards the historical structure. 'It's intact.'

Serah walked behind him but then he stopped. 'I think we are looking at two different times. I had a feeling my answer was within the walls and I was right because now I can hear whispers. I am being told by the past and present that we need to go to the water.'

Serah concentrated but heard nothing. They walked closer to the River Tay and that was when she heard a voice from below the water. Grabbing her husband's hand, she ran towards the sound as it grew louder.

'Who are you?' asked Serah as they appeared by the river's edge.

Ricardo looked around wondering if she was still seeing a different time as he couldn't see anyone.

A woman rose from the water. She was as blue as the sea. 'I am Taygete. I am the calm in the waters and the creator of Oceania. I am the one who mixed with the Atlanteans who provided the intelligence through a goddess in Egypt.'

'Can you see her?' whispered Serah to a stunned Ricardo who nodded his head as the woman turned into a serpent. 'Why do you think she is important? She has nothing to do with rocks or destiny.'

The serpent changed back to an acceptable form with high cheek bones and flowing hair. 'I have everything to do with what you seek, Ricardo. I am the one who holds the stone that will take you to your destiny.'

'I came across others who live in the waters when I was in Canada,' stated Serah who was interested in her knowledge.

'Canada shares its land with North America,' announced Taygete. 'My sister, Asterope mixed with the tribes long ago who still remember the star people who visited this planet.'

'Celeste should be here,' said Ricardo. He was not as interested as Serah who continued to encourage the woman from the water to speak.

'The daughter of the goddess you call Aerona is my mother. I, along with my six sisters, lived on another planet, but help was needed here so my sisters and I were put into a spaceship and sent to Earth. Our transportation had seven points that broke on impact. This created an impression on the humans as they believed that we came from the stars and as our craft looked like a star, they called us star people. They had no idea of our mission of integration and were more interested in what was left of our spaceship. My sisters, being the ones to remain on land, passed the stone that powered the ship onto me as I was to live amongst those in the water.'

'That's fascinating,' said Ricardo picking up interest with the mention of a stone.

'Who are your sisters?' asked Serah who was mesmerised by the woman.

'Maia; she chose to live with the people who resided in South America. She created a civilisation that thrived on her knowledge of the galaxy that has become known as the seven sisters' galaxy.' Taygete's tail thrashed in the water creating waves.

'And the others?' coaxed Serah who clung on to Ricardo.

Taygete moved in and out of the water, changing her appearance to now resemble a whale. 'Why do you think whales are intelligent?' she quizzed, changing back to herself.

'Did you integrate with them as well?' Serah wondered, standing back after the sight of the enormous mouth.

Her humanly form was easier to relate to and the couple listened as she explained about her other sisters, Electra, who integrated with Asians to advance technology, Calaeno, who toyed with mind control in Africa and Alcyone, who calmed everyone in Antarctica.

'There is one sister missing,' said Serah counting the names with her fingers.

'Merope is the answer to your destiny,' said the woman as she produced a large stone that looked extremely heavy. 'Serah, you wanted to know about your family, and your husband would have found out if you had let him go to the big rock in Australia. There are some there who know of a time in the past when my sister refused to integrate with the Europeans. Merope had fallen in love with a mortal but then again so had Asterope. She had created a civilisation that is remembered today but the people left when she did. Asterope felt a longing to return to beyond the stars and tried to take the stone away from me; she wanted to take the stone back with her but it had to stay here. She grew angry with me and returned to Egypt as she believed that parts of the stone were scattered throughout the land. When our spaceship crashed, there was some damage to the stone but it was minimal. However, my sister was determined to search and it paid off. She found out about a fragment that the goddess in Egypt kept hidden and tried to extort it from her. But her action caused a reaction. The goddess of creation passed the fragment of stone on to another to hide; a daughter of a Pharaoh by the name of Scota came here and gave the fragment to me.'

The history lesson fascinated Serah but she wanted to know what happened to Asterope.

Taygete rubbed the stone with her long fingers as she told of how Asterope roamed the land in search of another piece. 'Her travels took her far and wide and she only stopped searching when she met a man in Troy. He fell in love with her and convinced her to end her quest, but even he was unable to keep her on Earth so he watched as she jumped from a cliff top.

'Oh!' declared Serah. 'Am I a descendent from her? Every time I'm up high, I want to jump.'

Ricardo squeezed her hand as he shook his head. 'You have already been told that you are from Mary Magdalene. Remember I'm the Templar who protects you.'

A splash drew their attention. 'Asterope has the strongest

connection to the stars so therefore she has the strongest connection to the goddess in Egypt who controlled the stone. You may have picked up a part of her DNA during your life times but you are definitely a direct descendent from another line. Science is coming back to the humans and soon they will realise how to use the energy and live as they once did. There is no need for me to hold the stone any longer as the man who was destined to take it is here.'

All eyes were upon Ricardo as he wondered how he would pick up the enormous rock. Then a spark from the woman's finger shrunk it to fit into his hand. And as he held it, he felt the energy and received the message of where to go. 'Luckily I can use the energy to leave a message for my family,' he said as he focused on the lipstick that was left in front of his mirror in his bedroom. It was difficult at first to manoeuvre the make-up but with closed eyes he managed to visualise and orchestrate what he needed to do. Not being sure how it would write on the mirror, he kept it short by writing:

Have gone but will return
Love
Ricardo Knight
And
Serah Kohw

forty five

A sleepy Genevre woke to a quiet house. The clock that sat next to her bed showed that she had slept in. Trying to visualise her children already up and preparing the food at the restaurant was but a dream, so she stretched and pulled away the sheet that covered her husband.

'Time to get up,' she said, still in a sleepy state.

John groaned, but someone had to organise the food, so Genevre staggered to her eldest daughter's room and turned the handle in hope that she was up.

'Adona,' said Genevre as she crept through the door, 'are you here?'

'Yes,' said a faint voice. 'What time is it?'

'Time to get up,' explained her mother. 'We're late.'

Knowing that Adona was still in bed meant the others were as well, so she made her way to the room where Coco and Donata slept and, as she suspected, they were in a deep sleep. Not knowing how she was going to wake them, she decided to take off the sheets that covered them.

'You're still in your dresses,' observed their mother. She then told them to get up as she made her way to the room that belonged to Ricardo.

Her fingers rubbed the door and she wondered if she should tap but then there was Serah to consider and it had been their wedding night. So, deciding to leave them alone, she woke up her sons who would undoubtedly provide the noise required to wake up their eldest brother.

As they sat around the table with their breakfast discussing the night before, Genevre stood up and made a tray of food.

'You're not going to disturb them, are you?' said Enzo sipping on his coffee.

'They must be hungry,' said his mother, 'and they can't possibly be asleep with all of you making such a noise.'

'Leave them,' said John pulling on a stool for her to sit.

Genevre shook her head and took the tray to knock on the door.

Placing her ear against the wood, she expected to hear a sound but there was silence so she gently turned the handle. Thoughts went through her mind of her own wedding night so she contemplated leaving the tray by the door, but the door had already swung open. Deciding to leave the tray on the cupboard, she tiptoed backwards to look at a mirror with unusual writing.

Not knowing what it read, she turned to the empty bed and screamed.

'What is it?' called out Angelo.

Donata choked on her orange juice. 'Probably caught them in bed.'

'Ughh,' said Angelo wincing at the scenario.

'Don't worry,' said Coco getting from her stool. 'I'll go.'

Coco entered the room expecting to see her brother and his wife but there was only her mother who was trying to read what was written on the mirror.

'What do you think?' said Genevre taking a bite from the toast on the tray. 'You think he would care enough to leave me a proper message.'

Coco looked at the lipstick squiggled on the mirror. 'You know what Ricardo is like. He's mysterious. He searches for stories from stones so what do you expect. Besides I think he does care. If you look at the message it seems some letters are prominent because they are in capitals and you know how enticed he is with the letter, K. I bet you it's a code and he will come back one day with another surprise.'

'What do you mean?' said Genevre wiping the tears and putting the toast back on the plate.

'He left a note when he went to Canada and came back with a fiancée so who knows where he's gone now, but he'll probably come back with a pregnant wife,' said Coco giving her mother a hug. 'You know what he's like. He has spent his whole life searching for something.'

Genevre nodded her head as she looked once more at the writing on the mirror before rubbing off the lipstick that read:

nruter lliw tub enog evaH
evoL
thginK odraciR
dnA
whoK hareS